# STATE OF LIFE

A Virgil Jones Novel—Book 12

## THOMAS SCOTT

For information contact:

ThomasScottBooks.com

Linda Heaton - Editor

**HIGH ROAD PRESS**

**VIRGIL JONES SERIES IN ORDER:**

State of Anger - Book 1

State of Betrayal - Book 2

State of Control - Book 3

State of Deception - Book 4

State of Exile - Book 5

State of Freedom - Book 6

State of Genesis - Book 7

State of Humanity - Book 8

State of Impact - Book 9

State of Justice - Book 10

State of Killers - Book 11

State of Life - Book 12

State of Mind - Book 13

State of Need - Book 14

**JACK BELLOWS SERIES IN ORDER:**

Wayward Strangers

Updates on future novels available at:
ThomasScottBooks.com

*For Sam*

*Life*

/līf/

*noun:*

The condition that distinguishes animals and plants from inorganic matter, including the continual change preceding death.

———

*"As heads is tails, just call me Lucifer, 'cause I'm in need of some restraint..."*
—Mick Jagger

———

*"There's more to this case than you can imagine."*
—Mason Jones

# CHAPTER ONE

**DECADES AGO:**

It was odd the way the life of one man could affect the lives of so many others with little to no forethought. Odd because no one would ever be able to say how far back it went...the bent, twisted gene that made him who he was, the same one that would turn his own children into who they would ultimately become. The whole thing was like a neglected apple tree that had never been trimmed, the branches slumping and sinking toward the earth, the apples themselves kissing the ground while still on the limb, their skins wilted with the heat of the summer, then browned by the sting of an early autumn frost. A few people might have noticed what was happening, yet no one seemed to care all that much...not back then anyway.

But later they would. The apples were tasty if you

weren't all that picky about the soft spots. The killer wasn't and never had been. In fact, it was the soft spots that drew him in. They were, in their own way, Golden Delicious. It was like sneaking a piece of mom's apple pie.

As long as the old man wasn't around.

———

THE OLD MAN'S NAME WAS DICK WHITTLE, AND HE WAS rotten to the core. He learned early in life that with a name like his, he was going to be ridiculed and laughed at forever. It began in grade school when the teachers would call out the student's names while marking the attendance sheet. The names were listed in alphabetical order, last name first, first name last.

Day after day, year after year, it was always the same. "Whittle, Dick." The younger students would giggle because it was sort of funny, and during recess, they'd all run around and say things like, *Hey, there's a Whittle Dick,* which eventually turned into, *Hey, there's a little dick,* which ultimately led to fistfights, bloody noses, and that one terrible day right after the high school graduation ceremony when Dick Whittle lost control and beat the living daylights out of two fellow students, one of them a pretty blond girl who snickered as he walked by, turned to her boyfriend and said, "Hey, there goes a little dick."

Whittle turned around and slapped the girl hard in the face and she fell to the ground, the back of her head bouncing off the pavement. The boyfriend, one of the school's football players had about a fifty-pound advantage over Whittle. What he didn't have was the immediate ability to process what he'd just witnessed. He was still staring at his girlfriend who was out cold when Whittle unloaded on him with two quick punches to his solar plexus that bent him over, and one wicked punch to his jaw as he was going down.

Then he started kicking. By the time two staff members managed to pull him away, both of Whittle's victims had multiple broken ribs, and bruises that would last all through summer.

The first police officer on the scene was a rookie sheriff's deputy named Mason Jones. He got the cuffs on Whittle, then radioed for an ambulance. Later, during his arraignment—mostly because the kids had survived and times were different back then—Whittle was offered his choice: three years for aggravated assault, or five years in the Army. The Vietnam war was winding down, so Whittle went with the Army.

On the first day of boot camp, the drill sergeant got right in his face and began screaming at him. "Whittle, Dick? Whittle Dick? What kind of fucked up, hillbilly, jack-off name is that...?"

If Whittle wasn't messed up going in, by the time he got out five years later, he was all but gone.

———

BUT NOT COMPLETELY. THE FIRST THING HE DID WHEN he got out was use his GI Bill money and enrolled at Indiana State University on the government's dime, where he took business classes and studied animal husbandry. Whittle had a thing for chickens. Every gook he ever saw when he was in the war was always walking around with a chicken. And why not? They cost pennies to feed, they gave you eggs every day, and when they could no longer do that, you could eat the damned things for dinner.

During his last year of college, he met a young woman named Evelyn Morgan. Evelyn's mother had recently died, and her father, who wasn't getting any younger, had a small farm in south-central Indiana, which he was getting ready to sell so he could spend his retirement years in Florida. Morgan, a pretty brunette with soft doe eyes and curves in all the right places began dating Whittle, and after six months they were married. Exactly nine months later to the day, their first child was born, a girl named Karen.

Whittle and his wife had worked out a deal with Evelyn's father...they'd buy the farm on land contract, and Whittle would turn it into a chicken ranch.

"Not much money in chickens," Bob Morgan said. Bob was Evelyn's dad, an ancient relic of a man who could no longer run the farm himself. "Hogs or beef, I'd be on board with you. Don't see it with chickens, though."

Whittle nodded at him like the old man was handing out sage advice for free. *What a dope,* Whittle thought. "Maybe not right now, but industrial farming is the future of livestock, and chickens would be the easiest and quickest way to get started."

Morgan looked at his daughter, and said, "Are you on board with this idea, Evelyn?"

"I am. Dick has a degree in both business and animal husbandry. I believe he knows what he's doing."

Morgan looked at them both. "Well, I hope you're right. As long as I get my check every month, I'll be fine. If it ain't paid off by the time I croak, the rest of the debt is canceled, and the place is yours."

And Whittle thought, *Perfect.*

————

EXCEPT IT WASN'T. BOB MORGAN LEFT FOR FLORIDA, and the Whittles soon discovered that in addition to the cost of the chickens, the feed, the refurbishing of the barn, the land taxes, and all the other expenses—not the least of which was their daughter, Karen—money was more than tight...it was practically non-existent.

Whittle ended up working two full-time jobs, plus the farm just to keep them even. He averaged four hours of sleep a night, and exhaustion became a way of life.

Then, when Karen was barely six months old, Whittle returned home late one afternoon and found Evelyn standing in the kitchen, staring at nothing, tears streaming down her cheeks.

"What's wrong? And what's for dinner? I've got to eat and get back to work. Grab me a beer." When Evelyn didn't say anything, Whittle said, "Are you gonna answer me, or not? And where's the god damned beer I just told you to get me?"

Evelyn took a deep breath, then said, "I'm pregnant. Again."

Whittle hit her so hard he knocked two of her teeth out.

---

HE NEVER LAID A HAND ON EVELYN AGAIN, MOSTLY because he knew if he did, she'd leave him, or he'd go to jail, or both. Besides, there were other targets of opportunity over the years, and all Whittle had to do was bide his time. They had two more children—a boy they named Sam, and another boy named Don—and despite his mean streak and constant emotional and physical abuse, as time went on they somehow managed to see themselves as a family. But underneath it all, even as the children grew, and the farm became a success, Evelyn Whittle and her children were the only ones who really ever knew the type of monster that lived inside Dick Whittle.

They knew because he reminded them on a daily basis. The kids got the worst of it—though when they were older, Sam, in particular, thought maybe there were things his father had done to his mother that none of them would ever know about. Karen, the oldest, was expected to keep the house not just clean, but absolutely spotless. Whittle would actually put on a white glove and run his fingers across the fireplace mantle—or some other obscure area—to check for dust. If the glove came away with as much as a speck, Whittle would beat her and scream in her face until she curled up on the floor, shaking and crying like a little dog.

When he was fourteen years old, Sam was put in charge of the chicken business. He had to get up every morning before school and collect the eggs, make sure that the water lines were running properly, carry the buckets of feed, and clean the shit from the pens. When he returned home from school, he'd do it all over again, before going inside to eat dinner, do his homework, then fall into bed, exhausted. The weekends weren't any better. In addition to the chicken business, there was a lawn to mow, weeds to pull, fencing to fix, siding to replace, and anything else the old man could think of. And like his sister, Karen, nothing was ever good enough. Too much feed. Not enough feed. Too much water. Not enough water. Broken eggs. An actual fox in the hen house. There was always something wrong, and never anything right. Dick Whittle just couldn't quite figure out what it was. So he took it out on his kids, over and over, making little monsters in his own image.

Except for Don. Don somehow became the golden boy who could do no wrong. He didn't have to work in the barn, or help with the house, or do anything that Karen and Sam were expected to do. No one could ever figure out why. Some said it was because he was the youngest, while others said it was because old man

Whittle took out all his hate and anger and abuse on Karen and Sam. And while some of those things may have been true, Don figured out how to become a survivor amid the constant abuse and dysfunction.

He became a pleaser.

The madder Whittle got, the happier Don became. He'd tug at his father's sleeve during one of his outbursts, then hand him a beer, or he'd say, "Hey, Dad, let's go play catch." And for some reason, Whittle found it impossible to say no to his youngest son. As Don grew up, he began to see himself as the leader, a savior of sorts, the one who could make everything okay for everyone else...no matter how bad it all was.

Looking back, everyone always thought that Sam and Karen—especially Sam—had gotten the worst Dick Whittle had to offer. As it turned out, Don would have his own demons to face. He just didn't know it at the time.

# CHAPTER TWO

The killer, alone, out in the black of night. He knew the route because he'd been here before, right on the edge of the woods line, but he had to pick his spot with care. Not too dense, or he wouldn't be able to maneuver, yet not too open because he didn't want to be seen. Plus, the spot had to be close enough to where his van would be parked.

So many things a killer has to think about.

He carried a small penlight, the lens taped over just enough to keep the light from exposing him should anyone be watching, though out here at this time of night, no one would be. Still, better safe than sorry. He walked the route a few times, got his bearings, then went back to his van and retrieved an eighty-pound bag of sand. He carried the sand back to where he thought the perfect spot might be, leaned it against a tree near the edge of the path, then waited until his heart slowed and his breathing returned to normal. He pulled a stopwatch from his pocket—a single-handed chrome dial with a bug-winder of a knob at the top—took a deep breath, punched the button on the watch, then...

He ran toward the bag of sand, punched it twice, then hefted it up over his shoulder and ran as fast as he could back to his van. He opened the side door—he'd left it cracked to save a few precious seconds—tossed the sandbag inside, then slammed the door, and checked his time.

Start to finish, twenty-nine seconds, give or take.

That'd work.

———

COACH WAS THE GUIDANCE COUNSELOR AT THE HIGH school in French Lick, Indiana. He told everyone to call him Coach because while he enjoyed his paying job as a guidance counselor, what he really loved was something he did for free. He was the coach of the girl's cross-country team. There was something special about being called Coach. He liked it, and the kids did too. They'd walk into his office and say things like, "Hey, Coach, got a minute? I'd like to talk about my college choices." Or they'd see him in the hallway and shout, "What's up, Coach?" To him, it was a badge of honor. Like being called Doctor, or Captain.

The match today was against one of the teams from Indianapolis, and since Coach's girls were the visiting team and running on unfamiliar terrain, he wanted to get there early and make sure everyone knew the course. It was situated in one of the parks just outside the city limits, and nearly half the course was wooded, so there'd be some obstacles to contend with. All that aside, the weather was perfect, the girls were in top physical form, no one was out sick, and that all added up to victory.

He walked out onto the field, near the starting line, and watched his girls loosen up. He wore gold shorts, a black pullover team shirt, and a whistle on a lanyard around his neck. When the girls were ready, he blew the whistle and gathered them together.

He used his coaching voice on the field, not his counseling voice. There was a distinct difference. "All right ladies, now that everyone is warmed up, let's walk the course."

A series of muffled groans filled the air.

"I don't want to hear it," Coach said. "Almost half of this course is through the trees, this is the first meet of the year, and I want each and every one of you to know exactly what you're getting into."

One of the girls put her hands on her hips and cocked a knee the way high school girls often do, then said, "Coach, in case you've forgotten, we've been running through wooded courses all summer getting ready for today, and the flags and streamers are set up to guide us the whole way."

"Nice try, young lady. I haven't forgotten, but in case you have, a storm came through up here over the weekend, and it might have done some damage. I don't want anybody getting hurt because they tripped over a fallen limb. We're one of the best teams in the state, and the last thing we need is someone out for the season with a busted ankle." Then, before anyone else could say anything, Coach blew the whistle and shouted, "Head out!"

The team turned and began walking the course. They didn't actually walk...rather they jogged. Fast enough to get it over with, but not so fast that they'd wear themselves out. It was all part of the process.

Twenty minutes later the other team began showing up. Most were on a school bus, but a few of the older girls followed in their own cars. Once they were on the field, their coach, a harsh-looking woman with short black hair and muscles in her face, walked over, said hello, then asked about the condition of the course.

"You might know better than me, but I think it's in pretty good shape," Coach said. "There are a few places where it might be a little slick, especially on the hills. I was watching the weather, and that storm looked like it was pretty intense."

"It was. Nice day today, though."

Coach looked up at the sky, and said, "Sure is. Anyway, my girls are walking the course now. Looks like they're about finished. Feel free to send yours out whenever they're ready."

She gave him a tight nod, said, "Thanks," then walked away.

Coach smiled to himself. Tough to know you're going to lose before you even got started. With nothing better to do, Coach thought he'd walk part of the course himself to make sure the wooded areas had dried out. He thought they must have. It was windy, and the sun had been shining all day.

---

THE KILLER HAD PARKED HIS VAN IN THE EXACT SAME spot as before. The sliding door was unlatched, the path was clear, and he was ready to go. Risky? Yes. Worth it? Absolutely. He could practically taste her already. He stood well back in the tree line. If he was spotted now, he'd have to abort. The girls—some jogging, some walking —all went past without even glancing his way. Over the years he'd taken seven girls. This would be number eight, and the anticipation was almost too much to bear. The killer had to be careful, and he always was, especially today, as he'd never actually taken one from a cross-country course. What he usually did was find his victims by cruising the mall, or any number of fast-food joints late at night. He'd pick out his target, follow her home, and once he knew where she lived, the rest was basic research. He'd follow her to and from work, watch her at sporting events, take note of who her friends were and where they lived, and eventually an opportunity would present itself.

The trick was, to be ready when it did, and the killer was always ready. It wasn't that hard if you knew what you were doing.

But this time was different. He'd be more exposed, and while there was an increased risk, there was also a heightened sense of urgency that made the taking almost as exciting as what he'd do once he had her.

Almost.

He'd have to wait for the last girl, whoever she was, something he knew going in. At first the idea of not knowing who he'd get bothered him, but the more he thought about it, he considered this particular change of pace a nice little surprise. Sort of like Christmas...you never really knew what you were getting until you unwrapped your gift. The fighters were the best.

---

HE SAW HER COMING AND KNEW SHE WAS THE ONE. A redhead—not his favorite—the freckles were a little much sometimes, but it wasn't like he could afford to be choosey. Besides, redheads were a feisty bunch, so she'd probably want to fight. She was walking along, looking at the ground, chewing on one of her fingernails, paying no attention whatsoever. When she passed by the killer, he took a careful quiet step forward, made sure there was no one else coming, then made his move.

He was on her like a cat. She heard him coming at the last second, turned, and when she did he punched her in the gut to take the wind out of her. Then he hit her again, this time on the back of her neck, his arm wrapped around her midsection so she didn't fall all the way to the ground. She was stunned, but not completely out, and she grabbed his arm and tried to break free. She struggled and scratched at him, and the killer felt some blood on his arm where she'd ripped his skin. She began kicking and moaning, and the killer, now bleeding and furious with himself for not hitting her harder, grabbed her by the neck and smashed the back of her head into a tree. She collapsed in his arms, out cold. He threw her over his shoulder, ducked back into the woods, and headed for his van. It took longer than his practice run, but he got it done. He dumped her in the back of the van, stuffed a rag in her mouth, covered it with a piece of duct tape, then wrapped her wrists behind her back with the same roll of tape. When he had her secured, he slammed the door and turned to make sure no one had seen him. No one had. He looked at the scratch on his forearm and saw that it wasn't nearly as bad as he'd thought it was in the moment. He untucked his shirt, spat on his arm, and wiped the dried blood away. Couldn't even tell he'd been cut. More like a bug bite than anything.

*Bitch could kick, though.* He laughed at himself. He was so caught up in the moment he never noticed that when she was kicking, she'd lost a shoe.

Coach watched as the girls finished their final warmups, and when everyone was ready, he took out his starter's pistol, made sure all eyes were on him, and was just about to pull the trigger when the other team's coach stopped him by blowing her whistle three times.

Coach turned and gave her a curious look. All the runners relaxed out of their starting stance. "What is it?" Coach asked.

The female coach held up her finger and did a quick count. "I'm missing one," she said. "Has anyone seen Mary?"

All the girls turned and looked around, the French Lick girls having no idea who Mary was, or what she looked liked. The girls on the Indy team all shook their heads, then one of them said, "She was walking the course, but she didn't want to run it. She was sort of falling behind."

"That sounds like Mary," one of the other girls said.

Coach, as was his nature, took charge right away. "Okay people, we may have an injured runner out there. I want half of you—let's say the Indy girls because you know the course best—to walk it backward, and my girls, take it from the starting line. She might have slipped and sprained an ankle or something. Let's go help her out."

Ten minutes later, they found Mary's shoe.

Twenty minutes after that, the cops started showing up.

BECAUSE THE COURSE ITSELF WAS OUTSIDE THE CITY limits, it made the case a county matter. The shoe was left in place, with an evidence marker next to it on the ground. The Marion County cops conducted a full search of the park but came up empty. The meet was canceled, and the sheriff had all the girls sit on the grass in a circle. He looked at both teams' coaches and said, "Are we sure everyone else is accounted for?" He was told that they were. After questioning all the girls as a group, asking what they saw, if anything, he discovered that while plenty of girls had seen Mary go into the woods, none of them actually saw her come out.

"And her last name is Adams," the sheriff said.

"That's right," the Indy coach said. "Mary Adams. Redhead, she's a Junior, weighs about ninety pounds, probably five-four, maybe five-six. I'm not exactly sure."

The sheriff was taking it all down in his notebook. "Boyfriend?"

A few of the girls looked at each other, but they all shook their heads. One of them said, "I'm not sure she's ever had a boyfriend."

Sheriff Mason Jones looked out across the park and shook his head. This was the last thing he needed right now. His sons were off fighting a war in the Middle East, and his wife was at home fighting cancer. He hoped his boys would be okay. He knew his wife, Elizabeth, wouldn't be. He'd already turned in his retirement papers so he could spend more time with her. He looked at both coaches and said, "Okay, listen, let's get your girls back home. Keep them off the phone until I can notify the parents. The last thing they need to hear is that their daughter is missing. The second last thing they need is to hear it from someone besides one of my men. Understood?"

They both said they did. As the coaches were rounding up their girls, a crime scene tech came jogging over with the shoe in a plastic bag. "Pretty sure it's her shoe, Sheriff. If you look inside, under the tongue, you can see her initials written in ink. M.A."

Mason swore under his breath. Then he turned and pointed at the group of girls. "I meant what I said. Stay off your home phones. If anyone calls the Adams residence, you'll be in big trouble."

The girls, who at first were mildly amused by the whole thing—like maybe Mary had just decided to run off —were now scared. Mason could see it on their faces.

"You won't have any trouble from my girls, Sheriff," Coach said. "None of them were friends or even knew who Mary was until we couldn't find her."

Mason nodded, his anxiety beginning to grow. "You're team...you're uh, from French Lick?"

"That's right," Coach said. "If there's nothing else, I guess we'll wish you the best of luck and get out of your hair."

"Have a safe trip back," Mason said. Then he quickly thumbed through his notebook, and said, "In all the confusion, I don't believe I got your name."

Coach felt sorry for the man. It looked like he was

struggling with more than just the prospect of dealing with a missing teenaged girl. He let out a little chuckle and said, "You probably didn't, because all anyone ever calls me is Coach." He stuck out his hand to shake and said, "My name's Don. Coach Don Whittle."

Sheriff Jones shook hands with Whittle, then "Appreciate your help today, Coach." Then he turned and got back to work, the whole time thinking about his sons, Virgil and Murton...praying for their safe return. And his wife...praying that she wouldn't suffer in the end, an end that seemed to be coming at them like a double-header locomotive that'd lost its brakes, screaming through the night on a downhill slope, headed toward certain destruction.

With those types of thoughts going through his head, Mason made a mistake that would haunt him, even after his own death. He just didn't know it at the time.

# CHAPTER THREE

**PRESENT-DAY:**

A cool weekend, high cirrus clouds drifting about in no particular direction, a fish toying at the end of his line causing the bobber to wiggle and make concentric circles on the water's surface, the kids running and playing in the backyard with Larry the Dog, the women at the farmer's market getting fresh vegetables for dinner, a lawnmower buzzing from across the far side of the property. The scent of the cut grass drifted his way and mixed in with the aroma of the pond water and the brisk, sharp, freshness of the air.

For Virgil Jones, lead detective of the state's Major Crimes Unit, it should have been one of those weekend days where everything was right with the world, where life and those who lived it were happy, content, and free—at least temporarily—from the worries of the job, and the grief, stress, paperwork, and the politics that came with it all.

But still...Ron Miles. Dead and gone.

Maybe free in his own way. Then again, maybe not. Virgil didn't know, though clearly he should have. He only knew the heaviness he carried around with him after everything that had happened, and he felt like the weight might be crushing him on the inside, like a piece of dead-wood smashed underfoot in the forest of his soul.

Life. The great cosmic mystery. Here one minute, and gone the next. He hadn't seen his father since Ron's murder...yet another thing tearing him apart. He looked at the cross next to him and said, "Are you there anymore? Were you ever?" When he got no response, he pulled the fish from the water, took the hook from its mouth, and set it free. If only everything was that easy.

---

VIRGIL'S PATH FORWARD FELT THIN, RAZOR-SHARP, crooked, and chaotic. It was a switchback of sorts, a dividing line between the man he knew he was, and the man he couldn't seem to find no matter where he looked or how hard he tried. He felt like a fractal of a being, broken inside, which is exactly what he'd told his wife, Sandy, a number of months ago. Virgil had lost himself, and now, at the tag end of a cool, crisp summer, he was trying to balance the fact that he'd lost both a friend and an advisor of sorts. Ron Miles was dead, and Virgil knew who was to blame, no matter what anyone else said.

Virgil's life was coming at him in pieces...little dribs and drabs that made no sense whatsoever. Ron's death had hit him hard—and to a lesser extent, though he was ashamed to admit it—so did the death of Sheriff Ben Holden. And because he hadn't seen or spoken with his dead father since the deaths of Miles and Holden, the whole thing left him feeling...apart from himself. It was a feeling Virgil knew well but handled poorly.

Work was dragging him down, and it wasn't long before everyone began to notice. What started as supportive hugs or words of encouragement, turned into tight nods, the meaning sympathetic, yet the words unspoken. As time went on, he began snapping at his coworkers to the point where if they happened to see him walking down the hall, they'd suddenly realize they'd forgotten something, turn around, and walk the other way...or duck into their office until he'd left the building. When they'd all finally had enough, somebody whispered into Cora's ear, and Cora LaRue—both Virgil's boss and the governor's chief of staff—said something to the lieutenant governor, who, as it happened, was Virgil's wife. After a few staffing questions regarding current caseloads and the MCU's ability to function, Sandy assured Cora that she'd handle it.

And she did...in her own unique way.

THE WEEKEND HAD COME AND GONE, AND WHEN Monday morning rolled around, Virgil got up early and ran three hard miles to try to clear the thick, dense fog inside his own head. He'd been through this before...the junkyard of thoughts tumbling down into the basement of his brain. His friend, Patty Doyle, had been through it as well. She once described it to Virgil as a thought tornado. And that's exactly what it was. But no matter how he or anyone else described it, the bottom line was this: Virgil was once again suffering from PTSD, brought on by his own actions which ultimately cost Ron Miles his life.

He quietly showered in one of the guest bathrooms, then dressed in his usual: jeans, a white T-shirt, and half-top boots. He grabbed his badge, gun, and truck keys, and tried to sneak out of the house before anyone else was up. Virgil loved his family more than anything in the world, but lately, if someone even looked at him the wrong way, he'd snap and say something he'd later regret.

The sneaking out didn't work. Sandy was waiting for him in the kitchen.

---

"TRYING TO LEAVE WITHOUT SAYING GOODBYE?" SANDY said. Her blond hair was sleep-tangled, and she wore an oversized light blue sweatshirt that did little to hide the curves of her body. Her feet were bare, her toenails painted a deep shade of red so dark they almost looked black. She was leaning with her butt against the counter, her arms crossed. Her voice was pleasant enough, but when she smiled it didn't show in her eyes.

"I wanted to get down to the office a little early today," Virgil said. "There's some paperwork that Cora wanted—"

Sandy hip-checked herself off the counter, walked over to her husband, and placed her hands on his chest. "You were going to the cemetery again, weren't you?"

Virgil raked his teeth across his bottom lip and didn't answer. Sandy simply stared at him and waited it out. Finally, he said, "It's on the way. I thought I'd put some fresh flowers on Ron's grave."

"Virgil, the gesture is nice, but you can't keep going there all the time. I don't think it's helping you. In fact, I'd say it's making things worse."

"I don't see how it could possibly be any worse. I sent the man to his death."

"And now this is your penance?"

Virgil took a step back, and Sandy's hands fell from his chest. "What if it is? What's wrong with that?"

"I just told you what's wrong with it, Virgil. I think it's making things worse. You've got to find a way to get out of your own head."

"So you're the expert now?" The words were no sooner out of his mouth when he saw a mask of hurt and frustration wash over his wife's face. "I'm sorry," Virgil said. "I didn't mean that the way it sounded. Yes, I was trying to sneak out of the house. I didn't want to hurt you by saying the wrong thing...again."

Sandy let it go. "Do you remember what I said after the whole ordeal at the speedway?"

"I remember the catsuit," Virgil said with a slight grin. A brief moment of love expressed at what had the potential to turn into yet another argument.

Sandy took the compliment but held on to her question. "That's not what I asked."

Virgil looked down at his wife's feet for a moment, then said, "Yes, I remember. Your mind was made up and you were going to wave that flag and do your thing no matter what. After Mok's men died and Baker got shot, you said it felt like it was your fault."

"And what did you tell me?"

"Sandy..."

"Say the words, Virgil. You need to hear yourself say them."

"I was speaking about you, not me."

"Say it," Sandy said, a little bite in her voice.

"I said it wasn't your fault." He practically shouted it at her.

"So...was it true, or were you just trying to make me feel better?"

Virgil had walked right into the trap. If he said it was true for her, then that meant it was true for himself as well. If he said it hadn't been true, then he'd be putting a burden back on his wife...one she didn't deserve. He ran his fingers through his hair—he wore it long for a cop—and finally said, "It was true then, for you...but that was different."

"How? How is it different, Virgil?" Sandy was getting a little loud herself. "Are you different from the rest of us? Better? Wait, don't bother answering. I'll just say it: You're not. You didn't kill Ron anymore than I killed Mok's men. You've got to find a way to let this go."

"I'm trying." Still loud.

"Try harder," Sandy said. She put some teeth into her statement.

Virgil looked at his wife for a few seconds, then walked over toward the back door. He put his hand on the knob and said, "I'm giving it everything I've got."

"Wrong," Sandy said, her finger pointed straight at him. "You're not giving yourself, or anyone else for that matter, one single inch."

Virgil yanked the door open but Sandy wasn't done. "Mac wants you and Murton in his office at nine if you can pull yourself free from the cemetery."

"That's a shitty thing to say." He slammed the door on his way out.

Sandy let her chin rest against her chest and thought, *He's right. It was a shitty thing to say. What was I thinking?* She was about to chase him down and apologize when she heard the sniffling coming from the other room. When she turned, she saw one of their sons, Jonas, standing there, tears running down his cheeks. "Why are you and Dad yelling at each other?"

*Probably because we're both scared out of our minds,* Sandy thought. She went to Jonas and wrapped him in a hug. "It's okay, sweetheart. Your daddy is just sad because of what happened with Mr. Ron, and sometimes when people are sad, they get angry."

Jonas wiped his eyes and said, "He looked so mad I didn't even bother with the swear jar."

Sandy nodded, and despite herself, let out a little chuckle. "That's probably for the best. We'll let him have this one, okay, big guy? Give mommy just a second and I'll get you some breakfast." She walked to the front door and pulled it open just in time to see Virgil's truck fishtail out of the drive and head down the road.

---

VIRGIL AND SANDY HAD TWO BOYS, THEIR ADOPTED SON Jonas, and their biological son, Wyatt. Since Sandy was the lieutenant governor, and Virgil's job had the potential to take him anywhere in the state at a moment's notice, they also had a live-in nanny, a wonderful woman named Huma Moon.

Huma was in love with a man named Delroy Rouche, who was a Jamaican bartender, one who Virgil and his father, Mason, had hired years ago to help run their bar, a joint now called Jonesy's Rastabarian. After Mason died, his will stipulated that Delroy, and another Jamaican, Robert Whyte, along with Virgil and his adoptive brother, Murton Wheeler, would all own a piece of the bar together. It worked out well for everyone. Delroy and Robert ran the bar, while Virgil and Murton ran down criminals for the state.

When Delroy and Huma began dating, then managed to quickly fall in love, Virgil and Sandy added an entire wing onto the house so Delroy could move in. They didn't want to lose Huma. She was, they knew, worth her weight in gold. Plus, there was quite a bit of history there, with Huma, whose entrance into their lives wasn't exactly what anyone would call accidental.

---

WITH VIRGIL GONE AND THE ENTIRE HOUSE NOW awake, Huma took over feeding the kids so Sandy could get ready for work. As it happened, there were plenty of kids to feed. Delroy and Huma had a child of their own, a little girl they'd named Aayla. Virgil and Sandy had also hired a young lady named Sarah Palmer as their house-keeper. During one of Virgil's previous cases, Sarah's boyfriend had been brutally murdered, and with nowhere to go, she ended up staying with Virgil and Sandy. Sarah had a little girl of her own, named Olivia, who everyone called Liv.

When Sarah finally managed to move past her grief regarding the loss of her boyfriend, she happened to meet one of Virgil's coworkers, Andrew Ross. They soon became an item, and Sarah moved out of the house, and in with Ross, though she and her daughter Liv still showed up nearly every day...Sarah to help Huma with the cooking and cleaning, and Liv to play with the other kids. From the outside, it probably looked like overkill, but Virgil and Sandy not only liked it, they could afford it.

As it was, Virgil and Sandy had some money.

Actually, they had a lot.

---

SANDY'S DETAIL DRIVER—A FORMER MILITARY FIGHTER pilot—was a no-nonsense state cop named Emily Baker. When Sandy saw her turn into the drive, she gave all the kids a quick hug and a kiss, told Huma and Sarah that she'd see them tonight, and gave Larry the Dog a scratch on his noggin.

Sarah caught her just as she was going out the door. "I thought maybe I'd make something special for dinner tonight for Virgil. Thought it might help him feel better... or something. Any suggestions?"

Sandy smiled at her and said, "Don't bother. If I have my way, Virgil won't be eating here for a while." She winked at Sarah and walked out the door.

Sarah turned and looked at Huma. "Is it that bad?"

Huma shrugged. "Yes and no. Did you catch that wink?"

"I did."

"I tink the boss has something up her sleeve."

"You're starting to sound more and more like Delroy."

Huma smiled and said, "Tank you."

## CHAPTER FOUR

Sandy climbed into the back of the car, said hello to Baker, then asked, "Was he there?" She was speaking of Virgil and the cemetery. Sandy had asked Baker to do a quick drive-by to check on her way over.

Baker nodded. "Yes, he was. He was sitting with his back against the tombstone. He looked...tired."

. "Did he see you?"

"With all due respect, ma'am, I don't think he would have seen me if I happened to be standing right in front of him."

"I'm not surprised," Sandy said. "We had a little blow-up early this morning."

"Again?"

"I'm afraid so. Let's take a little detour and run over that way. We've got a few minutes to spare, but I want to make sure he's gone to work. He has a meeting with the governor this morning, and it's one he can't afford to miss."

"Yes, ma'am."

"And listen, Baker, how many times do I have to ask? Enough with the 'ma'am,' already. You took a bullet for me."

Baker choked out a laugh. "Not exactly on purpose. Besides, you ended up saving me."

"Regardless of how it went down, after everything we've been through together, it's Sandy, okay?"

"Yes, ma'am." Then: "Sorry. It's the military training."

---

VIRGIL WASN'T AT THE CEMETERY WHEN THEY WENT BY, and Sandy was relieved. She checked her watch and saw they were a little tight on time. "Let's step it up, Baker. I've got a meeting myself."

Baker increased her speed, and as she did that, Sandy took out her phone and made a call. When it was answered, she said, "I'm on my way right now. Where are you?"

"Sitting in the cafeteria drinking the worst cup of coffee I've had in quite some time, and eating a bagel with what could only be described as some rather questionable cream cheese. When do you want me?"

"I'll shoot you a text a few seconds beforehand. It

won't be long. We're almost there. Cora knows you're coming, so you should be able to wait in her office, then walk right in. Everybody else will already be there. And listen, when you come in, I need an *entrance*."

"Don't worry. Entrances are one of my specialties."

"I can't tell you how much I appreciate this," Sandy said.

"For you guys? Anything. Always." Then, *click*.

Baker touched eyes with Sandy in the rearview mirror. "Wheeler?"

Sandy smiled. "No. Someone better...I hope."

———

Murton Wheeler, Virgil's brother and partner, stuck his head into Virgil's office and said, "Did you hear we've been summoned to bend a knee or kiss the ring, or whatever? Nine sharp if my intel is correct."

"Yeah, I heard. Sandy told me this morning right after we chewed each other out. What's the deal?"

"How would I know?" Murton said. "It was your argument."

"Please Murt, don't start with me."

Murton gave his brother a big toothy grin. "I'm not starting anything. I was simply answering the question you asked. Maybe if you polished up your syntax a little, we'd be on the same page." Murton checked his watch. "Anyway, we better hit it if we're going to be on time. And to demonstrate my brotherly love, I'll let your syntactical error slide. In other words, I have no idea."

"Then why do you have that look on your face?" Virgil said.

"What look?"

"The one that says you're up to something."

Murton ignored his brother and said, "Are you driving, or am I?"

---

VIRGIL AND MURTON WALKED INTO CORA'S OFFICE AND discovered she was nowhere to be found. Murton looked at Virgil and shrugged, then headed for the door that connected Cora's office with the governor's.

"Maybe we should wait for Cora," Virgil said. "Mac might be in a meeting or something."

"You worry too much, Jones-man. Mac and Cheese said nine, which, if you look at the clock right over there, you'd see that it is currently two minutes past the appointed time. They're probably in there waiting on us right now."

And they were.

---

LIKE THIS:

Murton walked over to the connecting door, put his hand on the knob, and said, "After you."

Virgil shook his head, walked through the door as Murton pulled it open, then stopped dead in his tracks. He stopped so quickly that Murton bumped into him, then gently shoved him all the way into the room.

A knot of people—every single one of them Virgil knew and loved—all looked over at him. Then, with a dull, almost cynical sarcasm, they all simultaneously said, "Surprise."

Despite himself and the way he was feeling, he shook his head, let out a little chuckle, and said, "Guys…"

---

The governor took charge. "Jonesy, take a seat. That's not a request." Then he took note of the sport coat Murton wore, tipped a finger at him, and said, "We'll discuss that another time."

Murton smiled. "I'm available anytime, sir."

Virgil took a seat at the conference table, looked at Sandy, and said, "What's going on?"

Murton's wife, Becky, made a rude noise with her lips and said, "I'm surprised you have to ask. It's called a PPI. That stands for personal and professional intervention."

The governor took a seat behind his desk, kicked off his shoes, put his feet up on the corner, and wiggled his toes. His socks were dark blue with little gold sailboats stitched in an intricate pattern. "The thing is, Jonesy, we're all worried about you."

"Mac—"

Cora pointed a finger at Virgil and he shut up.

"Now," the governor said, "as I was saying, we are worried about you, both personally and professionally, although to be honest, I think Becky made up the PPI acronym. Anyway, after consulting with my chief of staff —who I know for a fact, you do not want to piss off—and everyone else in this room, we've collectively decided that enough is enough. It's time to get your head on straight, and we are here to help you, out of both love and respect."

Virgil wasn't quite annoyed, but he didn't want to be bullied into seeing a shrink or some damned thing. He'd worked his way out of this condition before, and he'd do it again, on his own time, and in his own way. He looked the governor in the eye and said, "Well, Jesus Christ, Mac, what are you going to do? Fire me again?"

The governor didn't flinch. "If I have to, although I don't think it'll come to that." He swiveled his chair and said, "Sandy?"

Sandy sat down next to her husband, then leaned close and whispered into his ear. "I'm sorry about this morning. You're right. It *was* a shitty thing to say."

Virgil gave her thigh a squeeze. "So what's the deal?"

Sandy leaned back and said, "You've really got nothing going on at the moment, and I know you've got about three billion weeks of vacation time in the bank. We've worked out a plan..."

Virgil was immediately suspicious. "What sort of plan?"

"I think that's what she's trying to tell you right now, Jonesy," Becky said.

Sandy waited until she was sure she had her husband's full attention. "The plan is simple enough. We thought it might be a good idea if you and Murton took a trip down to the island for a week or so. Spend some time getting your head together."

Virgil loved Jamaica, but he was already shaking his head. "Sandy, I don't think—"

"Virgil. Stop. You're not thinking...or you're not thinking straight, anyway. Consider it a brother's escape. It's something you guys could do together."

"Ah, I don't know."

"That's the problem, Virgil. You don't know. You don't know what to do and you're driving everyone crazy around here. Do it for yourself, Virgil, or do it for the rest of us. Frame it any way you like, but just do it. You need this. Get away. Get some fresh Jamaican air into your lungs. Get some sunshine on your face."

In other words, get out.

———

THEY ALL TALKED IT BACK AND FORTH FOR ABOUT HALF an hour. Near the end, Virgil said, "What about our caseload?"

Cora waved him off. "Ross and Rosencrantz are on top of the Tate case, and I'm sure they can handle anything that comes along. You're only looking at a week."

Virgil looked at Sandy. "And the boys?"

"The boys?" Sandy said. "Look Virgil, I'm not trying to be harsh with you, but when you left this morning, Jonas overheard our...discussion, and it left him in tears. And let's be honest, some of your cases? You've been gone longer than a week."

"It feels selfish," Virgil said.

"It is selfish, Virgil. That's the point. You need to start taking care of yourself."

"What about the bar?"

Murton laughed. "The bar? What about it? When was the last time you were even in the bar? Delroy and Robert run the show, and they do it better than anyone. You know that."

Virgil was running out of excuses and he knew it. He played one last card. "Look, I know we can afford it, but I don't want to sit in an airliner for four hours next to some snot-nosed kid. I'd probably be sick the entire time I'm down there."

As soon as Virgil started talking about the travel, Sandy pressed the Send button on her phone. He'd no sooner finished his comment about getting sick when the governor's office door opened, and Nichole Pope walked in like she owned the joint. She went straight to the governor's desk, leaned over, and kissed Mac on the lips, letting the kiss linger. "I just wanted to pop in to say goodbye...and thank you." She turned back and faced the room. "Hi everybody." Then to Virgil: "I heard that you and Murton are thinking of spending some time on the island. I've got plenty of room on the jet if you guys are looking for a ride."

"Beats the hell out of business class," Murton said.

Nichole gave him a dull smile, and said, "I wouldn't know, I'm sure."

---

VIRGIL FINALLY GAVE IN. THEY WORKED OUT SOME quick details, and once everything was set, Nichole gave the governor another lingering kiss, told Virgil and Murton that she'd meet them at the airport in a couple of hours, then headed for the door.

Sandy stood, and to no one in particular said, "Excuse me for just a minute." She followed Nichole out to the hallway and lightly touched her elbow.

Nichole stopped and turned. "Yes?"

Sandy felt her face redden slightly. "It's none of my business, but are you and Mac...?"

Nichole stuck her tongue in her cheek and said, "You ask for an entrance, you get an entrance. Tell Virgil and Murton two hours. Million-Air FBO. The jet will be ready."

"Nichole, I can't thank you enough. Virgil...he needs this."

"Like I said, for you guys, anything...anytime. Leave Virgil to us. In a week, he'll be back to his old self." Nichole pecked her on the cheek, and said, "It was good to see you again." Then she turned, gave Sandy a little finger wave over her shoulder, and walked away.

———————

BACK IN THE GOVERNOR'S OFFICE: "I DON'T KNOW HOW many times I have to say it, sir, but you really should just go ahead and concede." Murton and the governor both took their wardrobe seriously, and although they both had very different styles, the governor always seemed to be on the defensive.

"Think what you want, Wheeler," the governor said. "But I concede nothing. My socks probably cost more than that jacket you're wearing."

"Ah...cynicism. The last stand of the weary warrior."

"I am not being cynical," the governor said.

"Maybe not," Becky said. "But you've got a small hole on the bottom of your left sock there, Mac. It's almost like you're not even trying to stay in the game."

The governor grabbed his left foot with both hands and examined the sock. He shook his head and slipped his feet back into his shoes without saying anything. Murton seemed to be staring at nothing.

When Sandy walked back into the room, she looked at her husband and said, "You and Murton better head home and get packed. Baker and I will be there in about an hour. We'll all ride over to the airport together."

Everyone stood, and Murton said, "Sounds like a plan. You ready, Jones-man?"

Virgil nodded, then said, "Almost. If I could have a word with Mac in private?"

---

ONCE EVERYONE WAS OUT IN THE HALL, VIRGIL LOOKED at his friend, the governor, and said, "Mac, I'm sure it's none of my business, but are you and Nichole Pope...?" He let the question hang.

The governor kept a straight face, looked Virgil right in the eye, and said, "You're right. It isn't any of your business. Besides, a gentleman doesn't kiss and tell."

Virgil squinted an eye and chewed on the corner of his lip. "Okay, I get it. None of my business. Say, uh, could I borrow a quarter?"

"A quarter?"

"Yeah, you know...it's a silver coin that equals twenty-five cents."

"I know what a quarter is. Why do you want one?"

"I don't. Not really. But I couldn't help notice that you've got a roll of them in your pants pocket." Then, "That was some kiss, huh?"

The governor very quickly and quite unceremoniously moved back to his chair and sat down. "I see the prospects of a week in Jamaica has someone feeling better already. I think your wife is waiting for you."

Virgil took the hint and moved toward the door.

The governor called out to him at the last second. "Hey, Jonesy?"

Virgil stopped and turned, "Yeah, Mac?"

The governor opened his mouth to speak, but no words came out. They looked at each other until the governor broke eye contact.

"I get it, Mac. Thank you. I'll be fine. See you in a week, huh?"

# CHAPTER FIVE

Virgil and Murton went home to pack, and an hour later, Baker turned into the drive with Sandy and Becky. They brought the limo so there'd be plenty of room for anyone who wanted to ride along to the airport to say goodbye. As it happened, everyone did.

With Baker's help, Huma and Sarah got the kids loaded up and buckled in while Sandy and Becky inspected their husbands' luggage. Murton had a small leather carry bag that looked like it was made from the hide of an exotic bird found only in the northern Horn of Africa.

Virgil had a green canvas duffle with a mustard stain on the side and a frayed drawstring the color of dirt. Sandy looked at the bag and simply said, "No."

"What?" Virgil said. "It's just a bag. Who cares?"

"C'mon, inside," Sandy said. "This will only take a

minute." To everyone else, she said, "Wait here. We'll be right out."

Sandy led her husband back to the master suite, and Virgil began loosening the string on his bag. "I still don't see what the big deal is," Virgil said. He had his back to Sandy. "I'm not trying to impress anyone with my luggage."

"What are you doing?" Sandy said.

"I'm unpacking. Would you grab the suitcase out of the closet for me?"

"Virgil?"

"Yeah?"

"*Virgil?*"

Virgil turned around and saw that Sandy had stripped out of her dress. She stood there with her hands on her hips, wearing absolutely nothing at all. "I don't want you to unpack," Sandy said. Then she pushed him back on the bed, climbed on top of him, and said, "I want you to *impress* me. And you better make it quick before someone comes looking for us."

———

TEN MINUTES LATER—BECAUSE VIRGIL WAS QUICK— they were back outside and ready to go. Murton looked at Virgil's duffle bag, took note of Sandy's slightly disheveled hair, opened his mouth to say something, and got punched in the arm by Becky. "Shut up," she said.

Murton tipped his head at his wife and said, "Well, if I'd have known there was going to be time to repack..."

Becky kissed him on the cheek. "It's only a week, baby. I think you'll survive. We'll repack when you get back home."

As they were climbing into the limo, Virgil looked at Murton and said, "What? The suitcase had a broken handle." He tossed the duffle in the back and they were off.

---

WHEN THEY ARRIVED AT THE MILLION-AIR FACILITY AT the Indianapolis Airport, the gate slid open and Baker drove right up next to the Bombardier Global 6500 jet. Becky looked out the window and said, "Nichole sure likes to travel in style, doesn't she?"

"Looks exactly like the last plane we were on when we came back from dealing with Brenner," Murton said. Roje Brenner had been a drug kingpin on the island, and a few years ago when Nichole needed their help, Virgil and the entire MCU had flown down and taken care of business.

"I think it is," Virgil said. "We should be down there in time for a late lunch."

They all piled out of the limo, then Virgil and Murton spent a few minutes saying goodbye to everyone. Virgil got down on his knees and hugged his boys, promised them he'd call, and generally tried to make up for his behavior over the last few months in the span of ninety seconds. He kissed Sandy goodbye a second time, told her he loved her, and that he'd see her soon.

Sandy grabbed his T-shirt, bunched it in her fist, looked Virgil in the eyes, and said, "I love you too. Do whatever it takes, but bring my husband back."

"I will. I promise."

Ten seconds later, Virgil and Murton were on board, and the door was closed. Fifteen minutes after that they were in the air, and once past the 250-knot speed restriction of ten thousand feet, everyone settled in and rode comfortably at nearly the speed of sound.

Virgil looked at Nichole and said, "So, you and Mac?"

. Nichole just smiled.

———

VIRGIL HAD BEEN RIGHT. THEY DID ARRIVE IN TIME FOR a late lunch. When Nichole walked them into the guest house, her chef was ready and waiting, just putting together the final touches of their meal. Once that was done, he and Nichole left the men to eat and relax. As she was walking out the door, Nichole said, "Virgil, you know the phones and all that. I'll let you explain everything to Murton. Anything you need, just let us know. Wu said he might stop in tomorrow morning and say hello...among other things." Then she was gone.

The guest house wasn't new to Virgil—he and Sandy had stayed there before—but it was the first time Murton had ever seen the place. He spent a few minutes looking around, then turned to Virgil and said, "You know, being your brother does have its advantages."

Virgil let that go and said, "What do you think Nichole meant about Wu?"

Murton shrugged. "Beats me. She said he wanted to come down and say hello."

"She also said, 'among other things,'" Virgil said. "What's that about?"

"You're asking the wrong guy. C'mon, let's eat. Look at the size of those lobsters." Murton opened the fridge and said, "Want a beer?" Then he turned and glanced at the liquor cabinet. "Wow. This place is stocked better than our bar."

"I'll be sure and let Delroy know your feelings on the subject. And yeah, I'll take a beer."

Murton cracked the tops on two bottles of Red Stripe, then said, "What did she mean about the phones?"

Virgil explained: "Your cell phone won't work down here, even if you have the international plan. Don't ask me why. There are satellite phones on the table behind you. There's a blue phone in the kitchen without a keypad. It rings directly to the head chef. Someone is on duty in the kitchen twenty-four hours a day, and all you have to do is pick it up and let them know what you'd like to eat. The phone over by the sofa rings to the main house. Why are you looking at me like that?"

Murton held up his fork in a wait-a-minute gesture, chewed, then swallowed a bite of lobster. "Oh man, I might be in heaven. I mean, I love Becky with my whole heart, but now I'm sort of hoping it'll take more than a week to get your head straight."

———————

AFTER THEY FINISHED THEIR MEAL, MURTON GRABBED A bottle of over-proof rum, two glasses, and both men walked outside next to the pool. They stripped out of their shirts, poured themselves a drink, and stared out at the hills and the ocean beyond.

"I'll tell you something," Murton said, "this place, this way of life, it could be habit-forming, and I've only been here for a couple of hours."

Virgil nodded without responding.

Murton tried again. "I can see why you come down here almost every year. I'm half surprised you ever make it back."

Another nod.

Murton let a few minutes drift away to wherever drifting minutes tend to go, then said, "Talk to me, man. It's why we're here."

Virgil topped off his drink without responding.

Murton wasn't a quitter, though, and he kept pressing. "I want to tell you something, Virgil, and I need you to hear me."

Virgil turned and looked at his brother.

"Over the last few months, the way you've been struggling with Ron's death...I get it. I really do. Hell, I feel the same way."

"Except you're not the one who screwed up and sent the man to his own execution."

"Look, this is going to sound crass, or whatever, but the man went out happy, on top, doing what he wanted to do. You arranged for him to be sheriff, and I don't think he was ever happier than he was right there, at that moment, doing his thing. But you know what? None of that really matters until you decide to get your balls out and tell the rest of the story."

"What the hell is that supposed to mean?"

"It means that if you want to you'll work your way past Ron's death and any part you think you played in it, but only if you're willing to tell yourself the truth. The whole truth." Virgil started to respond, but Murton put his hand up. "Tell me about your last conversation."

"Why?"

"Because I'm asking. Because I'm trying to help."

"He said he needed a favor and asked if I'd have Becky look up the owner—"

"Stop it," Murton said. A little bite in his voice.

"Stop what? I'm trying to answer your question."

Murton jabbed a finger at his brother. "That's not the question I'm asking and you damned well know it. We all miss Ron. It's sad. It's tragic. It can't be changed. But if I had to put a number to it, I'd say that's only half of the equation, at best. Now, answer the fucking question."

Virgil looked at his brother for a long time before he spoke. "It was before we all went out to dinner that night. He told me he was in a place of peace, and he hoped that

I'd ultimately get there too. He had this look on his face, one I don't believe I've ever seen before. At first I thought it was shock, but then I landed on something else. I asked him if he was disappointed in me."

"And what'd he tell you?" Murton said.

"He said that he'd never been disappointed in me. Not one single time in my entire life. Then I pressed him and asked if it was about the case, but I wouldn't let him answer. I told him to forget it or something because it all worked out. He stared at me hard...I mean hard, Murt, then he said he had to go...that he was being called to do something."

"What was it?"

Virgil shook his head, then put his face in his hands. "Murt, my dad...our dad, he's left me and I think I know why."

This time it was Murton who remained quiet for a beat. Eventually, he said, "Tell me."

"He told me I was going to be asked to do something and I had to refuse."

"I know that," Murton said.

"Yeah, except I didn't refuse, and now Ron is dead, and my dad is gone. What if I never see him again? The whole thing is tearing me up inside."

---

THEY SKIPPED DINNER, DRANK TOO MUCH, TALKED OFF and on, argued about things that didn't really matter, and even had the brief, occasional laugh. Murton thought he might have made some progress, but he knew it was too soon to tell. Eventually, the day caught up with him, and as the stars twinkled in time with the lights scattered across the hillside, he told Virgil he was going to bed. When he didn't get a response, he looked over and noticed that his brother was asleep. He went inside, grabbed a blanket, and covered him up.

Once he was alone in his room, Murton did something he rarely did. He asked for Mason's help. If there was any kind of response, he didn't hear it.

# CHAPTER SIX

YEARS AGO:

A s the killer drove home—he lived in Prospect, Indiana, just north of the Lost River—he kept his speed limit where it belonged and let his mind wander. He wouldn't be going directly to his house in town. He'd go to his other place...a plot of land northeast of Highway 56. There, he kept a modest two-bedroom hunting cabin tucked neatly into the woods, not visible from the road. When he found the land, he couldn't afford it at the time, but he managed to talk his father into buying it, and he made the payments to him. He worked hard on the property, tearing down the ancient farmhouse that had long ago gone to seed, then building a new cabin in its place. The cabin was meant for his father with the hope that maybe one day he'd move a little closer...or perhaps even move in permanently, but that had never happened. The old man didn't want to hunt or be out in nature. He wanted to sit around in his big empty house in French Lick, all by himself, and do nothing but drink.

Except the old man's house wasn't exactly empty. The truth was, it was stuffed to the gills with high-end furnishings that were probably valued in the hundreds of thousands, stacks of bearer bonds in the safe worth nearly a half million, and roll after roll of Canadian Maple Leaf gold coins valued at almost two million, give or take, depending on the market. The old man had done well for himself over the years, and the killer knew it. The problem was, so did his siblings.

Thus, the cabin. But no matter how hard he pushed the idea, his father wouldn't budge, so now he was reduced to stopping by and visiting with the old man every few days. It was a pain in the ass, but also a necessity because his sister—rotten bitch that she was—lived in West Baden Springs, which was a bit closer to French Lick, and she'd go over twice a day...once in the morning to check on him, then once in the evening to take him his dinner. It made the killer sick. She was working the old man for his money, and the cranky old coot seemed to be buying into the whole enchilada.

If the killer didn't know better—and he wasn't completely sure he didn't—he thought she might be blowing the old man to keep him happy and satisfied. She'd do anything to get her hands on the money.

The killer's mother had died of cancer exactly nine years ago today. He shook his head at the thought of how time flew by. After she died, everyone knew—though no one said anything—that it really wasn't cancer that took her...it was the old man's emotional and mental abuse that finally took her down. It caused her body to turn on itself, to wither and die as a means of escape from the horrors of her everyday life.

And that, he thought, was why he took the girls. Something had snapped inside him the day he lost his mom. He felt the need to somehow save someone so they'd never have to experience what his mother had been forced to endure. He'd do it in her honor.

It took him a full year to plan and prepare for the first one. He'd done everything exactly right, and on the anniversary of his mother's death, he took his first. But the taking wasn't enough. He had to explain to the girls what he was doing and why. He had to let them know that there were monsters everywhere, men who would physically and mentally abuse them for no reason other than the fact that they couldn't conquer their own demons without ripping themselves apart...something none of them seemed able to accomplish. He had to explain that he was actually saving them from a life of pain, misery, and suffering.

As a child, he'd done everything right. He kept the old man off his mother, kept him preoccupied and as happy as he could. He became a pleaser. But it was never enough. His work was never done. He was a savior, and so he did what he'd always done. It was what was expected of him. Unspoken, but expected, still.

He was, after all, the golden boy of the family.

Don Whittle.

Guidance counselor.

Coach.

Killer.

---

HE TURNED INTO THE DRIVE AND MADE HIS WAY BACK through the tree line, and when he pulled around to the rear of the cabin, he saw his sister, Karen, leaning against her car. He swore under his breath, parked by the detached garage, got out, and said, "What's going on? Is Dad okay?"

Karen waved him off like it was a stupid question. "Yeah, yeah. Not getting any better, but right now he's okay. Blood pressure is up, he won't take the meds...says they give him headaches. Plus the doc told him he couldn't drink if he takes the pills. Even with all that, knowing our luck, the bastard will probably outlive us both."

"Hate to see that happen," Don said. "Sam would get everything."

Karen bared her teeth. "Fuck Sam, the hotshot writer. He thinks he's king shit because he sells a few novels. He lives less than a half-mile from Dad, and I don't think the two of them have spoken in over two years. At least that's what Dad tells me."

"What does Sam tell you?"

"Almost the exact same thing, but I haven't seen him in a while, myself. Plus, you know how it was with those two. I don't think I've ever seen a father more disappointed with a child, or a child more disgusted with a parent."

"Look who's talking," Don said. "It wasn't exactly a cakewalk for you, the way I remember it."

Karen seemed to soften. "No, it wasn't. But it wasn't all bad, either. You remember that, don't you?"

"What? You're talking about Christmas? They were all a joke."

Karen pointed a finger at him. "They were not."

Don actually laughed. "Yeah, Karen, they were. Don't you remember how extravagant everything was? How there were so many presents on Christmas we had to take breaks while we were still opening everything? And the way Dad would make everyone wait and watch while one of us unwrapped a gift? We had to do it one at a time. It was almost sick. The gifts weren't for us. They were for him, so he could feel like king for a day."

"That's not true."

"Yeah, it is. If it's not, then answer this: How could the man spend the other 364 days of the year beating us to a pulp—physically, emotionally, mentally—then one day...one fucking day, he'd shower us with the most expensive gifts he could find? Or how about this: The way he'd get drunk and make a big speech about how much it all cost? What about all that?"

"It was just his way," Karen said.

"It was bullshit, is what it was. A bullshit way of apologizing. And guess what? It didn't work. Don't you remember the way mom would always say she was sorry each time one of us opened a present? *Sorry?* What kind of way is that to give someone a gift. She wasn't sorry about the presents. She was sorry about the way we were abused all year long, except on that one magical day when everything was right with our world, even though it wasn't. That's why she was always apologizing."

"He got her a lot of nice stuff, too," Karen said.

"Yeah, and he made damned sure everyone knew how much it set him back. Here's a news flash for you, Karen. All those diamond earrings and gold bracelets and ruby and sapphire necklaces he gave her...like she was his queen? He'd leave the price tags on them so she'd know how much they all cost. Those weren't tears of joy we saw on her face every year. They were tears of guilt, sorrow, and shame."

Karen shook her head and waved her hands in front of her face as if she could erase her brother's words from the air. "I don't want to talk about that anymore. You've got your opinion, and I've got mine. Let's just leave it at that."

Don shrugged. "Fine with me. I'm just trying to help... to get you to see the truth."

"Well, here's some truth, and you're not going to like it very much."

"What now?"

"He went out and bought a Mercedes," Karen said.

Don rolled his eyes. "So what? He's always liked his cars."

"Yeah well, this one is a brand new convertible SL, top of the line."

Don visibly swallowed. "That's not good."

"You've got that right. The question is, what are we going to do about it?"

Don thought for a moment, then said, "Nothing, I guess. It's his money."

Karen got right in his face. "No, it's not, dummy. It's our money. We've got to rein him in somehow. He's spending our inheritance right out from under us."

"Maybe we could get him committed," Don said. "Mental incapacity or something like that."

Karen was already shaking her head. "That won't work. Plus, I can't afford a legal battle right now. The casino has cut my hours, and with your gambling debts, I'm guessing you can't either. And even if we could, if we lost, guess who gets cut out of the will?"

Don looked at her for a moment. "Have you ever seen the will?"

"Of course I have. I'm the executor. I've got a copy at home."

"What's in it?" Don said.

When Karen told him, Don was so stunned he could hardly speak. "That's...that's...that's..."

"Shut up. You sound like a stuck record."

Don got his words under him and said, "That's not fair. That can't be right. *Can't be.*"

Karen didn't seem all that worried. "It is what it is. We'll deal with it when the time comes." Then she looked over at her brother's van. "You've got to stop doing that. You're gonna get caught." Karen knew what was in the van, and when she spoke, her words sounded as if she might simply be referring to the spare tire.

Don had made the mistake of sharing his secret with his sister after he'd taken the second girl, six years ago. He was drunk, and so overcome with grief on the anniversary of his mother's death that he simply blurted it out one day. Karen acted like it was no big deal. She knew her brother was bent...and she knew she was as well. "Someone has to save them," Don said. "I'm honoring mom."

"No, you're not," Karen said. "You're trying to kill yourself. You're just not very good at it."

"I'll tell you when I'll stop," Don said. "I'll stop when the old man finally croaks and I can get on with my life."

Karen laughed with her shoulders. "Like that'll ever happen." Then she got in her car and drove away without another word.

Don didn't know if she was speaking of the rapes and murders he'd committed over the years or their father's eventual death.

Either way.

———————

ONCE SHE WAS GONE, DON CAREFULLY OPENED THE van's sliding door, then quickly jumped back. He didn't want to get kicked in the face, a lesson he'd learned the hard way after taking the third girl. She was a fighter, that one.

The fighting turned his crank like nothing ever had. All those years of being a pleaser, being the savior of the family, the leader of the kids even though he was the youngest child...they wore him down. He'd let the girls out of the van, and with their hands still bound behind their backs, they all tried to run. He'd chase them down, then tackle them and beat them into submission. It wasn't that hard.

Once he had them subdued, he'd carefully cut their clothes from their bodies, spend a few minutes admiring them, then he gave them a chance. He told them that if they could fight and beat him, they'd be free. All they had to do was fight for their life, something his mother had never quite understood. So they fought. Two of them were actually pretty good. One even scared him, as she'd nearly kicked his ass. But so far, none of the girls had gotten away.

When he looked inside the van at number eight, he knew she wasn't going to get away either. He'd pushed her head into the tree trunk a little harder than he thought.

She was already dead.

Don Whittle sat down on the ground and cried. Eventually, he got himself together, lifted the girl from the van, and carried her like the child she was to his special place in the woods...the whole time saying over and over again, "I'm sorry, Mom. I'm so sorry. You should have fought. I did everything I could, but you should have fought. I'm so sorry..."

## CHAPTER SEVEN

PRESENT-DAY:

The next morning, Wu walked down to the guesthouse and around back to the pool area. He knew that Virgil had slept outside all night because he'd kept an eye on him via the security cameras. He hadn't listened in on Virgil and Murton's conversation...he wasn't spying on them, but he was watching, mostly to make sure that Virgil was okay.

Wu was many things, among them, computer coder, hacker, thief, fighter...and physical fitness freak. At five foot two, and ninety-five pounds, he looked like he could be blown away by the slightest of island breezes. But looks could be deceiving, as some of his past adversaries had learned the hard way.

He walked over to Virgil's chaise lounge and gave the chair a little kick. It was six in the morning.

When Virgil didn't stir, Wu gave the chair another nudge. Virgil mumbled something unintelligible and pulled the blanket tighter around his body.

Murton walked outside with a cup of coffee and said, "Morning, Wu."

"Morning to Wu too. I think Virgil has overindulged."

Murton smiled. "That might be a bit of an understatement. Can't believe he slept in that chair all night."

"We are to get his head on straight if my information is correct."

Murton took a sip of his coffee and said, "That's the plan. Any suggestions on how to start?"

Wu tipped his head to the side, and said, "PTSD is something that must be taken very seriously. Wu has never experienced it, but I have studied it."

Murton was impressed. "For how long?"

"Many years, actually. I once had a friend..." Wu shook his head. "A story for another time, perhaps. But, PTSD... many people think it is a made-up problem, like chronic fatigue. It is not. It is an actual physical and emotional disorder in which a person has difficulty recovering after experiencing or witnessing a terrifying event. It can change the brain's chemistry and is not to be taken lightly. I understand that he has been through it before."

Murton nodded. "He has. We both have, I guess, but for Jonesy...I don't know...he has trouble letting it go."

"That is because it is not something you let go of. It is something you rid yourself of. In many cases, if nothing is done, the condition may last months or even years, with triggers that can bring back memories of the trauma causing intense emotional and physical reactions."

"That sounds like our boy," Murton said.

"Tell Wu of his symptoms."

Murton took another sip of coffee and looked at nothing as he considered Wu's question. "He's been depressed, he overreacts to certain situations, he's easily irritated, and he's told me on more than one occasion that he can't quiet the noise in his head. He calls it a thought tornado."

"He has not tried any medications?"

"No, he's too stubborn."

"That mean Wu will have to do it the hard way."

"What, exactly, is the hard way?"

"Virgil's treatment will include different types of trauma-focused psychotherapy in multiple steps to help rewire his brain. Wu can do."

Murton raised his eyebrows. "You seem awfully sure of yourself, Wu. How many steps are there?"

"That not up to Wu. It up to Virgil."

Murton nodded. "Okay. Sounds simple enough. What's step one?"

"This," Wu said. He reached down and pulled the blanket away from Virgil, who was still sleeping.

Murton laughed quietly. "That's it? That's step one? Let him get a sunburn?"

Wu shook his head. "No. Sunburn is very bad for skin and can lead to complications later in life. Still, the removal of the blanket as step one marks the beginning of the process."

"Okay, I get it," Murton said. "It's more of a ritualistic thing."

"That is one way of looking at it."

"Is there another?"

"Yes. It is the prerequisite for the next step, of which we are now ready."

"What's the next step?"

Virgil was a big man. He weighed a tad over two hundred pounds—virtually none of it fat—and stood about a half-inch over six feet tall. Basically, he was twice the size of Wu. What Murton saw next made him wonder if he should laugh out loud, or run back inside, pack, and get the hell off the island.

Wu bent over, his arms and legs corded with muscle, and gently snaked one hand under Virgil's neck, the other behind his knees. Then he picked him up and tossed him into the pool. He looked at Murton and said, "That is step Wu. I will be back after breakfast. Chef will bring fresh fruit down shortly." Then he turned and walked away.

Virgil was thrashing about, trying to get his bearings, and he looked like a drunken sailor who'd fallen from the stern of his own ship. Murton laughed, then went inside to get a towel for his brother. And a cup of coffee. Maybe some aspirin as well.

VIRGIL GOT HIMSELF TOWELED OFF, PUT ON CLEAN clothes, took some aspirin, drank a cup of coffee, and through it all, was thoroughly pissed. "What the fuck was that?"

Murton, known for his big toothy grins, gave his brother one and said, "According to your sensei, that was step Wu."

"Very funny, Murt. Where is he?"

"Who? Wu?"

"Knock it off," Virgil said. "You sound like an owl. Yes, Wu."

"He said he was going to go get some breakfast, then he'd be back."

"Yeah, well, when he gets down here I'm going to wring his neck."

Murton tipped his head to the side, serious now. "Think you could?"

"We're gonna find out," Virgil said.

"Ah, lighten up, Jones-man. He's a friend. He's trying to help. It's why we're here."

"I came down here to clear my head, not to get thrown in the pool."

"It was sort of funny. I guess now we know what Nichole meant when she said, 'Among other things.'"

"Whatever. When he gets back, he's the one who's going in the pool."

"Wu you talking about?" Wu said.

Virgil spun around and when he saw Wu he headed straight toward him like a steamroller. Wu held his ground, stuck out his hand in a stop sign fashion, then held up a single finger and made a *ssst, ssst, ssst,* noise. It stopped Virgil in his tracks.

Wu smiled, did a polite little bow, and very formally said, "Good morning, Virgil."

Virgil pointed his finger at him. They were standing about two feet apart. "Nobody puts their hands on me, Wu. Nobody. Understood?"

Then before Virgil ever knew what was happening, Wu reached out—lightning quick—and lightly slapped Virgil four times...once on each shoulder, and twice on the sides of his neck. His hands were back at his sides before Virgil registered that he'd been touched.

"I think you are mistaken," Wu said.

Virgil shook his head, and said, "Oh that's it." Virgil didn't want to hurt Wu...they *were* friends after all, but he wasn't going to let him get away with anything. He moved to slap him, but when he did, all he caught was empty air.

"Too slow for Wu, it would seem."

Virgil, still pissed about being thrown in the pool, reached out to grab Wu. He was going to put him in a bear hug, toss him in the pool, and give him a taste of his own medicine. But when he reached out, Wu took one step back, turned his body just so, and when Virgil stepped forward, Wu slipped in behind him and tapped him on the back three times.

"If you do not like others to put their hands on you, it seems you would try harder to prevent such a thing from occurring."

Virgil was gritting his teeth. "Wu, I'm done playing. Knock it off." What Virgil didn't realize was that when he and Wu swapped positions, it put his back to the pool.

Wu smiled and held up his hands. "Wu apologize. It was wrong to throw you in the pool. I can see now that you did not like it."

"Would you?" Virgil said. He practically yelled it at him.

"Of course not. That is why it has never happened."

Virgil was beginning to calm down. "Yeah, well, that's because you weren't sleeping at the time."

"Are you asleep now?" Wu asked.

Virgil put as much sarcasm as he could into his voice. "Nooo."

"That is good," Wu said. "It is always better to be awake when you hit the water."

Then, quick as a cat, he stepped forward and pushed Virgil into the pool for the second time that morning.

Murton was laughing so hard he didn't notice Wu moving toward him. Murton ended up in the water as well.

———

Once they were back out of the pool and dried off again, Virgil looked at Murton and said, "Not so funny when it happens to you, is it?"

But Murton had never been one to let others get over on him. "That's where you're wrong, Jones-man. I thought it was funny. Besides, I was going to take a morning dip myself. I wasn't going to do it fully clothed, mind you, but it was refreshing."

Virgil was still annoyed. "You seem to think this whole thing is some kind of joke or something."

"Well, one of us does, that's for sure. Want to know who it is? Go look in the mirror."

Virgil pointed a finger at him. "Look, I agreed to come down here with you so we could spend some time together and I could clear my head. What I didn't come down for was to get man-handled by—"

"Hey, Virgil?"

"What?"

"Relax. Go with the flow. I had a little conversation with Wu while you were sleeping. I think he knows what he's talking about."

"Wu do," Wu said.

Virgil and Murton turned around in their chairs and saw Wu walking over. Virgil started to stand, but Murton put a hand on his arm and held him in place. Wu sat down and looked directly at Virgil.

"Wu give you his word on two things: One, I can help if you want me to."

"What's the other thing?" Virgil said.

"If you do exactly what I tell you, Wu not throw you in pool ever again."

Virgil stared at his little Asian friend for a long hard minute. He'd promised his wife and children that when he came back home, he'd be his old self again. And not only did he promise, Virgil knew they deserved it. He owed it to them. Finally, he said, "What did you have in mind?"

Wu spent the next twenty minutes laying out his plan. When he was finished, Virgil looked at Murton and said, "And you're on board with all this, because if I'm doing it, you are too."

Murton shrugged. "Why not? I like a good adventure. Besides, I could stand to clear a few cobwebs out of my brainpan as well. It all sort of sounds like that old Karate Kid movie. You know, Wax on, Wax off."

Wu laughed. "By the end of the week, you will both be too tired to wax off." Then he slapped his thighs like it was the funniest thing in the world.

# CHAPTER EIGHT

Wu worked them like dogs all week long, from sunrise to sunset. They ran the hills of Hanover Parish, eventually working their way up to ten miles a day. In addition to the running, he had them do manual labor around the estate—everything from cutting the grass, painting a few of the outbuildings, and replacing part of the roof on the guest house garage. They worked with Chef to prepare their own meals, and they labored with a construction crew to build a new home for a local family in Lucea. For some odd reason, they hand-shoveled an entire dump-truck load of dirt from one side of the drive to the other. They helped cater a large event, working as humble busboys, rebuilt two engines on a couple of Cushman scooters, and in general, whatever Wu told them to do. The only time they were allowed breaks was for water, to use the bathroom, have lunch, or meditate.

Virgil thought the whole meditation part was bullshit, but Wu made him do it.

By the fifth day, Virgil noticed he was waking up in the morning with a quiet mind, and a sense of calm he'd not felt in a very long time. He started looking forward to the meditation, doing it on his own every night before bed... box breathing and focusing on nothing except the end of his nose.

On the day before they were scheduled to leave, Wu asked Virgil how he was feeling.

"I'm exhausted, Wu. But if I'm being honest with you, I've never felt better."

"Wu told you. Relax your mind, work your body, rewire your brain. Your fog is gone?"

Virgil nodded. "It is."

"And your cerebral cyclones?"

Virgil gave him an odd look, then he immediately got it, and laughed. "You mean the thought tornados?"

"Yes. Wu being funny. It one of my many gifts. Just ask Nicky."

"That might be debatable," Virgil said. "But to answer your question, yes, the thought tornados are gone."

"Do you feel you are done?"

Virgil nodded. "I do."

Wu looked at Murton and said, "Today, you may do as you wish." Then to Virgil, "You are mistaken. You have one more task to complete."

"What is it?"

"Come. Wu show you."

They walked from the guest house, turned out on the road, and began climbing the hill that would take them up to the Brenner estate—a property now owned by the Popes. When they arrived, Virgil noticed that Brenner's house had been demolished, and the grounds had been turned into a park with a large community garden.

"It is beautiful, no?"

Virgil had to agree. It was almost artistic in nature. There were all sorts of tropical plants and flowers, fruits and vegetables, a large recreational area, shade trees with park benches, and a cement path that snaked its way through the various sections of the park.

"It is beautiful, Wu. Looks nothing like the last time I saw it." Then he got suspicious. "I'm not here to pull weeds or something, am I?"

Wu shrugged. "You may, if you wish, though I do not believe you will find many."

"Then why are we here?" Virgil said.

Wu shook his head. "Not we. You. Wu is leaving now."

"I don't understand," Virgil said. "You told me I had one more thing to do."

"You do."

"So what is it?"

"You tell me," Wu said. Then he reached into his pocket, pulled out a Pond apple and tossed it to Virgil before walking away.

VIRGIL FOLLOWED THE PATH DOWN THE HILL TOWARD the back of the property. The only things that remained of Brenner's presence were the small table and chairs next to the two Pond apple trees. Years ago, Delroy and Robert had buried Delroy's girlfriend and their infant child after a series of tragic events, then planted the trees above their graves.

Virgil sat down on one of the chairs, the shade of the trees blocking out the sun. A plate of fresh fruit had been set out on the table—by whom, Virgil didn't know. A small cooler filled with ice and bottles of water sat between the chairs. Virgil set the apple on the table, popped a bite of fruit into his mouth, opened a bottle of water, then wondered what, exactly he was supposed to do, other than eat breakfast by himself.

"I see you're back amongst the living," Nichole said. She came out from behind the trees and sat down with an apple of her own.

"Jesus, Nichole, you scared the hell out of me."

She placed the apple on the table and said, "Sorry." She gestured at the fruit on the table, and said, "I wanted to bring you a bite to eat and see how you're doing."

Virgil stood and pulled the other chair into position for her. "Have a seat." He grabbed a bottle of water from the cooler, handed it to Nichole, and said, "I was beginning to wonder if I was going to see you at all this week."

Nichole laughed, and said, "If you'd been paying attention, you'd have seen me plenty of times."

Virgil raised an eyebrow at her.

"You really shouldn't do that," Nichole said. "Anyway, I've been watching you all week."

"What? When?"

"Everywhere, Jonesy. I was the old lady you waved to every day when you made the turn at the end of the road while jogging. I bussed tables with you at the catering event. I was the one who delivered the engine parts when you guys were working on the scooters. I also drove the truck and delivered the shingles for the roof. You signed the delivery form I handed you...like that. A girl's gotta stay sharp."

Nichole's ability to disguise herself was almost legendary. "I'm impressed," Virgil said. "And I think you can rest easy. You're as good as you ever were."

"Thank you. So, what do you think of our little park?"

"It's gorgeous. You guys took a place that represented the worst this island had to offer and turned it into something beautiful. There's just one thing I don't understand."

Nichole cocked her head at him. "What's that?"

"Where the heck is everyone? I thought the place would be packed."

"It will be soon. But I've arranged to let you have it to yourself this morning for a little while."

"Why?"

Nichole stood, and said, "I'll be going now." Then she bent down, kissed Virgil lightly on the cheek, and said, "And you're right, this place is beautiful. Some might even say magical."

Virgil watched her walk away, thinking about the first time he'd ever met the woman, and how at the end of the investigation he'd told her he hoped to never see her again. And now, here he was, counting himself among those who called her a friend...and a good one at that, even though he'd shot and killed her father over twenty-five years ago.

"Makes you wonder about the state of life, sometimes, doesn't it, Son?"

Virgil had been so caught up in his own thoughts as he watched Nichole walk away, he didn't notice his father had taken a seat in the other chair. He felt the weight on his heart leave him as if someone had just removed a boulder from his chest. "Dad...I didn't think I'd ever see you again." His voice trembled when he spoke.

"Why not?" Mason said. He was bare-chested, as usual, a bar towel thrown over his shoulder. The scar where the bullet had punched through his chest and cost him his life was pink and fresh as if the wound had healed only days ago. He popped a piece of fruit into his mouth and gave his son a good-natured smile.

"It's been over three months," Virgil said.

"Has it?"

"Dad..."

Mason winked at him. "Okay, fair enough. I just wanted to make sure we didn't have to recap the whole time issue...again."

"Why did you leave me? It was tearing me up inside."

"I never left you, Virg. Not once. I've been with you all along. It's my blood that runs through the rivers of your heart."

Virgil turned and looked away from his father for a few minutes, mostly because he thought he might be hallucinating. When he turned back though, his father was still there.

"What were you thinking just now?" Mason said.

"I thought I might be imagining all this."

"You're not."

"If you've been with me all along, how come I haven't seen you?"

"Maybe for the same reason you didn't notice Nichole all week, even though she was practically right in front of your face the whole time. If you want to see, Virg, you've got to look."

"You're saying that all those times over the past three months when I needed you, you were there and I simply didn't know it?"

"Not exactly. As I recall, I told you I had something to do, and as a point of fact, you did as well."

"What's that?" Virgil said.

"In a word? Grieve."

"I've done plenty of that."

"Have you?"

"What's that supposed to mean?" Virgil said.

"I'm sorry about Ron, Son. But he's in a place of peace now. You better than anyone should know that. You didn't send him to his death any more than I did. It's time to stop feeling guilty about something you had no control over."

"But you told me I was going to be asked to do something and I had to refuse. I ignored that advice and now Ron is dead."

"That's not what I was talking about. It didn't have anything to do with Ron."

"Then what was it?"

"I'll let you explore your own past, Virg. I've been busy doing the same with mine."

"Why?"

"To examine my mistakes. To learn from them."

"Have you?" Virgil said.

"I'm whittling away at the truth...running down some clues, you might say."

"Care to explain what that means?" Virgil said.

Mason looked across the park area toward the front gate. "Looks like things are starting to pick up around here."

Virgil turned and noticed that people were beginning to show up. He turned back to his father and said, "You haven't answered my question."

"Of course I did. What was it Nichole said that day in the bar when she gave you the thumb drive? Something about the answer is somewhere in the middle?"

Virgil heard someone running hard on the path behind him, and when he turned and looked, he saw a young girl, maybe in her mid-teens, with red hair and a face full of freckles. She ran right up to him and said, "Excuse me, sir. I don't mean to intrude, but would you mind if I have one of those apples?"

He smiled at the young lady, and said, "Sure." Then, just to be friendly, he said, "My name is Virgil Jones. What's yours?"

"Nice to meet you, Mr. Jones. My name is Mary Adams."

Virgil smiled again and said, "Actually it's Detective. I'm a police officer from America."

"I know," Mary said.

Virgil tipped his head to the side, and said, "Do you, now?" When he turned to reach for an apple, he noticed his father was gone. He let out a weary sigh, picked up the apple, and turned back to the girl.

That's when Virgil noticed she was gone as well. In fact, the entire park was empty once again. When he looked at where the girl had stood, he saw a single shoe, the kind runners wear, in the middle of the path. He didn't know what to make of that, so he left it alone, and walked back to the guest house.

———

VIRGIL AND MURTON SPENT A WONDERFUL EVENING with the entire Pope crew, laughing and reminiscing about their past encounters, and catching up on the work they were doing, both with their foundation and their lives in general.

The next morning, Nichole came down to say good-bye, promised Virgil and Murton both that she'd see them soon—although the way she said it made Virgil just the tiniest bit suspicious—and waved them off as Lola drove them to the airport.

She talked the entire way. Neither Virgil nor Murton managed to get a single word in. Four hours later they landed in Indy, where Sandy and Becky were waiting.

After all the hugging and kissing, Sandy grabbed Virgil by his biceps, held him at arm's length, then said, "Did you keep your promise?"

"I did," Virgil said. "I am fully and completely here."

Sandy nodded once, like that was all she needed to hear. Then she took note of the physical transformation both Virgil and Murton had gone through. They were both leaner, tighter, their faces edgy, deeply tanned, and in short, they looked terrific. "Nichole kept us informed. I understand Wu worked you guys a little harder than you let on."

Murton laughed. "Well, he did me, that's for sure. But I think Virgil spent most of his time waxing off."

# CHAPTER NINE

SIX MONTHS AGO:

Sam Whittle was working in his home office, doing the final rewrite of his fifth novel—his editor told him she wanted the final draft by the end of the day if they were going to get it out on time—when his phone buzzed at him. He glanced at the screen and saw it was his brother calling. He thought about ignoring the call, but it'd been a while since they'd spoken, so he hit the Save key on his keyboard, pressed the Answer button, and said, "Hey, Don. How's it going?"

"It's going okay. Got a second?"

Don might have said it was going okay, but Sam knew him well enough to know by the sound of his voice that it wasn't going okay at all. "Yeah. What's the matter? You sound upset."

"Look, Sam, I know you don't want to hear this, but I

think you need to go over and see Dad. He's running out of time, man, and if the two of you don't get things worked out...well, I think you might spend the rest of your life regretting it."

"What do you mean he's running out of time? The last time I saw him he was running a chainsaw in the backyard. He seemed fine to me."

"Sam...that was over two years ago. I'm telling you, he's getting sicker by the day. I don't know what happened between the two of you, but if you won't do it for me, or even for him, I'm begging you...do it for yourself."

Sam shook his head at the sound of his brother's voice. The pleaser, the fixer of the family who just couldn't let it go.

Also the liar. Don knew exactly what had happened between him and their father, he just didn't want to hear it. It was easier to live in a fantasy world than it was to tell the truth. "I'll tell you something, Don...you keep saying you don't know what happened between the two of us, but I know you do."

"I don't want to get into all that right now. Just go see him, please."

"I'll think about it."

"Better think quick."

AFTER THEY ENDED THE CALL, SAM SAT AT HIS DESK AND tried to get back to work, but his mind kept taking him back to the past. Back to the time when his father used to beat him. Back to the time when he was running the entire ranch by himself, and so tired he was barely able to function. Back to that one awful winter when the blizzard hit and the roof of the barn collapsed. He barely made it out alive, the rafters snapping and falling like dominos as he ran for his life to escape the carnage. He wasn't hurt... until he got to the house, that is.

He threw open the kitchen door and found his father sitting at the table, a drink in his hand.

"The fuck you doing in here? You're supposed to be out working."

Sam was so out of breath, and shaking from the adrenaline flooding his system he could barely speak. "Dad, the roof of the barn just came down. It collapsed under the weight of the snow."

Dick Whittle looked at his son, his face a mask of both confusion and rage. "What? What the fuck are you talking about?"

"I didn't think I was going to make it out. The rafters were snapping like toothpicks."

Whittle jumped from his chair and grabbed his son by the sleeves of his jacket. "Did you get the chickens out? Did you?" He was screaming so loud that spittle dripped from his chin.

"The chickens?" Sam jerked away from his father. *"The chickens?* Did you hear what I just said? I almost died."

Whittle grabbed his boots and jacket and stumbled across the yard and out toward the barn. He was only halfway there when he stopped. The building had been completely crushed by the weight of the snow. He turned to Sam and said, "This is your fault. You should have gotten up there on that roof and shoveled that snow off. What the hell were you thinking?"

Sam was so stunned by his father's words, he couldn't speak.

"Well, what are you going to do about it?"

"I don't know. What should I do?"

Whittle put a mocking tone in his voice. "I don't know. What should I do?" Then, "My God, I don't think I've ever been more disappointed in anyone, ever. I'll tell you what you're going to do. You're going to get inside that fucking barn and find every dead bird you can. Thanks to you, we're going from a house full of hens to a freezer full of fryers. I want them butchered and cleaned proper. Don't come in until you're finished. Jesus Christ, what a piece of shit. This is your fault. Do you hear me? *This is all your fault.*"

———

AND THIS: WHEN HE WAS AN ADULT, HIS MOTHER DEAD and gone, God bless her, Sam married the woman of his dreams in their own backyard...a wise, intuitive woman named Danika. The invitations were sent, the tent put up, the catering in place, and the only single person who didn't show for the wedding or the reception—even though there were free drinks—was his father. The next day when Sam went out to check the mail before he and his bride would leave for their honeymoon, he found a crumpled Walmart bag in the box. When Sam looked inside the bag, he saw a check from his father. The amount? Twenty-five dollars. Attached was a note that read: *Congrats. Love is all that matters.*

Sam took the note and the check inside, tore them to pieces, threw them in the trash, then sat down and wrote his father a letter:

*Dear Dad,*

*It's too bad you couldn't make the wedding. I have a few things I'd like to say, and I guess now is as good a time as any. The short version is this: You've deeply hurt me and my wife. If you think that sounds harsh, I'm sorry you feel that way. Also, if history is any sort of marker, you'll probably disagree with what follows. Anyway, here goes:*

*Of everyone invited to our wedding, you were the only one who didn't show. Why is that? Are you so ashamed of your past behavior that you couldn't stand to see me happy and at peace? Are you that afraid of the truth?*

*I've had a lot of time to think about things over the years, about how I view my life, my past, my future, how much my wife means to me, and how I plan to continue to love and care for the people who want me in their lives. In the process I've come to realize something: I've spent my entire life trying to protect your feelings. What a colossal waste of time. It's a waste of time because I'm not responsible for your feelings. You are. I've learned that every time I try to protect your feelings (which everyone in this family has been doing all our lives, by the way) all I'm really doing is hurting you in a different manner...pushing the issue at hand further down the road until it is almost impossible to discuss, making things more difficult as time goes on.*

*I never meant to hurt our relationship by trying to protect your feelings, but that's how you raised me, so that's what I've done. I have to admit, I'm a little embarrassed that it's taken me so long to figure it all out. Want to know who taught me how wrong it was and why?*

*It was Danika.*

*I'm not sure how you feel about all this, (although if I'm being honest...I've got a pretty good mental picture in my head right about now) but whatever you feel, remember, you're responsible for your feelings, not me because all I'm doing is telling the fucking truth. If you don't want or can't handle that, or if you just want to have a pretend relationship, you'll have to do that with someone else, like Don and Karen. They seem up to the task. But don't expect me to continue to participate in the absurd lies and falsehoods that seem to keep everyone's motor running these days, yours in particular. Karen just sent me a picture of herself holding a chicken at the state fair the other day. Good grief.*

*I sincerely hope you're happy and well, though I doubt either of those things are true, and that fact saddens me to no end. I really do wish you nothing but the best, but please stop trying to find it at the expense of me and my wife. By the way, a mailbox is a poor substitute for a relationship. In other words, don't bother waiting for the check to clear. It's already in the trash.*

*Your son,*

*Sam*

*p.s. I'm profoundly ashamed of myself that I didn't have the courage to say this to your face, or at the very least stand before you as you read it, but it's the best I can do right now. The hypocrisy of leaving this letter in your mailbox isn't lost on me either. My only excuse is it's not wrapped in a Walmart bag pretending to be a gift.*

---

SAM FOLDED THE LETTER, TUCKED IT INTO AN envelope, and drove the half-mile over to his father's house. Once there he stuck the letter in the box and went back home. He hadn't seen his father since.

So...two years gone now, and his brother Don calling to say the old man was running out of time. Was he telling the truth, or was it the counselor in him trying to manipulate his older brother into doing something he really didn't want to do? Only one way to find out.

He picked up the phone, called his editor, and asked for a three-day extension. The editor said it wouldn't be a problem. "Is everything all right over there?"

*Not really...not when the old man is involved.* "Yeah, I've just got some family issues I'm dealing with."

"Not Danni, I hope."

"No, no, Danni is fine. And so am I."

"Okay, I won't pry, but Sam?"

"Yeah?"

"This one is going to be your breakout novel. I can feel it, and I don't want anything to get in the way of that. So...three days. And that's taking it right down to the wire."

"No more than that," Sam said. "I promise."

With that done, he grabbed his truck keys and headed for the door. At the last second, he quickly detoured into the kitchen and vomited into the sink.

---

DANIKA HEARD HIM RETCHING, CAME OVER, AND PUT her hand on his back. "Sam, what's the matter? Are you okay?"

Sam turned on the faucet, cupped his hands under the water, and rinsed out his mouth. Then he splashed his face and asked Danika for a towel.

She handed him the towel, and said, "Sam?"

He wiped his face, then turned to his wife. "Don called. He was practically in tears. He's asked me to go see my dad. Said he doesn't have much time left."

"Oh, sweetheart, I don't think—"

"I know," Sam said. "I don't think it's the best idea, either."

"Then why go?"

"Because while it might not be the best idea, it's probably not the worst. What if he really is sick?"

"You know what your brother is like," Danika said. "He lies and manipulates to get everything he wants, so *he* can feel better. I'm not saying you shouldn't go. I'm simply saying that if you do, make sure you're doing it for yourself. Not your dad, and certainly not for Don."

Sam nodded at his wife, gave her a quick hug, and said, "I won't be long."

# CHAPTER TEN

When Sam arrived at his father's house, he found him in his usual afternoon spot—sitting in his garage, a drink in one hand, a cigarette in the other. Dick Whittle looked at his son, set his drink on the workbench next to him, crushed out his butt in the tray, then stood up. "Wondered if you were ever going to come and see your old man."

"Nice greeting," Sam said. "Especially from the guy who didn't even bother to show up for my wedding."

Whittle ignored the comment, then he did something that surprised Sam. He walked over and gave him a hug. When he let go, Sam noticed his father's eyes were rimmed with moisture.

"You want a belt?" Whittle said.

Sam thought, *What the hell...why not?* He felt like he might need it. "What do you have?"

"Name your poison."

"I'd take a beer, I guess."

"You guess? Do you want a beer or not?"

"Yes, yes, a beer. Jesus."

Whittle walked over to the refrigerator he kept in the garage, opened the door, and handed his son a beer. Sam noticed that his father had definitely aged since the last time they'd seen each other. His hair was thinner and had turned from gray to white, and he didn't really walk...he sort of shuffled. Tiny, feeble steps that made him look like he could topple over any second.

"Let me get you a chair," Whittle said. He reached for a lawn chair that hung on the back wall, and couldn't seem to free it from the hook.

Sam walked over and said, "Here, Dad, let me."

Whittle brushed him away and said, "I've got it. This is my goddamned house. You think I can't get a lawn chair off the wall?"

Sam backed away and let the old man struggle. After a great deal of effort, he finally freed the chair from its hook and shook it open. He pushed it toward Sam, following it along like it was a walker. When he sat back down, his breath was ragged, his face flushed from the exertion. He lit another cigarette, took a drink of his vodka, then said, "Got your letter a couple years back."

"Yeah? What'd you think of it?" Sam said.

"Not much. Read it once, wiped my ass with it, then flushed it down the bowl. Probably didn't help my septic system, but it ended up where it belonged."

Sam actually laughed, though there was no humor

involved. "You know what? That sounds almost exactly like something you'd do."

"I worked you hard growing up. Don't think I don't know that. Tried to turn you into a real man, like your brother, Don. I must have failed though. Any puss can write a damn letter, but a real man would have told it to my face. I'm surprised you didn't show up here in a dress and high heels." Then, as if two different people lived inside his skin, Whittle said, "Book sales going okay?"

Sam knew it was one of his father's favorite tactics; throw out an insult or two, then pretend to show interest of a personal nature before anyone could respond to the way they'd just been disrespected. But Sam wasn't playing. "You didn't just work me hard, Dad, you abused me. You abused us all. Want to think of me as a puss for putting my thoughts in a letter? Go ahead. Like I told you, they're your feelings, not mine. I'd have told it to your face if I thought you would have listened."

"You gonna answer my question, or not?"

Sam shook his head. "Yes, book sales are going well. I'm finishing up my fifth manuscript right now."

"Waste of trees, you ask me," Whittle said. "I tried to read one of your so-called novels and didn't get past the first chapter before I tossed it in the trash. Hated to do it, mainly because I was embarrassed for the rest of the garbage in the barrel. Can't believe you make any money off that crap. You and Danni doing all right?"

"Yes, Danni and I are fine."

Whittle made a rude noise with his lips. "Danni.

What kind of a name is that for a woman? Sounds like a man's name. She one of them weirdos or something? I could see you marrying someone like that."

"Her name is Danika, Dad. You know that. And, as for your previous question, not everyone is going to like what I write. Art is subjective."

Whittle let out an old man's cackle. "Art? You call that art? More like fart, you ask me. I'll tell you what you need to do...you need to go out and get a real job, like your brother, Don. My pride and joy, that young man. Want a smoke?"

"I quit after mom died. I told you that."

Whittle nodded and seemed to be lost in his own thoughts. "That woman, your mother, I loved her with my whole heart. Maybe if she would have quit smoking, the cancer wouldn't have got her."

*The cancer is sitting right in from of me,* Sam thought.

"What was that? I don't hear so good anymore."

"I said the cancer isn't what killed her. Someone sucked the life out of her."

"Any thoughts about who that might be? Maybe if you'd have done your job as a child and been a better kid, like Don, she might have lived longer, or at least she might have been happier. What do you think of my car?"

Sam glanced at the car. "Yeah, nice. Mom told me a story once about the time when she told you she was pregnant with me. She said you hit her so hard she lost a couple of teeth."

"Nice? *Nice?* Do you have any idea how much money

that thing cost? Damned near a hundred grand. Reminds me of all the money I spent on everyone during Christmas. Christ, if I had that money now, I'd be living large. I'll bet I dropped over fifteen grand every year for nearly twenty years. What's that? Three hundred K? I'd like to have that back, I'll tell you that. You know what it was? It was wasted money on a waste of flesh. You and that wife of yours going to spit out a grandchild for me before I croak?"

*Good God, I hope not.*

"Why are you looking at me like that?" Whittle said.

"Are you sick, Dad? Don seems to think that you haven't been doing very well lately."

"I ain't sick. I'm old." He pointed a crooked finger at Sam and said, "Let me tell you something, boy, getting old ain't for pussies like you. Based on what I've seen over the years, you'll be lucky if you make it to fifty. Here's some advice: Pick out your own funeral dress now. There's still a few of your mother's nice things in the closet." Then he laughed like it was the funniest thing anyone had ever said. When the laughter stopped, he said, "Goddamnit to hell, it's good to laugh with you again, boy."

"You mean at me, don't you?"

"What are you talking about? We're having a nice visit. Don't be such a stick in the mud. You see, that's always been your problem...you can't find the good in anything. Always bitching and moaning about this isn't good enough, or that is good enough. I'll tell you what was never good enough...it was you. Always doing everything half-assed around the ranch. Letting the eggs rot, letting the fox through the hole in the fence, letting the roof collapse that one winter. Want to know how much that set me back? Over a quarter million, and it was all your fault. Sometimes I'm convinced the better part of you went running down your mother's leg. Either that or the nurse dropped you on your head when no one was looking and didn't bother to mention it to anyone. How's that new house of yours holding up? Everything okay there?"

"Never better, Dad."

Whittle huffed. "Well, I hope you're keeping it clean. Christ, when you were a kid, it'd take your mother half the night to get the feathers and the chicken shit smell out of the house. About to gag me to death. Every time you walked inside, it was like you were dragging the entire barn in with you. You stunk the place up so bad, I thought I was going to have to kick you out. You get a new haircut? Looks different...like you finally might be trying."

"Yeah, a couple of days ago."

"Probably went to Sally's Perms and Curls, didn't ya? Get yourself a nice set and a do to finally come over and see your old man? Did you lift your skirt while you were there and spread your legs so they could staple a sack on you? Maybe help you write another letter? You know your mother used to go there back in the day. Different owners, I think. Can't keep track anymore. Don mentioned you got a dog. Some kind of purse dog or something. One of them ones that always shiver. Since you seem to have forgotten your purse, I'm guessing you didn't bring it with you. Don't forget, you've got to get it started on the heart-worm meds and all that."

"I know Dad, I know."

Whittle waved him away. "Yeah, yeah, you think you know everything, don't you. Let me tell you something: You don't know shit about fuck. That dog even looks at you crooked, you got to kick him around for a while, show him who's boss. And I'm not talking about pointing your finger and saying, 'bad dog,' I'm talking about taking the boot to it, hard. You let an animal get on top of you and it's over. He's probably pissing on your carpet as we speak. A dog ever pissed on my carpet, I'd put a bullet in him. Say, you never did answer me...When am I going to get a grandchild? I'd sure like the chance to be someone's grandpa before my time is up."

"Danika and I have decided to wait until the time is right. I've got a book tour coming up, and my agent says he's got shops lined up all along the east coast."

"Mister Big Shot, huh? More like big shit. Well, let me tell you something Mr. Big Shit, ain't no right time to have a kid, that's for damned sure. When you came along it flat-out ruined my life. Thank god we waited a few years to have Don. That boy was something special, right out of the gate. Did you hear his cross-country team has won the state championship two years running? I'm telling you, I'm so proud of that boy, I could spit. And a counselor to boot. Now there's a man who knows how to make something out of his life, unlike the rest of my pathetic children, present company included. Say, you want another beer? I've got plenty."

LIKE THAT.

SAM WENT HOME, VOMITED IN THE KITCHEN SINK FOR the second time in less than an hour, turned to his wife, and said, "What was I thinking?"

"That bad?" Danika said.

"He hit all the highlights, that's for sure."

Danika led him into the living room, and after they were sitting down, she said, "Tell me."

They spent the next hour talking about the visit, and Sam's past, most of which Danika knew, some of which she didn't. As they were winding down, Sam's phone rang. He looked at the screen, then at his wife. "It's Don...again."

"Let it go."

"He'll just keep calling until I answer. Might as well get it over with." He punched the Answer button and said, "What?"

Don sounded elated. "Sam...man, I don't know what you said to Dad, but I just got off the phone with him. He sounded happier than ever. He kept saying how good it was to see you, how you guys talked and laughed, and what a great time he had. I can't thank you enough, man. Really, you're a hell of a brother, you know that? Sam, hey Sam...are you there?"

"Yeah. Listen, Don, I gotta go. I'm in the middle of something. I'll catch you later, okay?"

"Sure, sure. I just wanted you to know how happy you made Dad."

And Sam thought, *Yeah, once again, at my own expense.*

# CHAPTER ELEVEN

PRESENT-DAY:

The MCU was located inside an old post office building just south of the city's not-so-infamous Spaghetti Bowl, a series of never-ending loops, on-ramps, exits, and city streets, that in years past when viewed from above, looked like an actual bowl of spaghetti. It didn't look much like a spaghetti bowl anymore, but everyone still referred to the area that way.

On Monday morning, Virgil walked inside the building and made his way to his office. He took the morning to get caught up on paperwork, clearing out his email, then spent some time going over the reporting that had been generated while he and Murton had been in Jamaica.

Ross and Rosencrantz were working a cold case out of Kokomo...a teenage girl had gone missing over three weeks ago, and no one had heard from her since. He made a note to himself to check on their progress when they got back to the shop. The father of the girl was a longtime acquaintance of Mac's, so...

He called his business partner, Rick Said, and asked if everything was going well with the sonic drilling units down in Shelby County.

"It's going just fine, Jonesy. How are you?" Said said.

"I'm well, Rick. Just got back from a week in Jamaica."

"I heard. Nichole said something to Patty, and she told me you were down there. Have a good time?"

Virgil wasn't exactly sure how to answer the question. "Good enough, I'd say."

Said, who was a businessman at heart, got right down to business. "Listen, Jonesy, we've got a new set of geological reports that came in while you were gone. There's a section of land that sits right on the border between the old Graves and Mizner properties. I'd like to get a couple of drill units positioned over there and see what we can see. The reporting looks *very* good."

Basil Graves and Angus Mizner, former owners of the land, and minority shareholders of the gas extraction business owned by Virgil and Said had been murdered during Virgil's last case. It was the same case that killed Ron Miles. "That seems a little...premature, don't you think?"

"Look, Jonesy, I know what you're thinking, but the fact is, neither Graves nor Mizner had any heirs. You, me, and Johnson have all agreed to donate what would have been their proceeds to the cultural center, so I'm asking myself, why not?"

"What'd Carl say about it?" Virgil said. Carl Johnson was their other partner and acted as the de facto foreman of the operation.

"He said it'd take a day each to cap two of the wells, then another four or five days to reposition and get everything set up."

"So we're looking at a week of downtime," Virgil said.

"Yes, but only for two of the units. The rest will remain operational. In fact, if we boost the output—Carl and the engineers all agree the pumps can handle it—then we shouldn't see any drop in productivity over that period."

"Okay, you want to get with Carl, or do you want me to call him?"

"I'll handle it," Said said. "Just wanted to get you up to speed. Hey, speaking of up to speed and all things Shelby County, did you hear that the mobile voting app is going to get a trial run?"

"No, I didn't hear anything about it."

"Probably because you were too busy sunning yourself down in the tropics. Anyway, after Ron's, uh...well, after Ron, the county decided to hold a special election. Ed Henderson is running for sheriff, and the app we've built is going to handle the votes. The whole thing is happening in less than a month."

"No kidding? That's great, Rick. Congratulations. I hope it goes well. Who's he running against?"

Said let out a little chuckle. "Does the name Carla Martin ring any bells?"

"You have absolutely got to be pulling my weenie." Carla Martin was a federal agent with the DEA, and she'd been instrumental in cracking Virgil's last case as well.

"Nope...and I'll leave the weenie pulling to the lieutenant governor. How is she, by the way? Sandy."

"She's well. But let me ask you this: Why would a federal agent with the DEA be interested in running for sheriff?"

"Why not? According to Rosencrantz, she started with the feds right out of college, she's got enough time in to take her pension, so if she wins, she'll have the nice double-dip."

"Huh."

"Anyway, get with Rosie and he'll fill you in, I'm sure. I get the feeling those two are something of an item these days."

"Huh," Virgil said again.

"Okay, you're starting to repeat yourself, so I'm going to get back to work. Talk to you," Said said, and then he was gone.

Virgil set his phone down, then picked it right back up again and called Rosencrantz. "Hey, Rosie, it's me. Are you and Ross up in Kokomo?"

"Hey, Boss-man, welcome back. Ross is up there going through the county's records. I'm at the bar with Becky."

"Why?"

"It's sort of a long story. If you're not doing anything..."

Virgil wasn't, so he headed for the bar.

———

He walked in through the back and spent a few minutes with Robert and Delroy before going upstairs. When he walked into the office, Rosencrantz looked up and said, "Man, you're looking good. Right down to your fighting weight, huh?"

"Something like that," Virgil said. "Good to see you. Hey, Becks. What are you guys working on?"

Becky mumbled hello to Virgil without looking up from her computer. She was typing away and had three different screens going, none of which Virgil understood. He raised an eyebrow at Rosencrantz.

"I know it's only your first day back, but did you get a chance to read the reports Ross and I have compiled so far?"

Virgil turned his palms up, then flopped down on the couch. "Not the details. I skimmed the summary pages. How about you lay it out for me?"

Rosencrantz took out his notebook and flipped through a few pages. "Okay, we've got this young girl, Lisa Tate, sixteen years old, resident of Kokomo. An only child, living at home with her parents, straight-A student, volunteers at the shelter, church every Sunday, school athlete, part-time job at the grocery store...like that."

"Sounds like an all-American girl," Virgil said.

"Yup. Except about three weeks ago she went to a cross-country meet, or match, or whatever they're called, and vanished. It was like she'd been snatched right off the planet. This was during the actual event."

"Leads?" Virgil said.

"Nothing. Her parents have some money, so everyone thought there would be a ransom demand, but nothing ever came of it. No call, no letter, no nothing."

"Sixteen," Virgil said. "Think she might have skipped?"

"Not unless she decided to do it with her purse, wallet, cell phone, and most importantly, her insulin kit locked in her car, which was sitting right there in the lot where the match was being held."

"Mmm, that doesn't sound good," Virgil said. "Boyfriend?"

"Yeah. Good kid, with a solid alibi."

"What's his story?"

"He was at the meet, sitting with Tate's parents."

Virgil shook his head. "Man, that doesn't sound good, either."

Rosencrantz nodded at him. "Tell me about it. She simply ran into the woods and never came out. Howard County conducted a search of the immediate area and when they didn't find anything, they had their crime scene people go through the woods inch by inch. They didn't find a single shred of evidence."

Becky sat back and stared at her screen for a few seconds. "Whatcha got, Becks?" Virgil said.

"A seriously depressing set of facts."

"Let's hear it," Rosencrantz said.

Becky puffed out her cheeks and said, "According to my data, and this is just the raw stuff mind you, Indiana is currently ranked 15th in the nation for missing persons. Last year alone—in our state—there were over 174 people reported as missing. Sixty-three percent of them were women, and of those, almost twenty percent were young women under the age of eighteen."

Virgil was trying to do the math in his head. "That's, uh...let's see..."

"Careful," Becky said. "I can smell the smoke coming out of your ears. The exact number you're looking for is twenty-two."

Virgil couldn't quite believe what he was hearing. "Twenty-two girls, eighteen or younger every year? How is that even possible?"

Becky gave him a sad shrug. "There are ninety-two counties in this state, Jonesy. Statistically, that amounts to about a quarter a person per county, per year."

"Yeah, except no one loses a fourth of a kid," Virgil said.

Becky held up her hands. "I know, I know. I'm simply doing the math. Look what happened a few years ago with Patty Doyle. If you hadn't gotten involved with that and found her, she'd be one of the missing women, and it might not have even registered with you."

"I'll bet it registers with the parents," Rosencrantz said. "In fact, I know it does. Ross and I interviewed the

Tates last week, and I'm telling you, they were sitting there staring at us like their daughter disappeared last night...not three weeks ago."

Virgil looked at nothing for a few seconds, then turned to Becky. "Where's Murt?"

"He's on his way over. We're having lunch together." Then she let her eyelids droop. "Or are we?"

Virgil gave her the wait-a-minute finger, then turned to Rosencrantz. "Can you get in touch with the Tates? I'd like to run up there this afternoon and hear it all first-hand."

Rosencrantz made a quick call, and when he was finished, said, "They'll be waiting for you. I'll text you the address. Want my case notes?"

Virgil shook his head. "No, I'll take a harder look at everything when we get back. I want to come at them cold."

Just then, Murton walked into the room carrying two plates of Robert's famous Jamaican Jerk chicken. He'd overheard Virgil's last comment. "Come at what cold?"

Becky looked at her husband and said, "Your lunch, among other things."

Virgil took the plates from Murton, gave one to Becky and the other to Rosencrantz. "It's on the house." Then to his brother, "C'mon, Murt. Time to get back to work."

"Where are we going?"

"Kokomo. I'll fill you in on the way."

Murton looked at Rosencrantz. "Enjoy my lunch."

Virgil said, "Becky, start getting a list together of all

open and active cases of teenaged girls missing in the state. Maybe we can find some commonalities."

"How far back?"

The question was a good one, and it stopped Virgil. If they didn't go back far enough, they wouldn't have sufficient data to work with. Too far, and they'd be overwhelmed with information, some of which might no longer be relevant. "Let's go back a full two years. That way we might get a picture of what was happening before she disappeared. It won't be that many more, statistically, but it could help."

"You got it, Jonesy," Becky said. "But do me a favor, will you?"

"What's that?"

"At least try to get my husband back in time for dinner."

"No promises, but I'll try. Murt, you ready?"

Murton dropped his head. "I just gave away my lunch, I'm standing right next to the door, and as usual, I'm waiting on you." He walked over and kissed Becky goodbye, then said, "See, this is what happens when a guy starts feeling better. I miss the slower, foggier Jonesy."

"Murt..."

"Yeah, yeah, I'm coming," Murton said. He snatched a piece of chicken from Rosencrantz's plate, gave him a wink, and they were out the door, headed for Kokomo.

# CHAPTER TWELVE

FIVE MONTHS AGO:

Sam's latest book was still being torn apart by his editor, which left him with two things to do on this bright and sunny Saturday...yard work, and research for his next book. He thought about tackling the research first, but he knew if he did, he wouldn't be as productive with the yard chores barking at the back of his brain. So, he'd do the yard first, then spend the afternoon doing the research. He went outside to check the lawn. If the grass was dry enough, he'd get it cut, then get back to his office.

He ran his hand through the grass, and it was indeed dry. He went back inside, changed into his work clothes, put on a pair of grass-stained tennis shoes, then grabbed a plastic bag and the pooper-scooper to clean out the back-yard before running the mower. He'd just finished picking up the piles of dog poop when he heard a siren off in the distance. It sounded like a cop car. He listened for a moment as the sound got closer, then it faded a bit, before going silent. It sounded fairly close. Less than a mile for sure. Something going on, somewhere nearby.

He tossed the bag of poop into the garbage can, then gassed up his mower. He was just about to crank over the engine when he heard another siren, this one a little different from the first. Maybe an ambulance, or firetruck.

The thought that went through Sam's head at that moment was, *Dad?*

He spent a few seconds debating whether he should drive past the old man's house or not, but he ultimately decided it was nothing more than coincidence. This wasn't the first time he'd heard a siren or two over that way, and he'd never gone before. Why now? He pulled out his phone, brought up some tunes, and plugged his headphones in before dropping the phone back in his pocket. Then he started the mower and got to work.

———

SAM AND DANIKA'S LOT WAS FAIRLY BIG...JUST A TAD over a half-acre, and by the time Sam had the grass cut, the driveway, sidewalk, and curb edged, the weeds pulled from the landscaping—the front anyway, he'd leave the back for next week—almost three hours had passed. He got everything put away, and was checking the bottom of his shoes before going into the house when his phone buzzed at him. He pressed the tab on the headphone's wire and said, "Hello."

"Sam? It's Don." His voice sounded hoarse and raspy.

"What's up?" Sam said. In the background, he heard a woman saying, '*no, no, no,*' over and over again.

"Sam, I'm at Dad's. You better get over here. He's gone, man. He died this morning."

Despite their struggles over the years...the fights, the nature of abuse inflicted upon him by his father, Sam felt his heart break at that moment. No matter how mean and cruel and thoughtless Dick Whittle had been to his children—each of them in different ways—he was still their father, and Sam felt an immediate emptiness inside his chest.

"Sam? Are you there? Did you hear what I said?"

"What happened?" Sam asked.

"I just told you. Dad's dead. He just...died."

"When?"

"Are you listening to me? Karen found him this morning. If you want to see him before they take his body, you better get over here."

Sam was shocked by the news of his father's death, but it didn't stop him from thinking about the sirens he'd heard earlier in the day. "What do you mean before they take his body away? When exactly did he die?"

Don, the pleaser, was running out of patience. "Sam, I don't know for sure. But the funeral home is on the way right now, so get over here, will you?"

"The funeral home?" Sam was shouting at his brother now. "What the fuck? Why are you just now calling me?"

Don began shouting back. "I'm not your personal assistant. Get off my ass. I'm doing the best I can over here."

Sam felt the tears running down his cheeks. "I'm sorry, I'm sorry. I'll be right there."

But his brother had already hung up.

———

DANIKA WAS IN THE KITCHEN, AND SHE HEARD HER husband arguing with someone outside. When she opened the garage door, she found her husband staring at the wall. "Sam? What's the matter?"

When Sam turned and looked at her, his face was wet with tears, and he had a particular expression on his face, one she'd never witnessed before. "My dad died this morning. We've got to get over there."

———

DANIKA PUT ON HER SHOES, GRABBED HER PURSE, AND they jumped into the truck and made it to Whittle's house in less than a minute. Sam expected to see the police, or at the very least, an ambulance. Instead, all he saw were his sibling's vehicles parked in the driveway, along with his father's car, which was also in the drive.

When he and Danika walked into the garage, they

saw Karen kneeling next to Dick Whittle, who was sitting in his garage chair. He wore only a bathrobe and slippers. His hair was freshly barbered, his face cleanly shaved, and his beard neatly trimmed. His head was tipped back, and his lips were slightly parted. His skin held a bluish cast, and his expression was peaceful, as though he'd simply fallen asleep. His morning newspaper and cup of coffee were sitting next to him on the workbench. He held an unlit cigarette in one hand, and his lighter in the other. Don was standing in the driveway, speaking with someone on his phone. Danika walked over and hugged Karen, then patted Dick Whittle's cold dead hand.

Karen picked up a hairbrush and began running it through her father's hair. She started speaking before Sam could say anything. "I called this morning and he didn't answer his phone. I guess he must have been in the shower. When I tried a half-hour later, he still didn't answer, and I started to worry, so I drove over. I found him just like he is now, sitting in his chair. He was already gone. It looks like he made himself a cup of coffee, went and got his paper, then sat down to light a smoke, and then...then..."

Don finished his call, then looked at Sam. "That was the funeral home. I'm trying to figure out what's taking them so long to get here."

Sam was instantly hot. "What's taking *them* so long? I live less than half a mile from here. Karen lives in West Baden Springs. You live in Prospect. What the fuck? He got right in his brother's face. How long have you been here?"

"Sam, calm down. I know where everyone lives, including myself. I've been here almost two and a half hours."

"That's my point. You live twenty minutes away. Karen is half that."

Karen stood up and put her hand on Sam's arm. "Sam, we're all upset. Please don't do this now. I called Don first because I know how you and Dad felt about each other."

"He was my father, too, Karen, and I don't care who you called first, even though I live about one minute away from here."

"Then why are you so upset?" Karen said.

Sam couldn't believe what he was hearing. "Why am I so upset? Okay, let me see if I've got this right...you discover Dad's dead body, call 911, then call Don, who rushes over, the cops and everyone else show up, and I get the call three hours later? That's bullshit."

Danika put her hand on her husband's arm and pulled him away from his siblings, out to the driveway. She leaned close and whispered in his ear. "Sam, ease up a little. Your brother and sister are simply upset. I'm sure they're doing the best they can, even if it doesn't look that way to you or me. They had a different relationship with your dad...much different from yours, even though you all share the same history."

Sam looked at his wife, gave her a slight nod, then whispered back, "Okay, you're right. I'm in shock or something. But I'll tell you this: Something is wrong here. Who are they to be the arbiters of my relationship with my own father? Why wait three hours to call me when I'm only one minute away?"

"You're right, of course. We'll figure it all out. Just take it one step at a time, Okay?"

Sam spent a few minutes calming himself down, then walked over to his brother. "Look, Don, I'm sorry. I'm just...in shock I guess. You did me a kindness by calling last month and asking me to come here to see Dad. And no matter the difficulties he and I faced over the years, I was glad I got to see him one last time before he died. I don't think I'll ever be able to repay you for that. Thank you. And I really am sorry. I didn't mean to lose my shit on you...or Karen."

Karen walked over and hugged Sam. "We're all upset. Don't worry, we'll get through this together."

Sam looked at nothing for a few seconds then walked over to his father and gently touched his face and arm. He was already stiff and cold. He turned to his brother and sister, and said, "Both of our parents are gone now." Then, when neither of his siblings responded, he said, "Did the cops or the EMTs give you any paperwork or anything? It seems like there should be a report or something."

Karen seemed to stiffen a bit. "Sam, you don't have to worry about any of that. Dad gave me power of attorney a long time ago, and I'm the executor of his estate. The three of us can make the arrangements together if you want, but I'll handle everything else."

Before Sam could reply, the funeral home driver and his assistant showed up to remove Dick Whittle's body. They expressed their condolences, then suggested that everyone go wait in the driveway until they had Whittle on the gurney. "It's usually something the family doesn't like to witness," the driver said.

---

AFTER WHITTLE WAS LOADED UP AND GONE, DON SAID, "I guess we should run over to the funeral home and figure out what we're going to do."

Danika looked at Sam, and said, "Would you mind dropping me at home before you go? I think this is something you guys should do together."

"I think that's a good idea," Karen said, not bothering to hide the disdain in her voice. Then she looked at Don and said, "You have Dad's wallet?"

Don reached into his pocket and pulled Whittle's wallet out. "Got it right here." He looked back at Karen and said, "You've got his keys?"

"I do," Karen said. "I've already locked the place up. Let's go, okay?"

Don walked into the garage and made sure the interior door was locked. It was. He and Karen exchanged a quick glance.

So did Sam and Danika.

---

ONCE THEY WERE IN THE TRUCK AND ON THE WAY BACK to their house, Danika looked at Sam and said, "Those two are up to something."

"I know," Sam said. "But listen, I can't think about that right now. I just need to process what's happening at the moment. I want you to think about it, though, and we'll talk more when I get back."

Sam turned into their driveway and let Danika out. "I'm sorry baby, but I've got to go. I don't want to be the last one to arrive at the funeral home. I get the feeling Karen is going to bulldoze over everyone—including Don —to get what she wants...whatever that might be."

"I get it," Danika said. "Be careful. Stay calm."

"I will. Or at the very least, I'll try."

———

SAM WASN'T THE LAST TO ARRIVE AT THE FUNERAL home...he was the first. He waited outside in the parking lot for his brother and sister, but when they didn't show after fifteen minutes, he decided to go inside. The receptionist had a phone pressed to her ear, and when she saw him, she pointed at a chair and mouthed, 'have a seat.'

Sam sat down and waited for her to finish her call. When she was finally done, she gave him a sympathetic smile and said, "Are you related to Mr. Whittle?"

Sam nodded and said, "Yes, I'm his eldest son, Sam. My sister and brother should be here any moment."

The receptionist nodded and said, "I'm having a little

trouble getting ahold of the funeral director, this being a Saturday, and all. I think he might—"

The outer door flew open and Karen and Don walked in. Karen looked at Sam and said, "What's going on?"

Sam tipped his head in confusion. "Nothing. They're trying to get in touch with the funeral director. I've been here for twenty minutes. What took you guys so long?"

"Never mind that," Karen said. "At least we're not here wearing grass-stained clothing. You should have changed before you came over." Then she quickly added, "I'm sorry. I didn't mean that the way it sounded. Don was upset, so we pulled over to talk for a few minutes."

Sam looked at his brother. He didn't look all that upset to him.

Don looked around the reception area, then said, "Okay what do we need to do here? I'd like to get this over with as soon as we possibly can. Is Monday too soon to do the funeral?"

And Sam thought, *What the hell?*

"I'm afraid that's out of the question," the receptionist said. "There's simply too much to do." She looked through her desk scheduler and said, "It looks like the earliest we could do the service would be Thursday."

Now Don really did look upset. "Thursday? What's the hold-up? He's already got a plot at the cemetery. He paid for it years ago when our mom died. Put him in the box, dig the hole and drop him in. It's not that complicated."

The receptionist wasn't offended by Don's comments.

She'd seen all sorts of unusual behavior over the years. "Well, it's a bit more complex than that. Why don't we set up an appointment with the funeral director first thing Monday morning? He'll walk you through the process."

"Shouldn't there be an autopsy?" Sam said.

Don shook his head in disgust. "Sam, I told you Dad wasn't well. There isn't going to be an autopsy because he was sick, old, and died alone in his own home."

The receptionist politely cleared her throat, and they all got the message. With no other choice, they set the meeting for Monday morning at nine, then left the building. When they walked out to the parking lot, Sam noticed that Karen and Don had driven over together in Karen's car. That meant Don's van was still over at their father's house. "Listen," Sam said, "I didn't get a chance to go inside the last time I saw Dad. Why don't we all go over there and take one last walk through the place as a family?"

Don started to say something, but Karen cut him off. "I think that's a fine idea, Sam. Let's do that right now. It might help you get some closure."

They got in their vehicles, and as Sam turned out of the parking lot, he glanced in his rearview mirror. It looked like Karen and Don were arguing about something.

*I don't need closure,* Sam thought. *I need to know what the hell is going on.*

# CHAPTER THIRTEEN

When Sam turned into his father's driveway, he was once again hit with an overwhelming sense of sadness...not necessarily because of his father's actual death, but over the loss of what could have been. His father had never liked or respected him, but deep down, Sam thought there must have been some sort of love for him, even if it didn't measure up to his own standards.

He walked to the front door and found it was locked. When he went to the back door, he discovered the same thing. The garage had a keypad to open the overhead door, and Sam knew the code. He was going to punch it in and raise the door but decided not to. He wasn't sure if Karen and Don were aware of the fact that he knew the code. So he simply leaned against the fender of his truck and waited for his brother and sister. He felt like an outsider...an interloper who didn't really belong, even though he did.

A few minutes later, Don and Karen arrived. Don put his back to Sam, punched in the code to open the overhead door, then Karen unlocked the interior door, and they all stepped inside. The house was almost tidy, and it smelled mostly of cigarettes, coffee, and microwaved dinners. The three of them walked through the entire house, looking everything over...the fine leather furniture, the eighty-inch flatscreen TV, the expensive end tables, and walnut cabinets. Dick Whittle had never been afraid to spend money, that was for sure.

In the master suite, they all stood and looked at their father's bed for a moment, then Karen moved to smooth out the pillows like she was making the bed for a guest. When she ran her hand under one of the pillows, she pulled out a pistol—an old .22. She said, "Whoa."

Don quickly moved her way and said, "I'll take that." He grabbed the gun, opened the cylinder, and let the shells fall into his hand. He put the shells in one pocket and the gun in the other like it already belonged to him. Sam didn't care. Don was the gun nut. He could have the damned thing. They all entered the master closet, and there it was.

The safe.

Sam let out a nervous laugh and said, "I hope someone knows the combination because I sure don't."

"I don't either," Don said. "Karen?"

Karen shook her head.

Sam sighed and said, "Well, how in the hell are we going to get it open?"

Karen bared her teeth at him. "Is that all you care about? The money?"

Sam shook his head, "That's not what I meant, Karen. Calm down, for Christ's sake. I was simply asking a question."

"Yeah, great time for questions like that, asshole."

Don got between them—ever the pleaser, the one who could make everything right—and said, "Hey, c'mon now. We'll get a locksmith or safe guy, or whatever they're called to open the thing up. Let's get the heck out of here. This isn't doing anyone any good at all. C'mon, guys. What do you say?"

———

THEY ALL WALKED BACK TO THE GARAGE AND SPENT A moment looking at the chair where Dick Whittle had taken his final breath. Then Karen locked the interior door, looked at Sam, and dropped the keys in her purse.

"Is that the only set of keys?" Sam asked.

"Yes. And as the executor, I'll be keeping them." Then before Sam could say anything, she turned to Don and said, "I've talked to Dad's lawyer, and since there won't be any probate, we should be able to get things wrapped up pretty quick."

"I'd like to see the will," Sam said.

Karen tossed her hands in the air. "Again, with the money."

But Sam wasn't backing down. "Karen, it's not about the money. I've got more money than I can spend. They just optioned my last book for a major motion picture. But if Dad wanted me to have something, I'm not going to turn it down."

"Okay Mr. Moneybags, here's what's in the will: I'm in the will, and so is Don. Because you treated Dad like shit, he wrote you out. Everything gets sold and divided up between me and Don. The house, the cars, the furnishings, the contents of the safe, all of it."

Sam wasn't surprised his father had taken him out of the will, but he was surprised by his sister's reaction. He held up his hands, palms out. "Okay, okay, Jesus, take a breath, will you? I'm just asking to see it...the will."

Karen ignored him and said, "Don, get the overhead door." Then she got in her car and drove away.

Once she was gone, Sam looked at Don, and said, "Have you seen it? The will?"

"Yeah," Don lied. He hadn't actually seen the will, but Karen had told him what was in it, and it was nothing like the little speech she'd just given before driving away. "Sorry he wrote you out, man. I don't know what to tell you."

Sam shrugged. "It doesn't matter, Don. As I said, I don't need the money. I wouldn't turn it down if I had something coming, but other than that, I'm not going to lose any sleep over it."

Don let out a nervous little laugh. "So you're not going to sue us, or contest the will?"

Sam shook his head. "No. Why would I? I'd rather have my brother and sister more than the stuff, or the money. Besides, if that's what Dad wanted, the way to honor him is to abide by his wishes."

Don smiled at his brother and thought, *What an idiot.*

———

WHEN SAM RETURNED HOME, DANIKA WAS WAITING for him, a yellow legal pad in her hands. When he walked up to his wife and gave her a kiss, he glanced at the notepad and saw it was full of bullet points, written in Danika's hand. "What do you have there?"

"In a minute," Danika said. "Let's go sit out back and you can tell me how it went. I think we might have some things to talk about, but I need to hear what happened with you guys first."

Sam was still sort of in shock, so he simply shrugged and followed his wife to the back patio. After they were seated, he looked at nothing for a few minutes, then told Danika about his siblings' late arrival at the funeral home, his brother's insistence that the funeral be held as soon as possible, and his sister's odd and mercurial behavior while they were at their father's house.

Danika listened without interruption, and when she was sure Sam was finished, she said, "Do you believe Karen...about the will?"

Sam turned his palms up. "If I'm being honest with you, I don't know what to believe. On one hand, it wouldn't surprise me at all if Dad wrote me out of the will, but on the other hand...knowing what I know about my father, it'd be more likely if he did one of two things: Leave me an equal share of everything as sort of a last-ditch, fuck-you kind of guilt-trip, or he'd leave me something that was a joke...a dirty ashtray or something stupid like that."

"Don't you think it's odd that she actually told you there wouldn't be a probate process? I mean, I get it, she's the executor, but she isn't the one who decides if probate happens or not...it's the laws of the state. And Indiana law says estates worth more than fifty thousand have to go through that process."

"Been doing some quick research?"

"I have," Danika said. "And some of the things your sister says don't add up."

"Like what, exactly?"

Danika flipped through her notes. "Okay, first of all, we already talked about the fifty thousand threshold law. I don't know how much money your dad had, but let's face it, we know it was more than that. He made a boatload of money when he sold the farm, and the house he has now? He's lived there for years. According to Zillow, its value is close to half a million, give or take. And what's in that safe? You said at one point he had a bunch of gold coins and bearer bonds...?"

Sam nodded. "Yeah, that's what he said, but that was

years ago...when we were still speaking with each other. And he was drunk at the time he told me, so who knows?"

"Did you ask Karen if you could see a copy of the will?"

"Yeah, but she ignored me."

"I'm not surprised. According to what I found, technically, under Indiana law, you only have the legal right to see the will once something called the Grant of Probate is issued, and it becomes a public document. That means if you ask to see the will before then, she could simply say no, which I guess is sort of what she did."

"I guess," Sam said. "I don't know how much it matters anyway. Don told me he's seen it, and Dad wrote me out."

"That could be, but you know your brother. He's a habitual liar. And your sister? It's never enough for her, is it? She could win the lottery and it wouldn't be enough."

Sam nodded. "I know, I know. But listen, we're not going to figure any of this out today. Let's sit on it, at least until after the funeral. I don't want to make any waves right now. They're my siblings and no matter their idiosyncrasies, I love them. And besides, we don't need one single dime from my dad, you know that."

Danika reached out and took her husband's hand. "I know, baby. Maybe we should forget the whole thing."

"That's not what I'm saying. If my siblings are trying to do an end-run on me...on us, no matter the nature of the relationship I had with my dad, someone has to stand up and honor his wishes. If he didn't leave me anything, so be it. If he did, we'll donate it to charity. But I'm not going to be lied to, or manipulated because I didn't want to have a pretend relationship with my dad the way Karen and Don did. All I want is the truth. Let's just get through the next few days and see what happens."

---

FOR REASONS HE COULDN'T READILY EXPLAIN, THE DAY after the funeral Sam went back to his dead father's house. He wasn't looking for anything, other than a connection...a way to make peace with himself and any part he played in the failure of his relationship with his dad. Once there, he punched in the code on the keypad for the overhead door, but when he did, nothing happened. He shook his head in frustration, thinking that either Karen or Don had changed the code to keep him out, but when he tried a second time, the door opened right up. *Must have got it wrong the first time,* he thought.

Once the door was open, Sam couldn't believe what he saw...or rather, what he didn't see. The garage was virtually empty. All the tools on the workbench, the refrigerator and freezer in the corner, the high-end zero-turn riding mower, the portable generator, the Mercedes Benz, the two-seat electric golf cart, a small flatscreen TV, and all the other miscellaneous things that had been in the garage were gone. The only thing left was the chair his father had been sitting in when he died. Sam was instantly furious. Karen and Don had cleaned out the garage, taking every single thing of value. He wondered if they'd cleaned out the house as well. When he walked over to the interior door and tried the knob, he found it was still locked.

Sam was so mad he was shaking. He thought about kicking the door in—and probably would have—but then a thought occurred to him: Maybe the old man had hidden a key somewhere inside the garage. It seemed likely, as Dick Whittle had never been one to acknowledge his shortcomings or admit his mistakes to others. If he'd somehow managed to lock himself out of his own house, he wouldn't want to have to ask Karen or Don for help.

Sam went through the garage practically inch by inch. He looked underneath the ledge of the workbench, under the doormat, and anywhere else a key might be hidden, but in the end, he didn't find one. He spent a few more minutes looking at the chair where his father had been sitting when he died. The ashtray and a half-full cup of coffee still sat on the bench. The coffee mug had the words, 'World's Best Dad!' written in big bold letters on the side.

He ran his fingers through his hair, then for no real reason, he sat down in his father's death chair and lit a cigarette from the old man's stash...the entire time wondering how everything had gone so wrong between him and his dad. The answers never came, and Sam suspected they probably never would. He crushed out his cigarette—the damn thing tasted like a dog turd—then wrapped his hands under the arms of the chair to pull himself up. That's when he found the key. It was taped under one of the armrests.

Sam peeled the key from the tape, unlocked the door, and when he stepped inside if he thought he was mad in the garage, he discovered he was absolutely livid once he was inside the house. It was empty. Everything of value was gone. The fine leather furniture, the giant flatscreen TV, the kitchen table and chairs, the bedroom furniture... all of it. Gone. He almost didn't bother to walk into the closet. He knew the safe—even though the damned thing weighed over two hundred pounds—wouldn't be there either.

Except it was. The door was hanging open and the safe was completely empty, save four things.

All of Sam's novels stacked neatly on the top shelf.

---

SAM GRABBED HIS BOOKS, AND MOVED TOWARD THE front of the house, mostly in a daze. Had his father kept his books in the safe because he considered them valuable? Or was it because he didn't want anyone to know he had them? Clearly, Karen and Don didn't put them there. In fact, they left them behind, because to his siblings, it appeared they had no value at all.

As he moved through the kitchen, he discovered his mouth was so dry it felt like he'd been chewing on sandpaper. He opened the refrigerator and saw a half case of bottled water, still wrapped in plastic. He took two of the bottles and emptied the first with one long drink. He walked back out to the garage and set the empty bottle on the workbench. That's when he saw the hairbrush Karen had been using on his father as he sat dead in his own chair. He thought, *why not?* He grabbed the brush—probably the only thing he'd ever get besides his own books— walked out to his truck, and set everything on the back seat. Then he walked back, locked the interior door, and closed the overhead. He was just about to climb into his truck when he heard the neighbor next door say his name.

"Sam? Sam Whittle? Is that you?"

He turned and saw an elderly woman walking out of her flowerbed and over toward him. She wore an over- sized hat to keep the sun off her face, blue jeans with dirty knees, green plastic garden boots, and a sweatshirt, even though it was a warm day. He couldn't remember her name, so he went with his manners instead. "Yes, ma'am. It's nice to see you again."

"And you, young man. My goodness, it's hot out here, isn't it?"

"It sure is," Sam said. "You've got to remember to hydrate when it's this warm. As a matter of fact, here—" He reached into the truck and handed the woman the other bottle of water he'd taken from his father's fridge.

"Thank you, dear. I was just about to go inside and get myself one when I saw you." She twisted the cap off the bottle and took a polite sip, then a larger one to quench her thirst, before setting the bottle down.

"I see the movers came and got everything," Sam said. "I wasn't sure exactly when they'd get here."

"Oh, yes, they were here yesterday. Worked hard and fast. Don and Karen really had them hustling. Anyway, I'll let you go. I didn't mean to intrude, I just wanted to make sure it was family over here, and not some sort of crook."

*No, the crooks have come and gone,* Sam thought.

"What was that?" The neighbor said.

"I said, no, I just wanted to come over and get my books."

The woman clapped her hands a single time like she might be trying to kill a gnat. "Oh, Sam, your books are absolutely wonderful. I've read every one of them. When is the next one coming out?"

"Thank you. I'm not quite sure. My editor has it now. Probably in a few months."

"Well, I can't wait, that's for sure. And, listen, Sam, about your father...I'm so sorry for your loss, but I hope you know how proud he was of you, and what you've made of yourself. It's all he ever really talked about."

And in that single moment of time, Sam had never felt more alone in his entire life.

# CHAPTER FOURTEEN

Virgil and Murton arrived at the Tate residence, a tan brick McMansion located in one of Kokomo's nicer subdivisions. The house itself backed up to the Wildcat Creek Golf Course. As they climbed out of Virgil's truck, Murton looked at his brother and said, "You ever think about trying golf sometime?"

Virgil gave Murton a dry look, and said, "I think golf is a complete and total waste of time."

"So you've tried it then," Murton said.

Virgil chuckled. "I wouldn't exactly call it that. I think they actually invented the term Mulligan when I was on the course."

Murton was about to take another poke at his brother when the front door opened. A middle-aged man with salt and pepper hair—trending more toward salt—greeted them with a sad smile. "Are you the detectives from the state?"

"We are," Virgil said. "I'm Detective Virgil Jones, and this is my partner, Murton Wheeler."

"I'm John Tate, Lisa's father. Thank you for making the trip up. Please, come in."

Tate led them through the house. It had a modern, open and airy design, tastefully decorated with just a whiff of money showing in the artwork and furnishings. They made their way into what Virgil thought must have been Tate's home office, a richly appointed room with bookshelves on three walls that stretched from floor to ceiling, a massive desk with two computer monitors, and a comfortable seating area with four high-backed wing chairs. The view from Tate's desk gave onto the golf course that bordered the backyard. Once they were seated, Virgil looked at Tate and said, "Will your wife be joining us, sir?"

Tate nodded. "She should be here any minute. She's rented a small office space downtown as sort of a command center. We have it staffed twelve hours a day with community volunteers who are trying to help us find Lisa. Putting up flyers around town, making phone calls, that sort of thing. Do you think it'll help?"

*Probably not,* Virgil thought. "It certainly can't hurt, sir."

Tate waved his statement away, and said, "Please, call

me John. Would either of you care for coffee or a beverage?"

"No, thank you," Murton said. "While we're waiting on Mrs. Tate, could you tell us a little bit about your daughter?"

"You don't have to wait on me," Tate's wife said. "I'm right here."

The three men stood when she entered the room, and John Tate made the introductions. "Gentlemen, this is my wife, Amy. Sweetheart, meet Detectives Virgil Jones, and Murton Wheeler."

They all shook hands, and Amy said, "A pleasure, I'm sure." She looked directly at Virgil and said, "I understand you lead the team that works directly for Mac."

Virgil kept his face neutral. If Amy Tate could refer to the governor of the state by his nickname, then they were indeed close. "Yes, Detective Wheeler and I are part of the Major Crimes Unit. We report directly to the governor through his chief of staff—our direct boss— Cora LaRue. Cora was once a police officer herself, and—"

"Yes, thank you, Detective. I'm aware of Miss LaRue's vitae. Yours as well. The detectives you had looking into our daughter's disappearance have been competent but I have to tell you, it's something of a relief to finally have the leader of the unit taking charge."

Virgil watched Amy Tate as she spoke. She was fashion-ably dressed, had short dark hair, and wore very little makeup. She wasn't exactly what Virgil would describe as pretty, but she was attractive, in an almost harsh sort of way. She held her hands in her lap, constantly massaging one with the other. Her fingernails had been bitten down to the quick.

"I can assure you, ma'am, my entire team will be focusing on Lisa's disappearance and using every resource at our disposal to close this case."

Amy's face reddened, and she said, "That's a very diplomatic way of saying you'll work it until something bigger comes along, isn't it? Well, let me tell you, Detectives, I won't stand for it. Our daughter, our only child has been missing for three weeks and no one seems to care."

Murton cleared his throat. "Mrs. Tate, that's simply not true. The governor cares, your community cares, and I can assure you, we care. And, we're good at what we do." He leaned forward slightly in his chair, and said, "*Very* good. But we're going to need your help. That's why my partner and I are here today. We need you to tell us about Lisa...what kind of girl she is, who her friends are, what she does with her free time outside of school. The smallest of details, even if they seem inconsequential to you, could be of great importance to us."

"Don't you people keep records, for God's sake? We've been through all that with your other two detectives, Ross and, um, the other one...Rosebush."

"That'd be Rosencrantz, ma'am," Virgil said. "And to answer your question, yes, we do keep records. I've looked at their preliminary reporting, but we wanted to hear the facts straight from both of you. It's one thing to read it on paper, it's another to gather the information first-hand."

Amy seemed to relax a bit, then said, "Our daughter's name is Lisa Ann Tate. She turned seventeen last week. I say that because I believe she is still alive, even though we missed her birthday. She is a straight-A student who volunteers at the homeless shelter, she attends church every Sunday, she's an athlete—both soccer and cross-country—she has a part-time job at the grocery store..."

———

VIRGIL AND MURTON SPENT OVER TWO HOURS WITH the Tates, gathering every scrap of information they could regarding young Lisa Tate, and when they'd gotten everything they could, Virgil gave them his card and said, "Someone from our squad will keep you updated as often as necessary. We'll have follow-up questions as the investigation progresses, so you'll be hearing from us on a regular basis. Our researcher's name is Becky Wheeler, and she's Murton's wife. She is also extremely good at what she does. Expect to hear from her more than anyone. When something breaks in this case—"

"You mean if, don't you, Detective," Amy said.

"With respect, ma'am, I do not," Virgil said. "Please do not put words into my mouth. When something breaks, you'll be the first to hear it. I give you my word."

Amy Tate looked away and didn't respond. Then she

walked out of the room without bothering to say goodbye.

John Tate walked them back through the house and out the front door. Once they were outside, he looked at Virgil and Murton, and said, "I'd like to apologize for my wife's demeanor. She's one of the kindest, most caring people I've ever known, and I find myself honored to be her husband." Then he let out a sad little laugh, and said, "And believe it or not, she's actually quite charming. But all this...well, it's taken a toll. I hope you'll forgive her."

"It's not necessary to apologize," Murton said. "We completely understand."

Tate finally let a little fear of his own show, his voice feathered with anger. "*Understand?* Do you have children, Detective Wheeler?"

Murton remained calm. "No, sir, I don't."

"Then you couldn't possibly understand what this has been like for me and my wife."

"With respect, John, I do. More than you might imagine. The man standing next to me isn't only my partner, he's my brother. He has two young sons—my nephews—whose individual lives were threatened on two separate occasions. I not only found the men responsible for trying to cause them harm, I also took them off the board, if you get my drift."

Tate turned and looked at nothing for a few seconds. When he turned back, he said, "She's a diabetic and needs to take her insulin every day. She's been gone for three weeks. We missed her last birthday. She should be getting ready for college." He paused for just a moment, then finished with, "She's dead, isn't she?"

When neither Virgil nor Murton answered, Tate turned around and went back inside his house, closing the door softly behind him.

Virgil and Murton walked down the steps and over to Virgil's truck. Just as Virgil rounded the front fender, he saw Tate running back out of the house, straight for Murton. Virgil looked at his brother and shouted, "Murt, on your six."

Murton spun around as Tate grabbed him by his arms and pushed him back against the truck. Virgil started to move around to the other side of his truck, but when he saw that Tate wasn't a real threat, he simply stopped and watched. Tears were streaming down Tate's cheeks, and spittle flew from his lips as he screamed at Murton. "You find these motherfuckers and do for my daughter what you did for your own nephews. Do you hear me? Do you understand what I'm saying?" Then he let his whole body collapse into Murton, as if grief, misery, and sorrow were somehow a mechanical function of his knees. Murton held Tate up, then helped him back to the front door, Tate's arm around Murton's shoulders, like a wounded warrior.

Virgil watched as the two men stood there for a moment, the front door hanging open. Murton leaned close and said something into Tate's ear. Tate listened, gave Murton a tight nod, and went back inside.

Once they were in the truck, Virgil looked at Murton and said, "What'd you say to him?"

"I told the man we'd find his daughter."

Virgil knew that wasn't all that was said. "What else? Hey, Murt...?"

---

ON THE WAY BACK TO INDIANAPOLIS, VIRGIL PUNCHED in Ross's number on the truck's main display. "Where are you, young man?"

"Hey, Boss. Headed back to Indy. Almost there as a matter of fact."

"Did you get anything out of Howard County's records?"

"Not a thing. Or, I guess I should say nothing we didn't already know. Sort of a wasted trip."

"Did they give you copies of their investigative reports?"

"Yup. Got them boxed up and sitting right next to me."

"Okay, Murt and I just left the Tate residence. We're headed back as well. Get ahold of Rosie and Becky. I want everyone at the MCU in an hour. Time to come up with a plan."

"You got it, Jonesy. Say, I heard that little Wu guy threw you in the pool...twice. Is there any truth to that?"

Virgil thumbed the button on the steering wheel and ended the call without answering Ross's question. Then he looked at Murton, and said, "Was there anyone you didn't tell?"

Murton tipped his head in thought. After a few seconds, he said, "A few people might have slipped through the cracks, but I'm pretty sure I covered everyone who matters."

———

ONCE THEY WERE ALL IN THE MCU'S CONFERENCE room, Virgil, Murton, and Becky listened to Ross and Rosencrantz give their account of both their interview with the Tates and what they'd done in the meantime.

"It sounds like your interview went pretty much the same way ours did," Virgil said. He turned to Becky and said, "Do we have case notes yet for all the other missing girls?"

Becky shook her head. "Not yet. We've got some...a little over half, I'd say. Probably have the rest by the morning."

"Okay. That's great, Becks. The quicker the better."

Murton looked at Virgil, and said, "Isn't that what Small always tells you?"

Virgil ignored him. Then Becky said, "By the way, I'm putting a program together that's going to take all the relevant data we can gather on the victims, and sort through everything to find any commonalities. And before you ask, no, it's not ready yet."

"I wasn't going to ask," Virgil said.

"Uh-huh. Well, before you ask *when* it's going to be ready, the answer is I don't know."

"Why not?"

Becky gave him an eye roll. "Jonesy, I can't write a program if I don't know what the parameters are."

"That's why we're here right now...to figure out what we need, and what we don't. Let's use Lisa Tate as our, uh, control subject, I guess you'd say." Virgil pulled out his notebook. "Here's what we know: Lisa Ann Tate was a straight-A student who volunteered at the homeless shelter, she attended church every Sunday, she was a school athlete, and she had a part-time job at the grocery store." He turned to Ross and Rosencrantz. "Tell me, specifically, what you've done so far."

Rosencrantz took out his case notes. "We've got the names of all her teachers, every student she knew at her school, and everyone she volunteered with. We also have the names of her pastor and her coaches...she did both soccer and cross-country. We've got her boss at the grocery store, and her co-workers as well. We've done preliminary interviews with all of them. It was a long week, and so far, nothing is jumping out at us."

"My hope is, it's about to," Virgil said. "We're not going to just run the victims and look for commonalities, we're going to run every single person who has ever been interviewed as well...for all of the victims." He turned back to Becky. "Those are your parameters. We're going to do that for Lisa Tate, and once we have all the rest of the case files for the other girls, we'll run them too."

When Becky heard that she went a little pale. "Jonesy, that's a fine idea, but statistically, we're talking about a lot of girls. It'll take a month just to input all the data from every significant person these girls knew or had contact with."

Virgil smiled at her. "Get those case files from the other counties. Interview notes, all of it. Every single scrap. We'll have all the information in the system and ready to analyze in less than a week. Go write your program." Then he stood up to leave.

"Where are you going?" Murton said.

"To see my wife."

# CHAPTER FIFTEEN

Virgil called Sandy at the statehouse and told her he was on his way. "I need a few minutes with you and Mac. Can you make that happen?"

There was a pause and Virgil could hear his wife clicking away on the computer. "I should be able to. When will you be here?"

"In about twenty minutes," Virgil said.

"There's no rush, then. He's wrapped up for another half hour. We've both got time after that. What's up?"

Virgil smiled. "Maybe nothing. Or maybe a little extortion."

After he ended his call with Sandy, Virgil punched in another number.

Virgil didn't take his time, he hurried. He needed to speak with Cora as well. When he walked into her office, she looked at him like he was some sort of alien. "Your island tan really makes those white T-shirts pop. You look a little skinny, too."

Virgil smiled at her. "Got a few minutes? I've got a meeting with Mac, but I wanted to run something by you first."

Cora frowned at him, then checked the governor's schedule on her computer. When she looked back at Virgil, she was still frowning. "I thought we agreed—not that long ago, mind you—that you weren't going to make a habit out of this."

"Twice hardly constitutes a habit, Cora."

"As your little friend Wu would say, potato, tomato. Speaking of Wu, I heard he put you in the drink...twice."

"Yeah, yeah. Anyway, I won't...make it a habit. I was speaking with Sandy and just for the sake of expedience, I asked her if Mac had any open time. She said he did."

"Uh-huh. Just like last time, right?"

"Yeah, so?"

"So, that makes it a habit."

Virgil held up his hands in defeat. "I'm sorry. Won't happen again. Really." *Unless it has to,* Virgil thought.

"What was that?" Cora said.

"I said I need to talk to you, too."

"About what?"

"I need a small increase in the discretionary budget."

"Why?" Cora said.

"If you keep frowning like that, you're going to get a permanent line."

"If you don't answer my question, you're going to get a permanent fine," Cora said. "Now spill it. How much, and what for?"

Virgil tried to do the math in his head but failed. "I uh...don't really have a solid number yet."

"Well, uh...get back with me when you do. What's it for?"

"I want to put together a statewide task force. Did you know that on average over twenty-two teenaged girls go missing in this state every year...?"

---

SANDY WALKED INTO CORA'S OFFICE AS VIRGIL WAS wrapping up his speech. She walked over, gave her husband a peck on the cheek, winked at Cora, then, to Virgil, said, "Ready? Mac's waiting."

"I think so. Cora?"

"Yes, yes, get out of here. And for the love of God, please stop trying to invent ways to spend the state's money, will you?"

Virgil turned his palms up. "Think positively, Cora. And remember, it's for the children. Besides, if I get my way, we might not have to touch the discretionary budget at all."

"Yeah, like that'll ever happen. Now go."

WHEN THEY WALKED INTO THE GOVERNOR'S OFFICE, Mac stood, smiled at Virgil, and said, "I heard you let a ninety-pound Asian man throw you into the pool. Twice."

Virgil let his eyelids droop. "Yeah, yeah, you're only about the twelfth person to remind me. Is there anyone who doesn't know about it?"

The governor smiled. "What can I tell you? Word gets around."

"Whatever. And technically, he only threw me in once. The second time he pushed me."

"Well, if that was part of his plan, it seems to have worked. You're looking fit. Ready to rumble, as they say." Then, right down to business. "Speaking of rumbling... where are we with the Tates?"

"I understand you're close. You and the Tates," Virgil said.

The governor seemed to consider the question. "John and Amy Tate have made a considerable investment in my political career over the years."

Virgil tipped his head and said, "Ah." The governor was speaking of big money donors.

"In any event, I'd like to find a way to bring them some closure regarding their daughter, Lisa."

"That's why I'm here, Mac. We've got a plan that's coming together as we speak. I'd like to put a statewide task force in place to gather every scrap of information we can about all the missing teenage girls going back two years. If what we have planned works out, we'll be able to go back further, potentially solving a number of current and cold-case files, not just Lisa Tate."

"What do you need from me?"

"Other than your permission, nothing."

The governor shook his head. "Jonesy, you're among the highest-ranking law enforcement officials in the state. You don't need my permission to start a task force. Work out the budget issues with Cora and get it done."

"I've already started that process, Mac. And you'll have to forgive me, but that isn't why I needed your permission."

"Then what are we talking about here?"

"The amount of data we'll be collecting is too much for us to process alone. Becky simply can't do it by herself. It would take months to input all the data and find any connections. I'd like to bring in some outside talent for a week. Maybe two."

The governor let his chin drop to his chest. When he looked back up, he said, "You're not talking about..."

"They are the best we could ever hope for. This is what they do, Mac."

The governor shook his head. "Jonesy, every time the Pope crew has access to our system, we're at risk."

"It didn't stop you from using them before," Virgil said.

Sandy touched her husband on the arm. "That was to benefit Murton, and you."

"I know that," Virgil said. "And I'm grateful. But if I'm

not mistaken, we all benefitted from that in one way or another."

"Be that as it may, I'm not entirely sure I want two world-class hackers in our system...again," the governor said. "Look what happened with the lottery."

Virgil shook his head. "Ancient history, Mac. You know that. Nothing was ever proven, and in the eyes of the law, no crime was ever committed. I know these people. We can trust them." When the governor didn't respond, Virgil continued with, "And based on what I saw a little over a week ago, it seems you do too."

The governor pointed a friendly finger at Virgil. "That's personal. Nothing to do with the state. And, not to put too fine a point on it, my private business."

"What was that you said a few minutes ago?" Virgil asked. "Something about word gets around?"

Sandy's face went pale. The governor looked at her and said, "Have you been giving your husband lessons on the methodology of political maneuvering?"

Virgil laughed. "Mac, you've been doing that to me ever since we met."

The governor chuckled. "I suppose I have, in one way or another." Then he slapped his thighs, stood, and said, "Okay, if they'll do it, we'll have them. But the responsibility is on you, Detective."

"Thanks, Mac. I won't let you down."

"I know you won't," the governor said. Then: "Lisa Tate is dead, isn't she?"

Virgil bit into his lower lip and nodded. "If it weren't

for the fact that she needs daily meds, I'd tell you it could go either way. But when you factor the insulin into the equation, I'm afraid I'd have to say she's almost certainly gone. Mrs. Tate is still holding out hope on some level, but John seems to have acknowledged it in his own way. But we'll find who did it."

"I hope you do," the governor said. He walked Virgil and Sandy to the door, then said, "How long did you say all this will take?"

Virgil tugged at an earlobe, then said, "A week. Maybe two. I wouldn't think any longer than that."

"When do you think they can be here and get started? Nicky and Wu?"

Virgil smiled. "They're already on their way. I called them before I came over here."

"Get to it then," the governor said. He opened the door and let them out, looked at Cora, and said, "Approve whatever funding is necessary for the MCU's task force."

Once Virgil and Sandy were gone, the governor walked back into his office, picked up the phone, and made a call to a number very few people in the world knew of. "I hope you're on the plane as well."

"What do you think?" Nichole said.

———

THE GOVERNOR STUCK HIS HEAD BACK OUT OF HIS office, looked at Cora, and said, "Clear my schedule for the next week, please. Completely. And make sure anything scheduled for the following week is flexible."

Cora stuck her tongue in her cheek, then said she would.

"Why are you looking at me like that?"

"No reason," Cora said. *Except...word gets around.*

---

SAM AND DANIKA HAD SPENT THE LAST FIVE MONTHS trying to decide what—if anything—they were going to do about Karen and Don. Initially, after Sam had discovered that his siblings had cleaned out his father's house prior to the reading of the will, he was furious. He was no longer certain that he'd been written out of the will as his brother and sister had told him. What he really felt was they were punishing him for the nature of his relationship with his father.

"Who are they to judge?" Danika asked him one night. They'd both just returned from Sam's latest book tour. They were tired, but happy. The book was being called a literary masterpiece, and the publisher had already paid out an advance for Sam's next novel.

"They're nobody," Sam said. "They went in, cleaned the place out, lied to my face, and ultimately decided that they'd rather have the money and the stuff instead of their brother."

"You know what I don't understand? Why wasn't

there a probate process? Indiana law says there has to be if the estate is worth more than fifty thousand."

"That's just it, Danni. Technically, it wasn't. At least that's what the lawyer told me. Karen had power of attorney, and she refinanced his house right before he died. Where that money went is anyone's guess, but I'll bet her bank account is pretty fat right now. Don's too. Anyway, the house is out, and the furnishings—no matter how much they're worth—are considered garage sale value, and liquid cash of any kind held by the deceased at the time of death, including gold coins, or bearer bonds, aren't included."

"What about any bank accounts he had?" Danni said.

"Same story. Karen had power of attorney and listed herself on all of the accounts. When Dad died, the banks cut her a check."

"Will we ever know what was in the will, or the safe, for that matter?"

"We'd have to sue them, and as I've said, I don't think I'm up for that. We don't need the money—hell, I don't even want it. All I ever wanted was my family, and now they're gone too. I guess it doesn't take too much imagination to figure out what they think of me."

"It doesn't matter what they think of you, Sam. You're a good and decent human who decided that you were no longer going to put up with your father's abuse. You were the one in the family who always told the truth. You. Not Don the liar, and certainly not Karen, the money-grubbing..."

"You can say it."

"Bitch," Danni said. "Because that's exactly what she is." She stood and moved over to the bookshelf and grabbed all four of the novels Sam had removed from his father's safe. She waved them in the air and said, "I'll tell you this: If these books were in the safe, that meant he valued them, at least on some level, even if your brother and sister didn't. It also means that no matter your past, your upbringing, the difficulties you faced, or the abuse... the fact that he kept these books means he loved you. It might not have been perfect, but I guess he did the best he could. At the very least, he respected you in his own warped way."

"Well, that's certainly one way of looking at it," Sam said. "Maybe the rose-colored glasses version, but I'm at the point where I don't know what to think anymore."

Danika walked over to replace the books on the shelf —they hadn't been moved since Sam brought them home over five months ago—and that's when she noticed what looked like a bookmark stuck between the pages of the fourth book. But it wasn't. It was a sealed white envelope. She pulled it free.

"Hey, Sam?"

"Yeah?"

"Look at this."

"What is it?"

She handed her husband the envelope. Written on the outside was Sam's name, and under that, a date. The date was two days before Dick Whittle's death.

Danika visibly swallowed, then said, "Is that your father's handwriting?"

Sam was biting into his lower lip so hard he thought it might soon start to bleed. "Yeah, it is. I guess my dad's not done with me yet."

## CHAPTER SIXTEEN

Danika sat down next to Sam, gently took the envelope from his hands, then set it on the table.

Sam looked at his wife, and said, "What?"

"Are you going to open it?"

Sam knew the question held a validity all its own, one where the borders might as well have been written in smoke. If he opened the envelope and discovered it was simply another devastating tirade from his dead father...a way to taunt him from the grave, Sam wanted no part of it. He'd made some progress after his father's death...had managed to find some peace, and even forgiveness for the way he was raised and how he'd been treated throughout his life. He also knew he still had a lot of work to do in that regard. Maybe a lifetime of work. On the other hand, if the envelope contained something that could help him heal and move on, its contents needed to be seen.

"Sam?"

"I don't know, Danni. You know my dad. I'm not sure looking at the contents of that envelope could be good for me. In some ways, I think it might destroy me, or at the very least, set me back about six months."

They both stared at the envelope for a few minutes, then Danika said, "Would you like me to open it?"

"Yeah, maybe you better. If it's something you know I don't want to see, I'll deal with it when I'm ready."

Danika wasn't exactly sure if that logic was sound or not, but she trusted her husband and his instincts when it came to dealing with his own father. She grabbed the envelope, carefully peeled back the flap with her index finger, and pulled the contents out. There were three sheets of paper. When she looked at the first one, a single tear trickled down her cheek. When she looked at the other two, her hands began to shake.

Sam watched his wife's face turn red with anger, something he wasn't used to seeing. "Danni? You're shaking. What is it?"

Danika wiped the tear from her cheek, then handed Sam the first page. It was a short handwritten note:

*Sam,*

*If you're reading this, that means I'm probably trying to have some sympathy for the Devil right about now. In other words, I've kicked the bucket. I'm sorry I wasn't a better father to you. Maybe you won't believe this, but I did love you. The problem was, I didn't know how to love myself. I really wish someone had taught me, just like Danni has done for you. I've read every one of your books at least twice. Not only are they good, but I'm amazed by what you've accomplished. I'm proud of you, Sam. I always was. You alone ended up with your mother's heart.*

*Love—such as it is, I guess,*
    *Dad*
    *p.s. I can't put my finger on it, but there's something not quite right about Don. And, if you let her, Karen will take every plug nickel I ever earned. Don't let them get away with any of it, son.*

Sam read the note three times, his heart filled with an odd combination of anger, joy, and regret. His father had been a bitter, mean-spirited abusive man who never had the nerve to be vulnerable...to put himself out there for others who might have been able to show him how to love and be loved.

He looked at Danika, waved the note in the air, and said, "I'm not sure what to make of this. Why now? Why couldn't he have been different? Why couldn't he have loved me the way he writes in this note? I don't get it."

"I don't either," Danika said. She handed the other pages to Sam, then said, "But this is something to think about."

Sam took the other pages and read through them, quickly at first, then more carefully a second time. By the time he finished, his face was red, his own hands were shaking, and he was just as furious as his wife.

---

THE OTHER TWO PAGES FROM THE ENVELOPE CONTAINED Dick Whittle's last will and testament, along with a detailed listing of all his assets, the contents of the safe, and his bank account balances. Sam did some quick math in his head, and the total amount added up to nearly three million dollars. The will itself was direct and to the point. It said that the contents of the safe were to be split three ways, and the house and everything in it was to be sold, with the proceeds divided equally between Sam, Don, and Karen.

Danika looked at Sam, and said, "I think we should get back in touch with our lawyer. If we don't, we're looking at giving up almost a million dollars."

Sam nodded. "Yeah, that's the second thing I'm going to do."

"What's the first?"

"I'm going to go have a word with my siblings." He kissed his wife, took the will, and walked out the door. Karen lived the closest. He'd start with her.

---

KAREN LIVED ON ASH STREET IN WEST BADEN Springs, in a small bungalow-style house. Sam knew right away she wasn't home, because the house was dark.

He went to the front door anyway, rang the bell, knocked, and got no response. He walked around to the rear and tried the back door. It was unlocked—like so many small-town houses, and he stepped inside. When he turned the lights on, he almost couldn't believe what he saw.

Karen had gotten rid of all her own furnishings, and replaced them with things from his father's house. The fine leather furniture and end tables were crammed so tightly into the living room it was hard to walk around. The kitchen table was so big the refrigerator door wouldn't open all the way without moving the chairs aside. He wanted to look through the rest of the house, but he knew he needed to get out. Snooping around where he didn't belong—after dark, no less—would only lead to trouble, so he went back outside, got in his car, and headed north, toward Prospect, where his brother lived.

When he arrived, the result was the same. Nobody home. Except his brother had the good sense to keep the place locked up. Before he left, Sam peeked in through the front window and saw more of his father's furniture, along with the eighty-inch flatscreen TV. When he looked through the window of the side garage door, he saw his father's car and most of the things that had been in his garage. He was so mad and disgusted he almost forgot that Don had a second property—the hunting cabin tucked back in the woods—no more than five minutes away.

———

When Sam got to the cabin, he was surprised to find his brother and sister both there, standing next to their vehicles as if they'd just arrived, or were about to leave. He got out of his car, walked straight toward them, and before either of them could say anything, Sam balled his fist and hit Don with a solid left-handed jab that snapped his head back. Don stumbled back and fell to the ground. When he put his hands up to his nose, they came away bloody. He started to get up, but Sam pointed a finger and said, "If you get up, I'm going to kick your ass."

"That'll be the day," Don said. "I hope you've got good dental insurance. You're going to need it."

Karen took a step back, then turned to Sam and said, "Have you lost your mind? What the hell are you doing?"

Sam spoke, but he didn't look at her. He was watching his brother, who was pulling himself off the ground. "Shut up. Is this where you guys are hiding the money? Wait, don't bother answering. It'll just be another lie. If you weren't a woman, I'd knock the hell out of you too."

Don wiped his bloody nose on his shirt sleeve, then ran toward Sam, his face a mask of rage and embarrassment. When he was within striking distance, Sam turned slightly and kicked him in the balls as hard as he could.

Don's face went pale, and he bent over and vomited, both his hands holding his groin. Sam pushed him down, and said, "I told you not to get up."

Then he turned to Karen. "You thought you could get away with it, didn't you?"

"Get away with what? What are you talking about? You come racing in here like some sort of crazy man and start beating on your little brother? For what?"

Sam shook his head in disgust. "For what, she says. I'll tell you for what." He reached into his pocket and pulled out the copy of his father's will. "For this. It's Dad's will. He left me a copy, Karen. Everything was supposed to be split equally between the three of us, but you and that cherry-picking asshole in the dirt over there decided— against Dad's wishes—that it was going to be a two-way split."

"That's a forgery," Karen said.

"The hell it is. I thought you guys were my family. I guess I just found out how much I'm worth to both of you. About five hundred grand each." He turned his head and spat next to her feet.

"Sam, Dad gave me power of attorney, and made me the executor of his estate."

"Yeah, yeah, you've been throwing that line around for months. Well, guess what, Miss Executor, you're about to get your ass handed to you. Don too. The two of you have cheated me and Danni out of almost a million bucks."

"That's bullshit," Karen said. She had her teeth bared at him now. "There were only three copies of the will. I have one, the lawyer has one, and Dad had the other. I know what it says, and it isn't what you're telling me."

"I see Don has taught you how to lie almost as good as he does." He waved the will at her again. "This is Dad's copy. He left it for me. I just now found it. Actually, Danni did. Want to know where it was? It was inside one of my books. That's right...five months ago after the two of you went in there and stole all the loot, you made the mistake of leaving my books behind in the safe."

Karen was shaking her head. "Sam, listen to me, will you? Your books were the only thing in there."

"Not according to Dad. He left me an inventory sheet. The house, the furnishings, the gold coins, the bearer bonds, all of it."

Karen shook her head violently. "Shut up, shut up, shut up. There is no money."

"That's bullshit, Karen, and you know it." They were screaming at each other now.

"No, it's not. The estate didn't go to probate because it was valued at less than fifty thousand. That's the law."

"Right, and you made sure of that by stealing the contents of the safe, cramming your house with Dad's belongings, and giving a bunch of it to Don...yeah that's right, I went to both your places before I came here. You should lock your doors. I couldn't get into Don's but I looked in the window. I saw the furniture, the flatscreen TV, and the Benz in his garage. The car alone makes the estate worth more than fifty thousand, Karen. And you've got so much of Dad's stuff in your house you can't even open the refrigerator door all the way."

"You were in my house? *My house?*"

"Like I said, you should lock your doors."

"I can't believe you," Karen said.

"Yeah, that sounds about right. *You* can't believe *me*. Well, guess what, I can't believe you...or Don about anything anymore. Here are your choices: Write me a check for a million dollars, or I'll take both of you down. I'll file suit against you and Don. I'll also file against Dad's lawyer for letting you get away with everything. Now, what's it going to be?"

"Sam, listen to me. There is no money. Maybe it wasn't right that Don and I took Dad's stuff without offering you anything. I'm sorry. Tell me what you want, and you can have it. The car? It's yours. Whatever. But there is no money, and because I was the executor, I had the legal right to decide who gets what. Maybe if you'd been nicer to Dad all these years, I would have cut you in."

"Fuck you, Karen. I think you've actually gone crazy. No really, like a clinical thing. I think you're insane. Who the hell do you think you are to go against a deceased person's written wishes after their death?"

Karen smiled at him. "Check the law, asshole. I guarantee you, it's on my side."

"I already have, Karen. You're not only breaching a fiduciary responsibility to me, you're breaking practically all the laws in the book. I'll spend every last dime I've got to get what's mine, and in the process, I'll make sure you and Don go broke spending the money you stole from me."

Sam was so caught up in arguing with Karen, he didn't notice Don approach. He had a gun in his hand and he pressed it into Sam's ear at the same time he pulled the hammer back. The sound froze Sam.

"That's right," Don said. "Not such a tough guy now, are you? You've got ten seconds to turn around and walk away. If I ever see you again, I'll kill you...brother."

"You don't have the balls," Sam said.

Don pressed the gun harder into Sam's ear. He was applying so much pressure, Sam's head was tilted to the side. "I don't have the balls? Who do you think killed—"

Karen screamed at her brother. "Don!"

Don pulled the gun away, looked at Sam then shoved him toward his car. "Get out, and don't ever come back."

Sam looked at the two people he'd grown up with, suffered with, played with, and at that moment, he knew they were no longer his family, and never would be again. He barely recognized them...or perhaps he was finally recognizing them for who they really were. He shook his head and walked back to his car.

# CHAPTER SEVENTEEN

True to his word—or at the very least, his estimated timeframe—Virgil's task force was up and running a week later. Thanks to Nicky, Wu, and Becky, they had digitized every single detail of over twenty missing teenaged girls, along with anyone who knew them either casually or intimately. Once that was done, they let their program compile the data sets over the weekend, and first thing Monday morning, everyone sat down in the MCU's conference room to look at the results.

Virgil looked at his team, including Nicky and Wu, and said, "I want everyone to understand something: We're doing this to try to find out what happened to Lisa Tate. But as a point of fact, there isn't one single girl who is more or less important than she is. We'll follow every lead and try to narrow the results as much as possible but if it helps any of these young girls or their families in addition to Miss Tate, then we've done our job. That's confidential, by the way. The Tates are friends of the governor, so we'll want to keep that in mind."

Ross, who could be very direct at times, said, "You're suggesting Tate is our main priority, but we also want to find out about these other girls as well, all without letting the Tates know what, exactly, we're doing or how we're going about it. Do I have that right? Because if I do, and just for the sake of argument, let's say we find a bunch of kids, but none of them are Lisa Tate. Then what?"

"Let's not go there right now," Virgil said. "We'll cross that bridge if and when we need to. My hope is we won't have to do that."

Nicky and Wu weren't really paying attention. They weren't cops, and they really didn't care about the politics or procedures Virgil was discussing. They were both working at temporary computer stations that had been set up in the conference room. Their job—at least in the moment—was to search for all the girls who might still be alive. They were scouring every database they could—all across the country—to find out how many of the girls had either run away with a boyfriend or simply decided to go and live their lives elsewhere. It happened, and they all knew it. As a matter of fact, over the weekend, Wu had found five, and Nicky had found three. They had a little competition going, and Nicky was desperately trying to catch up.

"It no use," Wu said. "I am better than you."

"Yeah, yeah, keep talking," Nicky said. "While you're running your mouth, I'll find the next one."

"Keep after it, guys," Virgil said. "You're doing great. The more you find, the better off we all are...especially the girls."

"Wu will do. Cannot speak for Nicky."

Nicky ignored him.

Virgil turned back to his people. "We started with twenty-two girls. So far, we know eight of them are alive."

"That sort of creates a problem all by itself, doesn't it?" Murton said. He walked over to Nicky's station and said, "Can I see that list?"

Nicky handed Murton the list, and he looked at it for a few minutes, then said, "Based on the birth dates of the ones they've found so far, as of this moment, all but one of them have turned eighteen or older. In the eyes of the law, they're adults now. Three are in Vegas, two are in LA, one is in Miami, another is in Seattle, and the one who isn't yet eighteen is living in Mexico. That'd be Mexico, the town in Indiana, not the country."

"What's your point?" Rosencrantz said.

"My point is," Murton said, "there really isn't anything we can do about it. I'm not sure we'd want to, even if we could."

"Explain that," Becky said.

Virgil shook his head. "He's right, Becks. These girls, or young women, I guess I should say, took off for a reason. Maybe they were being abused, or whatever. If we reveal their locations to their parents or whoever they ran from, we might be putting them right back into a bad situation."

"What if they're in a bad situation right now?" Becky said.

"Your point is valid, but the bottom line is this: They're adults."

But Becky wasn't ready to let it go. "So the parents of these missing girls have to wonder where their child is, whether they are dead or not, and we have actual proof that they're alive and we're supposed to keep that information to ourselves? That's nuts."

"We're not going to keep it to ourselves," Virgil said. "Not exactly."

"Meaning what?" Murton said.

Virgil looked at his brother. "Know of a high-ranking official in the state who used to be a cop, and has a degree in psychology?"

Murton smiled. "You're speaking of Small?"

"He is," Sandy said. She'd just walked into the room. "I'm going to have Cool fly me to the different counties where these girls were from. First I'll interview the investigators who initially worked the case, then based on my assessment of their findings, I may or may not go and speak with the parents or guardians of these young ladies."

"So you'll have the final say?" Ross said, letting his directness fly around the room.

Sandy smiled and winked at him. "You're cute when you get right to the point."

"No, he isn't," Virgil said. Then to Ross: "And as a member of the MCU, you'll be accompanying my wife as her protective detail."

"That's fine," Ross said. "What about Baker?"

"She's on vacation this week, so you were going to get the job no matter," Sandy said.

"I don't mean to get all political on everyone," Rosencrantz said. "But if Mac is off...uh...well, I mean Nichole is in town and all that, and if you're flying around doing assessments of the victim's families, who exactly, is running the executive branch of our state government?"

Murton snorted. "Probably the same person who always does. Cora."

Becky looked at Sandy and said, "Do you want to punch him, or should I?"

———

DON AND KAREN WEREN'T EXACTLY PANICKING, BUT they were close. "I don't know why we have to keep meeting out here," Karen said. "I hate this place." They were inside Don's cabin, and while it was neat, there was an odor of stale beer, cigar smoke, and microwaved pizza. "The things you've done out here are sick. You need to get help, Don."

"I told you I'd quit all that when Dad died, and I have."

Karen looked at her brother for a long minute. "Have you?"

"When you ask someone the same question after they've already answered, it's the same thing as calling them a liar."

Karen let her expression speak for itself.

"Yeah, well, fuck you too," Don said. "It's not like you didn't do a little killing yourself."

"You're just as guilty as I am," Karen said. "You're the one who bought the arsenic."

"Yeah, and you're the one who gave it to him, made sure it was in his coffee pot every morning, and his liquor bottle every afternoon."

"Look, Don, we talked about this months ago. We had to get rid of him. He was spending every last dime right out from under us."

"Buying a new car isn't exactly spending every last dime. I think we could have waited. He was going to kick the bucket sooner or later."

Karen shook her head in frustration. "It doesn't matter. What's done is done. We've got to focus on what we're going to do now. Sam isn't going to let this go. Maybe we should cut him in. He's got a list of assets. If it's accurate—and it probably is—then he's not going to just wait and see what happens."

"I'm not giving up a half million, especially to a guy who doesn't even need it. Besides, I spent my entire life earning that money."

"We all earned it, Don, in one way or another. Even Sam. Maybe especially Sam."

"Yeah, maybe. But I can't give up my share. I owe

some pretty heavy hitters, and you know it. If I don't pay up, these aren't the kind of guys who just shrug their shoulders and walk away."

"Sometimes I think you're deranged. You've killed and raped god only knows how many women, all while gambling your inheritance away. What's wrong with you?"

"There's nothing wrong with me," Don said. "Things just got a little out of hand."

"How far out of hand?"

"Almost the exact same amount I'd have to pay Sam. That means I'd end up with about a million, while you end up with almost twice that when you count the money from the sale of the house. We should have split that too."

Karen was shaking her head. She pointed a finger at him and said, "No. Dad always told me he wanted me to have the house. Me, and only me."

Don waved her words away. "First of all, that's bullshit, even if he said it or not. It's what's in his will that matters, and you know what the will says. Secondly, if you wanted the house so bad, why are you just letting it sit there? Sell the damned place."

"I don't have to sell it. I refinanced it before he died, you idiot. The mortgage company will foreclose, and I'll get to keep the money."

"Yeah, great plan, Karen. Do you think they won't come after you?"

"They can't. The lawyer made sure of that."

"Well, good for you," Don said. "That still doesn't get us anywhere when it comes to Sam."

"If we make an enemy out of him, things could start to unravel for us in ways I don't want to think about," Karen said. "You in particular, especially after everything you've done out here. Where are the bodies?"

"Why?" Don asked, suddenly suspicious. "Going to turn me in?"

"Of course not."

"Damn straight you're not. Because if you ever do, I'll go away for life. Probably get the needle." He walked over and got right in his sister's face. "And if that ever happens, I'll tell them what really happened with Dad, and what you did. Maybe they'd wheel in a double gurney and execute us both at the same time."

Karen edged away from her brother. She was the only one who knew her brother's secret, and she also knew that if Don killed her, all his problems would go away. *Time to reconsider,* she thought. "Listen, Don, I love you, and even though I'd hate to do it, if we give Sam his money, I think everything could work out. Let's do what he wants. I'll cover half your share if you clean up your gambling debts and address your other...problem. Go see a therapist, or whatever. If you do that, you'll still be out three-quarters of a million, but so will I. That makes us even."

"Not quite, Karen. You've still got the money from the house. I want half of that too."

"Don, you've got the car. Sell it."

"The car cost over a hundred grand brand new. I'd get fifty at best. Meanwhile, you're sitting on almost three hundred grand from the refi on Dad's house. That's hardly fair, and you know it."

"That's as far as I'll go, Don. Your problems are your own. I won't budge from that. Take it or leave it."

"I guess I'll take it then," Don said. "Take it right up the ass, is what it sounds like."

Karen was losing her patience. "Enough. There's something else I want to talk about."

"What now?" Don said.

"I've been watching the price of gold. It's higher now than it has been in a long time. I want my share. I'm going to cash it in."

Don laughed. "Bullshit. You're afraid I'll spend it."

"The reason doesn't matter," Karen said. "Open your safe and hand it over."

Don stared at his one and only sister with disgust. Finally, he moved to the center of the room and pushed the sofa aside. He bent down, pulled on the handle set into the hardwood, and opened a small hinged section that revealed his floor safe. He spun the knob a few times, entered the combination, and opened the door. When he reached inside, he pulled out exactly half of the gold coin rolls, then handed them to his sister before locking the safe and replacing the rug and sofa. "Satisfied?"

"Yes," Karen said. Then she let out a little laugh, and said, "Do you want to give Sam the check, or do you want me to?"

"You're the executor," Don said. "I'll let you handle it. I don't ever want to see that son of a bitch again."

Karen put the gold in her bag and moved to the door. Once they were outside, Karen turned to her brother and said, "This is all for the best, Don. We'll take care of Sam, and then neither of us has anything to worry about."

*That's one way of handling it,* Don thought.

"Why are you looking at me like that?" Karen said, not realizing the words she just spoke would be her last.

Don pulled out his father's gun and shot his sister in the head. He took the gold from her bag and ran it back inside the cabin. Then he went back outside, picked up his sister's body, and carried her back to his special place in the woods, speaking to her the entire time, as if she could still hear him. "I'll stop when I'm ready, and guess what, Karen? I'm not ready. In fact, I don't think I'll ever be ready. I took another one not long ago. And I'm getting ready to do it again. Bet you didn't know that...or did you? Oh, and fuck Sam. He isn't getting a penny, and neither are you. Do you hear me, Karen? Not one goddamned cent."

## CHAPTER EIGHTEEN

By the end of the day, Nicky and Wu had found three more girls living in various parts of the country, bringing the total number of girls still alive and well up to eleven. Sandy hadn't yet returned from interviewing the various investigators who'd originally worked the cases, and while they were waiting for her, Virgil, Murton, and Rosencrantz were still reviewing the data sets that Becky's program had churned out. They soon discovered that at the rate Nicky and Wu were locating the girls who'd simply gone off on their own, it was becoming increasingly difficult to find any commonalities between any of the girls and Lisa Tate.

"You know what we need?" Virgil said.

"I need a beer," Rosencrantz said.

Murton looked at his brother, and said, "If you say what I think you're going to say, you get to tell her. Not me."

"I'm not sure what else we can do, Murt," Virgil said. They were in Virgil's office, each of them with stacks of paper in their laps. "We need more data. Essentially half the girls we're looking at have been found. Nicky and Wu are confident they won't find Tate because they've been looking and haven't found one single thing that indicates she is alive, and none of the girls have anything that links them to any one particular person. We need to go back further."

"How much further do you think?" Rosencrantz said.

Virgil turned his palms up. "I'm not sure. I'd like to go back another three or four years. We'll put out a request to every county in the state."

"Then you're definitely telling her," Murton said.

"What's the matter?" Rosencrantz said. "Afraid of your wife?"

Murton gave him a dull look. "No, but why suffer the consequences of someone else's decision?"

Rosencrantz turned the corners of his mouth down. "I can see that."

Virgil hit a button on his desk phone, then said, "Hey Becks, see you in my office for a minute?"

"Sure. Be right there."

Murton stood up. "I'll be in the break room."

Rosencrantz stood as well. "I have to pee."

A few minutes later when Becky walked in, she said, "What's up?"

Virgil gave her his best nice-guy smile. "I've got good news and bad news."

Becky frowned and said, "Where's Murt and Rosie? I thought you guys were going through the data."

"We are. They, uh, just stepped out for a second. I'm sure they'll be right back. Anyway, the data your program is putting out is great. That's the good news."

"What's the bad?" Becky said.

"We need more of it because so far not one single shred of it connects Lisa Tate to anyone...at all. I'd like you to put out an immediate high-priority request to every county in the state for all case files on missing teenage girls going back four years."

Becky wasn't surprised. "Anything else?"

Virgil hesitated, then gave her the brow. "No, except, if I'm being honest, I thought you might blow a gasket or something."

Becky smiled at him. "You know me...I'm a go-getter. And stop with the brow, Spock. When do you need it?"

"The sooner the better."

"How's first thing tomorrow morning sound?"

"A little like a miracle," Virgil said. Then he lowered his brow and said, "What have you done?"

"Like I said, I'm a go-getter. I already put the request out. At the rate Nicky and Wu were turning up the missing girls—the live ones, I mean—I knew we'd need more information. Except I asked for five years, not four."

Virgil wasn't upset, but he was a bit of a control freak. "That's good thinking, Becky, but you probably should have told me first. I am your boss, after all."

"Jonesy, you're talking to the woman who once

convinced the state's National Guard I was the lieutenant governor. I'm not afraid to break a rule every once in a while. You're also my brother-in-law, so I get to push you around a little. It's one of the many benefits of being married to Murt. As benefits go, it's pretty much at the bottom of the list, I'll give you that, but a benny is a benny, right?"

———

THE NEXT MORNING SANDY SET OFF WITH COOL AND Ross to finish interviewing the investigators of the girls who'd been located. Becky was inputting more data into the system with Nicky and Wu's help. Rosencrantz, along with Virgil and Murton were still going through the data, trying to find a connection when Virgil's desk phone rang.

"Hey, Jonesy. It's Patty. How are you?"

"I'm well, Patty. How are you?"

Patty Doyle was Rick Said's niece, a young woman Virgil had once rescued from certain death after she'd been kidnapped and locked in the basement of an abandoned farmhouse. And because Virgil and Said were business partners in the sonic drilling operation, he and Patty had remained close over the years.

"I might need your help."

"What's wrong? Is your Uncle Rick okay?"

"Oh, yeah, he's fine. That's not why I'm calling."

"How can I help?" Virgil said.

Patty let out a sigh, then said, "When I was going to

school at IU, I had a part-time gig tutoring a young girl. She was ten or eleven at the time if I remember correctly. Anyway, we sort of stayed in touch over the years, and she and her family recently moved to Shelby County. I ran into her by chance about a month ago and told her what I was doing at the cultural center. She took an immediate interest, so I gave her the nickel tour, and by the end, she was so excited, I offered her an internship at the center so she'd have something substantial for her college applications."

"Sounds great, Patty."

"It was until she didn't show up a few days ago. When I called her house, no one answered. You've got to understand, this is a really responsible kid, so I chalked it up to some type of family emergency or something, and since I was pretty busy that morning, I didn't give it much more thought. Anyway, about an hour after I got home, her parents called me, and they were frantic. She's missing and hasn't been heard from since."

Virgil sat up in his chair. "What's her name?"

"Kelly Price. She's seventeen years old."

"What did Ed say? What's he doing about it?"

"Who's Ed?"

Virgil mentally palmed his forehead. "Sorry. Ed Henderson. He's the sheriff of Shelby County."

"Oh, yeah. Okay. According to Kelly's parents, they've been searching, but they can't find her anywhere. This isn't the type of kid to just take off, Jonesy. Someone has her. I've been through this before, and I know you know that. She's in trouble. I can feel it. I'm hoping you'll get with the sheriff and see what else he can do."

Virgil was nodding into the phone. "I'll do better than that. I'll get one of my men down there right away. Tom Rosencrantz."

Patty was quiet for a few seconds, then said, "Listen, I don't mean to sound disrespectful, but wasn't he the guy who couldn't find me when I was missing? I heard he wanted to give up. If it hadn't been for you..."

"Patty, you're not really going to want to hear this, but I got lucky. I was in a position to receive some information that simply clicked with me, and when it did, that's when I found you."

"Jonesy..."

"Listen Patty, I'll get Rosencrantz headed that way right now, as soon as we get off the phone. I'll have Murton go as well if that makes you feel better. I'll also call the sheriff myself and speak with him. We're working a statewide task force right now, looking into missing teenage girls, so we'll add her information to the data we already have and see what turns up. Fair enough?"

"Yes, I guess so. This is a good girl, Jonesy. You guys have got to help her."

"We'll do everything we can, Patty. I promise."

---

VIRGIL GAVE MURTON AND ROSENCRANTZ A QUICK briefing and sent them down to Shelby County. Then he had a thought, something that should have occurred to him earlier, but hadn't. He went to the operations room and sat down with Becky.

———

SAM AND DANIKA WALKED OUT OF THEIR LAWYER'S office feeling more dejected than when they went in. By the time they returned home, Sam was practically livid. "My brother and sister cheat us out of a million bucks, my brother puts a gun to my head and threatens to kill me, the lawyer wants a retainer for an amount that's so ridiculous he'd be the only one who makes any real money, and on top of all—"

That's when the doorbell rang. Sam looked at his wife and said, "Are you expecting someone?"

Danika said she wasn't, so Sam got up and went to the door. When he pulled it open, at first he couldn't believe who it was. Had Danika not followed him to the door, Sam probably would have beaten his brother to a pulp.

Don held up his hands, and said, "Sam, I'm sorry for what I did, and especially for what I said. Really, man, I'm sorry."

Sam shook his head in anger. "I don't care. You pulled a gun on me, asshole. Get the fuck out of here."

"Sam, you can accept my apology or not. I hope you do, but that's not the only reason I'm here."

"Oh yeah? Let me guess. Are you on the run? Did your

bookie catch up with you? The casino throw you out again?"

"Sam, shut up and listen. Karen is missing. She's gone, man. I haven't been able to reach her for days."

Sam gave his brother a nasty laugh. "The two of you screwed me and my wife out of a million bucks. You put a gun to my head. Do you actually think I give two genuine shits that Karen—who is now fat with cash, by the way—can't be found? Well guess what? I don't. The last time you and I spoke, you said if you ever saw me again you'd kill me. So I'm only going to say this one more time before I call the cops: Get the fuck out of here." Then he slammed the door in his brother's face.

---

ONCE SAM HAD CALMED DOWN, HE AND DANIKA continued with their conversation. Danika took her husband's hand and said, "Look, let's forget about the lawyer for a few minutes, okay? I'm more concerned about Don."

Sam gave his wife an odd look. "Don? Why are you concerned about Don? He put a gun in my ear, and not only that, he had it cocked and ready to fire. If Karen hadn't been there, he might have killed—"

When Sam interrupted himself, Danika said, "What? What is it?"

Sam looked down at the floor and held up his hand. "Hold on a second, please. I'm trying to remember something." After a few minutes, he looked at her and said, "Remember the day we found out my dad was dead?"

"Of course."

"When we arrived at his house, I was mad that they'd waited so long to call me. But you pulled me aside and during that moment, we both knew something didn't feel right about the whole situation."

"That's because it wasn't."

"I know," Sam said. "Except, with everything that was going on I was too overwhelmed to think clearly. But now that some time has passed, I'm getting a bad feeling about something, and it doesn't have anything to do with the money or the will or any of that."

"What do you mean?"

"I'll tell you in a second, but first, tell me why a few minutes ago you said you were concerned about Don."

"I misspoke," Danika said. "I meant to say that I was concerned about us, and what sort of manipulation Don was trying to pull off this time…with you. With us."

"Me too. And I think I know what it is." Sam looked his wife right in the eyes. "That night when I went to confront them…the night he pulled the gun on me, he was so mad I thought he was going to do it. He told me I had ten seconds to turn and walk away, and that if he ever saw me again, he'd kill me."

"I know all this. We've talked about it for a week."

"But I just remembered something, Danni. When he put the gun in my ear, I told him he didn't have the balls to do it. To kill me. That's when he said, 'I don't have the balls? Who do you think killed—,' but then Karen screamed his name and stopped him from finishing."

"Sam, are you saying what I think you're saying?"

"Yeah. I think Don or Karen, or both, killed my dad."

"Oh Sam, do you really think they could do something like that?"

Sam ran his fingers through his hair. "You tell me. Why wait three hours to call me after Dad died? Why was he still holding a cigarette in one hand, and a lighter in the other? Wouldn't the EMTs have tried to revive him? If they did, he wouldn't have been sitting there holding an unlit cigarette. Why did Don already have his wallet, and Karen the keys to the house? What took them so long to get to the funeral home that day? I waited twenty minutes. And why was Don in such a hurry to get him in the ground? When I asked about an autopsy, they looked at me like I was an idiot.

"The whole thing, Danni, start to finish was a stage play designed to make me think nothing was out of order, that Dad died of natural causes, and I wasn't in the will. Except we know that isn't true, don't we? If they lied about that, who knows what they're capable of? And Don showing up here, saying he can't find Karen? Do you know where Karen is? Because I'm pretty sure I do. Karen is dead, Danni. Don killed her and is cleaning up his mess after the fact."

"Sam, if that's true, we could be next. We've got to talk to the police. Maybe we should call the Orange County cops."

"We're going to, but first I want to get some advice from an old friend. If we're going to do this, we've got to do it right."

"Who are you going to talk to?"

"Remember my college roommate, Ed?"

Despite the nature of the conversation they were having, Danni let out a little laugh. "My God, I haven't thought of him in years. Why would you want to get his advice?"

"Why else?" Sam said. "He's the sheriff of Shelby County. He'll be able to tell us exactly what to do."

# CHAPTER NINETEEN

Ed Henderson was, in almost every way imaginable, exhausted. He'd been acting-sheriff of Shelby County ever since Ron Miles was killed, and since the county council decided to hold a special election, he'd been doing double duty. On one hand, he was expected to be present for his regular work schedule, and on the other, he needed to find time to run a campaign to keep the job he already had.

He wasn't happy with the council's decision to hold the special election, mainly because he didn't want to be the state's guinea pig for some new mobile voting app they were cramming down everyone's throat. What was wrong with doing things the old-fashioned, like showing up to the polling place and flipping a switch? In a word, nothing. And on top of that, the guy whose company had come up with the idea was the same person who was using some sort of sound technology to drill for natural gas. What a joke. No wonder Ben Holden had always been so grumpy. In addition, he was down in the polls to a former DEA agent, Carla Martin, who was not only cute, but she had a certain sort of federal dreaminess that everyone seemed to be eating up like it was a hot fudge sundae at the county fair.

That was Henderson's mood when Betty stuck her head into his office and said, "There are two state detectives from the Major Crimes Unit here to see you. A couple of the same guys who got Ben killed, if you ask me. And I don't care what anyone says, including you, that's the truth. They don't have an appointment. Want me to tell them to take a hike?"

Henderson sighed, shook his head, and said, "No, send them in."

Betty made a noise, one that Henderson couldn't quite put his finger on, then disappeared. A few seconds later, Murton and Rosencrantz walked in the door.

Murton stuck out his hand to shake, and said, "Sheriff, good to see you again."

Henderson shook hands with Murton, and said, "You too. Wish I could say the same about your buddy, here."

Murton tried to play dumb. "Why? What'd he do?"

Rosencrantz was making a concerted effort to look at absolutely nothing.

"His cute little federal girlfriend is flat kicking my ass in the polls, and he knows it. I'm running around trying to explain how I'm going to restore law and order to this county, and everyone's eyes start to glaze over. Meanwhile, our lovely Agent Martin is going door-to-door with this bubbly, aw-shucks bullshit, wearing cut-off jeans with cowboy boots, a shirt that looks like a Bob Evans tablecloth, and a gun strapped to her hip. Half the constituents think they're voting for Daisy Duke, and the other half don't care because they think she's the poster girl for the NRA."

Murton lit up the room with his big toothy grin and said, "Sounds like it's working."

Henderson made a funny noise with his lips. "Is it ever. She's the showgirl, and I feel like the dumb circus elephant that just knocked down the center pole on the main tent." Then, "Oh, relax, Rosie. I'm just busting your chops. No different from what she's doing to me."

Rosencrantz let out his breath and grinned. "It's my understanding that you guys have decided to run clean campaigns."

Henderson nodded. "We did, and we are. But how am I supposed to compete with what she's doing? It's like trying to run a race against a thoroughbred, and I can't even find a saddle blanket for my pony."

Rosencrantz raised his shoulders, and said, "Why not concede? From what Carla's told me, she wants you as undersheriff anyway."

"I'd love to. I'd do it right now if I could, but I can't. The county council has made it very clear that I am to run a full and complete race because Rick Said and the governor want to make sure this mobile voting app is the thing of the future."

Rosencrantz gave Murton a look, one that didn't need much, if any, explanation. Murton caught the look like a pro, turned back to Henderson, and said, "We need to talk to you about Kelly Price."

Henderson let his chin drop against his chest for a moment. When he looked back up, he said, "Look, I'll take all the help you can offer, but I want it on the record that young Miss Price works as an intern for the cultural center."

"We're aware," Murton said. "What does that have to do with anything?"

Henderson bobbed his head in a silent laugh. "You're joking, right? The cultural center is run by Patty Doyle, Rick Said's niece. Said and the governor are the ones pushing this voting app at everyone in the county, even offering to buy them smartphones if they don't have one. Said, the governor, and the leader of the MCU—your brother—are all either business partners or friends." He looked directly at Rosencrantz and said, "And your girlfriend is kicking my ass with a smile on her face, her thumbs hooked into her belt like she's about to start steppin' and fetchin,' all with a gun strapped to her leg like some sort of phallic symbol." Then to no one in particular, "Whew, end of rant. Sit down, both of you. I'll go get the Price file."

Once Henderson was out of the room, Rosencrantz

looked at Murton, laughed, then said, "And Jonesy thinks he has politics to deal with."

———

WHEN HENDERSON WALKED BACK INTO HIS OFFICE, HE carried an expandable file folder that wasn't very expanded. He sat down, tossed the file on his desk, and pointed at it with his chin. "That's what we've got. You can take it with you. Betty made a copy. But the truth is, there isn't much to go on."

"Tell us what you have so far," Murton said.

Henderson looked out the window for a few seconds, then turned to Murton and Rosencrantz. "Very little. Kelly Price was a busy young lady." He let out a sad little chuckle, then continued with, "Hell, I guess all teenaged girls are these days. It makes me feel like I'm getting old." He shook his head. "Anyway, she was a senior at Shelbyville high school and interned at the cultural center. I know you already know that. Her parents told us that on the day she went missing, she had an early dental appointment, then a couple of classes, and after that, she was scheduled to work at the center with Patty."

"Did she show at her dentist?" Rosencrantz said.

Henderson nodded. "She did. A copy of her dentist's sign-in sheet is in the file. She's been going there for years, the signature matches her driver's license, and the receptionist and the dentist both say she was on time, friendly as usual, didn't appear to be stressed, and spoke well of both Patty Doyle, and her internship at the cultural center, and her college applications. This was a happy young woman."

"What time did she leave the dentist's office?" Murton said.

"According to their records, she arrived at 7:30 in the morning, and was out by 8:15."

"What time was her first class?" Rosencrantz said.

Henderson shook his head. "I'm pretty sure that's where it all goes to shit. She wasn't due at the school until 9:45. You know how it is with seniors...they usually only have a few classes to take during any given day, especially the ones who worked hard through their first three years. So, that gave her ninety minutes to kill, and I think that ninety minutes got her killed instead. She never showed for her classes, at the center, or for cross-country practice that afternoon."

"So somebody snatched her during that ninety-minute timeframe," Murton said.

"It looks that way," Henderson said.

"What about her phone?" Rosencrantz said.

"We've tried it a number of times. Goes straight to voicemail, which is now full, by the way, because her parents kept leaving her so many messages."

Murton took out his phone and said, "What's her number?"

Henderson opened the file folder on his desk and recited the number. Murton took it down, then asked, "Do we know what cell provider she uses?"

"Verizon."

Murton let a small grin form at the corner of his mouth. Then he dialed Becky, back at the shop. "Hey, gorgeous. Do we still have access to Verizon's system?"

"Of course," Becky said.

"Let me give you some digits," Murton said. He read the number off to Becky, then said, "Get me all the data you can for the last week. Tower pings, call and text records, and precise locations if you can get them."

"Sure. When do you need it?"

"As soon as you can. Might want to tell—whoops, make that ask—Jonesy to get a subpoena going just to cover our rear, but get me the info right away, will you?"

"Sure. Are you guys on to something already?"

Murton let out a heavy sigh. "I'll let you know. Get back with me as soon as you can."

Becky said she would, then ended the call.

Henderson had an odd look on his face. Murton caught it and said, "What?"

"I should have done that...gotten a subpoena for the phone records."

"That's what you just did," Murton said. "By having our help. Anything else you can tell us before we go and speak with the parents?"

Henderson shook his head. "No. Other than the phone, that's it, really. Unless some maniac walks in and confesses, we don't have one single thing to work with." Then directly to Rosencrantz: "Forget everything I said earlier about your girl. She deserves this job a lot more than I do."

———————

IN THE CAR ON THE WAY OVER TO THE PRICE residence, Rosencrantz looked at Murton and said, "I think Sheriff Henderson might be a little out of his element."

Murton considered the statement for a moment, then said, "You may be right, but not every cop is an investigator. It takes a different mindset to catch a killer than it does to bust up a bar fight."

Rosencrantz nodded. "I hear you. In fact, Ed isn't the kind of guy I'd want to take on in a bar, or anywhere else for that matter. The guy looks like he could crush a brick if he put his mind to it."

Murton didn't respond to Rosencrantz's statement. He instead said, "Did you notice how he was already speaking of Kelly Price in the past tense?"

"Yeah, I did. It's hard not to. When Ross and I interviewed the Tates up in Kokomo about their daughter, Lisa, I had to constantly remind myself not to do that. You have to always speak of the missing in the present tense or you'll get your ass handed to you."

"Did Jonesy tell you what happened when we went up there? Right as we were leaving?"

Rosencrantz nodded. "He did. Said for a second he thought Tate was going to try to take you on."

"Ah, it was never anything close to that. The man was

simply trying to come to terms that his one and only daughter is dead."

"What about Price?" Rosencrantz said. "Think she's still out there?"

Murton gave Rosencrantz a look, one that didn't require an explanation.

They rode the rest of the way to the Price residence in silence, each man lost in their own thoughts regarding who was taking the girls. Murton, in particular, spent his time thinking about what he'd told John Tate on his front porch, and how he'd handle the killer if they ever came face to face.

---

FRANK AND LAURA PRICE, KELLY'S PARENTS, ANSWERED the door together, the looks on their faces suggestive of hope and surprisingly good news, like it might be Kelly herself ringing the front doorbell instead of two state investigators. Murton watched as their faces went from hope, to blank, then finally the stark realization that they'd managed to dupe themselves into a false sense of emotional freedom...the kind that comes from knowing your child is alive and well.

Once they were all seated inside, Murton looked at the Prices and said, "I'd like you both to know that the governor himself has taken an active interest in your daughter's disappearance. We're working with law enforcement agencies all across the state, gathering relevant data that can help us catch whoever has taken your child, and others."

Laura Price looked at Murton and Rosencrantz and said, "Is she still alive? Please tell me she's still out there."

Murton opened his mouth to respond, but no words passed over his lips.

# CHAPTER TWENTY

Don already had his next girl picked out. It hadn't been that long since the last one, but his urges were growing, and not only that, he found over the years that with the advent of the internet, his research was much easier than before. He no longer had to bother with scouting the malls and shopping centers or fast food restaurants, following this girl or that everywhere they went. And more importantly, he didn't have to run the risk of taking them from the actual cross-country meets as he'd done on a few occasions. *That* was simply too dangerous. All he had to do now was look them up on Facebook, Instagram, or Twitter. Thanks to modern technology, every scrap of information he needed was at his fingertips, twenty-four hours a day.

It went like this: As coach of the girl's cross-country team, he'd go to the meets and watch the girls from the opposing team. With the roster provided by the other coach, he'd pick one out before the event started. And when no one was paying any attention, he'd take out his phone and snap a quick picture. Once he had that, everything else was a walk in the park. With a name and a photo, a basic internet search on the various social media sites usually turned up his girl in about five minutes. He'd study their profiles, their sexy selfies with full pouty looks in the mirror, and when he'd seen enough pictures to fire his engine, he'd research where they worked, who they hung out with, and even find their home addresses. It wasn't that hard if you knew what you were doing. He'd stalk them online, then when he was ready, he'd make his move.

And later tonight, he'd be ready again. It was almost too soon to take another, but this one had to be done out of necessity, if nothing else. If he didn't take one of his own, the cops would start to notice a pattern. So tonight, it'd be one from his own team—a French Lick girl—which Don thought sounded appropriate, given what he had planned for her.

———

WHEN VIRGIL WALKED INTO THE OPERATIONS ROOM AT the MCU headquarters, he found Becky hard at work, her fingers flying across the keyboard. "What are you doing?"

Becky hit a few more keys, then turned to face her boss. "We need a subpoena for Kelly Price's phone records. Murt asked if you'd get the necessary paperwork started with Verizon."

"Okay, I'll get right on that," Virgil said, trying to hide the sarcasm in his voice.

"I'm just passing on the information," Becky said. "In other words, don't shoot the messenger."

"I thought Sheriff Henderson would have done that already."

Becky shrugged. "I don't know what to tell you, Jonesy. Murt asked for the subpoena, so I guess we better get it. Since I'm not technically a law enforcement official, that leaves you."

"Yeah, I get it. That's fine." Then: "Listen, I need to talk to you about something."

Becky snuck a peek at her computer monitor, then turned back to Virgil and said, "What's up?"

Virgil opened his mouth, closed it, then opened it again. When no actual words were spoken, Becky gave him three slow blinks, and said, "You sort of look like a guppy. If you've got something to say, say it."

Virgil puffed his cheeks, let out a breath, then said, "You have to understand, this isn't something that's easy for me to talk about."

Becky, nobody's fool, figured it out in about three seconds. "Your dad?"

Virgil tipped his head. "Yeah. How'd you know?"

"Women's intuition. That, plus the fact that you don't seem to have any trouble offering your thoughts on just about anything else. So, spill already."

"At least you're making it easy for me," Virgil said. "Anyway, after Ron died and all that, I was pretty messed up. Maybe I still am, but in a proper way, if that makes any sense."

"It does," Becky said, and she meant it.

"Well, one of the things bothering me was the fact that I hadn't spoken to my dad the entire time since Ron died. He simply quit showing up. I thought I'd lost him forever."

Becky raised her eyebrows and drew her mouth into a thin line. "And now?"

Virgil was surprised. "Murt didn't tell you? About what happened while we were in Jamaica?"

"Only that Mason spoke to you. Not the details."

Virgil nodded. That sounded like Murton, he thought. Loyal to the core. "I'm not sure the context of the conversation I had with my dad is relevant, but he did say some things that got me thinking."

"Like what?" Becky said.

"He told me he's been busy exploring his past, trying to learn from his mistakes. When I asked him if he'd made any progress, he said, 'I'm whittling away at the truth...running down some clues, you might say.'"

"What does that mean?"

Virgil actually laughed, and it made Becky smile. "That's just it, Becks...talking to my dad and figuring out what he's actually saying is a little like patting your head with one hand, rubbing your stomach with the other, and balancing on a beachball with one foot in the air...all while you're blindfolded."

"That's quite the analogy, there, Jonesy."

Virgil waved her statement away. "It's apt, I can assure you."

"So how about you answer my question?" Becky said.

"He said he was trying to learn from his mistakes. He said he was running down some clues. As that was happening, a teenaged girl came jogging through the park. She asked me for an apple. When I turned around to the table, my dad was gone. When I turned back to the girl, she was as well. Except she left one of her shoes on the path. It was a running shoe. I think he was trying to tell me something about his past...a mistake he made."

"On the job, you mean?"

"That was my thought," Virgil said. "I'd like you to pull all his old case files from his time when he was working Marion County."

Becky's shoulders fell. "Jonesy, do you know how long that will take?"

"I'm sorry," Virgil said. "I misspoke. I want you to pull all his unsolved cold case files. There aren't that many, I'm sure. I know it's a long shot, but there might be something there we can use. A piece of information that might help us find this nut who's taking these girls."

"Some of those case files won't be digitized, Jonesy. Most, in fact."

"I know," Virgil said. "But the index of the case

numbers should be. If you can get those for me, I'll go into the archives myself and dig them out."

"Okay," Becky said. She took another glance at her computer monitor. "I'll get what I can as soon as I'm done with this."

"What are you doing there, anyway?" He was looking at her monitor.

"I'm wiggling my way into Verizon's system. Better get that subpoena going..."

---

AFTER MURTON AND ROSENCRANTZ LEFT HENDERSON'S office to go speak with the Prices, Betty stuck her head in the doorway again, and said, "Guess who's here to see you now?" She was actually smiling, something that happened with the regularity of a heatwave at the South Pole.

"I'm sure I wouldn't know, Betty. How about you just tell me?"

"Because I'd spoil the surprise. I didn't know you were friends with someone famous."

Henderson smiled and stood up...a brief respite from the duties of his day. "Sam Whittle is out there?"

Betty, still smiling like a teenaged girl, said, "He sure is, along with his wife. How come you never told me you knew him? And look, I don't mean to be a bother, but I've got one of his books in my desk drawer right now. I hear they're going to be making a movie out of it. Do you think he'd be willing to sign my copy?"

"I'll see what I can do," Henderson said. "Show them in please."

"Right away. I'll get some fresh coffee going too. The good stuff."

Henderson's smile faded just a bit when he saw his old college roommate and his wife walk through the door. Sam Whittle looked like he'd aged beyond his years since the last time they saw each other. They all gave each other hugs, then Henderson asked them to sit. "I'm really sorry I missed your dad's funeral, Sam."

Sam waved him off, but Henderson wouldn't let it go. "No really. I know it's not much of an excuse, but I would have been there if I could. We've been so busy and so understaffed lately I simply couldn't get away."

"Don't worry about it, Ed. Really. You know how my dad was. I wasn't offended that you couldn't make it then, and I'm not offended now."

Henderson gave his friend a tight grin and a single nod. "I hear you're doing well."

Sam gave Henderson a half shrug and said, "We're squeaking by."

Henderson laughed out loud. "Squeaking by my ass. I'm told they're making a movie out of one of your books."

"It's not nearly as glamorous as it sounds. And at the rate they're moving, it should be in the theaters when I'm about ninety years old."

Danni laughed, looked at Ed, and said, "I hope you

know he's downplaying the glamorous part, and exaggerating the length of the timeline."

"I do," Henderson said. "It seems pretty exciting, you ask me."

"It is," Sam said. "I wish I had more control over the screenplay itself, but the producers want to do it their own way."

"Ah, who cares?" Henderson said, "Take the money and run."

"That I can do," Sam said.

"So what brings you two in today? On the run from the boys down in Orange County?"

Sam looked at his friend for a long time, then said "Not exactly..."

---

MURTON AND ROSENCRANTZ SPENT THE BETTER PART OF two hours with the Prices, going over their questions again and again, and in the end, they ended up with a decent picture of who their daughter was, but no actual information that was of any evidentiary value. As they were getting ready to leave, Murton asked if Kelly had a laptop or computer of her own.

Laura Price nodded. "The sheriff's department still has it."

"Do you know her passwords?" Rosencrantz said. "For the computer and any social media sites she was active on?"

"I don't know them by heart, but I know she keeps a written list in her bedroom."

"If we could take that with us, it'd be a big help," Murton said.

Laura stood and disappeared down the hallway to her daughter's bedroom. Once she was out of earshot, Frank looked at Murton and Rosencrantz and said, "If you find this bastard, I hope you string him up by his balls." He said it so calmly and matter of fact, that both men knew he was serious.

A few minutes later, Laura returned with a list of user-names and passwords. "I'm not sure if these were all the sites she was active on...there are so many these days, but here's what I've got. The first one on the list is for her computer. Do you think it will help?"

"Everything helps, Mrs. Price," Murton said. He gave them both his card, and said, "If you think of anything, no matter how big or small, call me day or night. We're doing everything we can."

The Prices walked them to the door, their expressions filled with resignation and sorrow. "We'll be in touch," Rosencrantz said.

"I sort of hope you won't," Frank Price said.

Murton tipped his head to the side. "Why do you say that, sir?"

"Because it means when you do, you'll have found her body. Until then, we're hanging on to the thinnest of threads, holding out hope that she's still alive. I guess that makes us a couple of damned fools doesn't it?"

Murton shook his head. "No, sir. It makes you human. We'll do our best. I promise."

———————

HENDERSON LISTENED TO HIS FRIEND'S STORY, THEN HE sat back and stared out the window for a few minutes, lost in thought. When he finally turned back to Sam and Danika, he said, "First of all, I want you to know how sorry I am that things have turned out this way for you and your family. That said, you're not going to want to hear what I say next, but you're my friend, so I'm going to give it to you straight."

"I'd expect nothing less," Sam said. "That's why we came to you first."

"All you really have are suspicions. And some of them are based on nothing more than a guess. No, no, wait, hear me out, please. For an executor, the proper handling of an estate is harder than it seems to someone who has never done it. And legally, there are just enough loopholes in the law to give that person ample room to maneuver and often manipulate the assets in such a way that probate isn't necessary unless one of the known heirs goes to court to force the issue.

"With regard to your sister, Karen...she's an adult. If she decided to take off to parts unknown without telling you or anyone else, that's her business. And what you said about Don being involved in her disappearance, and both of them being involved in the death of your father? That's pure speculation on your part."

Sam shook his head. "My own brother put a gun in my ear and threatened to kill me."

"Then go to the Orange County authorities, swear out a statement, and let them investigate the matter."

"I can't do that," Sam said. "Is he an asshole? Yes. But I was on his property and I instigated an assault. Any lawyer worth his salt would have my complaint tossed out in about two seconds. Besides, that's not the main issue. The death of my father is. I'm convinced, and so is Danni, by the way, that Don and Karen killed him. Don couldn't wait to get him in the ground, and when I asked about an autopsy, they looked at me like I was an idiot for even bringing it up."

"The problem, Sam, is you don't have any proof. Let me ask you this: Do you need the money or the stuff?"

"Of course not, Ed. You know that."

"Do you want it?"

Sam looked away for a second, then said, "No, not really. Danni and I talked about it and said if we ever did get anything, we'd donate it to charity."

"Well, unless you want to tangle yourself up in a legal battle that could last for years, and spend a truckload of money along the way, I'd think long and hard about letting it all go."

"Ed, I'm telling you...they killed my father."

"Prove it."

Sam knew he couldn't. Then he had a thought. "What

if they exhumed his body? What does it take to make that happen?"

"Something that rises to what we refer to as reasonable cause," Henderson said. "It doesn't sound like you have that. In fact, you're not even close. My advice, sue your siblings if you want to go down that road. Otherwise, let sleeping dogs lie, and all that. I'm sorry buddy, I wish there was something I could do for you, but there isn't."

# CHAPTER TWENTY-ONE

W hen Murton and Rosencrantz returned to the Shelby County Sheriff's office, they once again had to get past the keeper of the gate, and this time, she had no intention of interrupting the sheriff. "I know you state investigators think you're more important than the rest of us, but you're not. Sheriff Henderson is tied up with a couple of people at the moment, and I'm not sure when he'll be—"

That's when Ed Henderson opened his office door to show Sam and Danika out. Betty forgot all about Murton and Rosencrantz and grabbed her book and a pen. She walked right up to Sam, and said, "Would you mind very much? I'm a great admirer of your writing. You can say whatever you want as long as it starts with, 'To my dear friend, Betty.'"

Sam reddened slightly, took the book and pen, wrote a few words, then signed his name. He handed the book back, thanked Betty for her support, nodded to Murton and Rosencrantz, then took Danika's hand and walked out.

"Who was that?" Rosencrantz said.

Betty snickered, then said, "From what I've seen of your intellect, no one you would know, I'm sure."

Murton leaned close to Rosencrantz, and said, "Sam Whittle. Famous author."

Rosencrantz shrugged and said, "Huh. Never heard of him."

Betty gave everyone a dull look. "Like I said..."

---

ONCE THEY WERE BACK INSIDE HENDERSON'S OFFICE, Murton said, "What's up with Sam Whittle?"

"Ah, we were college roommates back in the day. His dad died about six months ago, and the family is fighting over the money. My buddy even thinks his siblings killed their own father to get the loot."

"Did they?" Rosencrantz asked.

Henderson shrugged. "Who knows? All they have are suspicions and intuition." Then, a little heavier: "And to tell you the truth, it's out of my jurisdiction, so that means it's Orange County's problem...not mine. I think once they get a few more months under their belt, the whole thing should die down."

"They usually do," Murton said. "Listen, we're getting ready to head back to Indy, but before we do, if you have a proper chain of custody form, I'd like to take Kelly Price's laptop with us. We might be able to get something from it."

Henderson snorted. "Good luck. We had one of our best guys try to crack the password, and he couldn't do it."

Murton genuinely liked Henderson and didn't want to embarrass him. Instead of saying they'd gotten the list of passwords from Kelly's mom, he told him about Becky and her computer skills. "If anyone can crack that thing, she can."

"I hope you're right," Henderson said. He filled out the form, signed it, had Murton do the same, then walked them down to the property room. Once Murton and Rosencrantz had the laptop, they told Henderson they'd keep him updated, and left the building.

---

As they were walking to Murton's car, his phone buzzed at him. He checked the screen, then hit the Answer button and said, "Hello wife of mine. Did you get a glimpse of Verizon's horizon?"

Becky chuckled and said, "I did. I'm sending everything to your email right...now. Price's phone is still active and pinging off a tower close to Shelbyville. The email I sent has the coordinates. I don't have the tracking history yet. That takes a little longer."

"Nice work, Becks. Get it to me when you can, huh?"

"I will. Are you going to make it back for dinner?"

"Unless we find a body attached to the phone, then yeah, we'll make it back."

"Well, here's hoping you don't find a body," Becky said.

And Murton thought, *Isn't that the truth.* He opened the email, sent a copy to Rosencrantz, then they headed over to where Kelly Price's phone was, not hopeful...just doing the legwork.

---

THE PHONE WAS PINGING TO A TOWER THAT WAS between the dentist's office and the high school, at almost the exact midpoint. When Murton and Rosencrantz arrived at the location, they found a small combination bookstore and coffee shop. The only available parking was at the rear of the store. They got out of Murton's car and began looking around.

"Seems like a pretty unlikely place for a kid to get snatched," Rosencrantz said.

Murton looked up at the corners of the buildings. "You might be right, especially if you look up right over there."

Rosencrantz turned and looked where Murton was pointing. A security camera was mounted on the back wall of a building across the alley. "Is that a liquor store?"

"Looks like it," Murton said. "Let's go have a talk with their employees."

They left their car parked in the back and walked

around to the front of the building. Inside, behind the counter was a middle-aged man, slightly overweight, balding, with reading glasses perched at the tip of his nose. He looked up at Murton and Rosencrantz and said, "You guys don't look like customers. You look like cops."

"Cops don't drink anymore?" Rosencrantz said. "I guess I missed that memo."

"How can I help you, gentlemen?"

Murton pulled out his phone and brought up a picture of Kelly Price. "Have you ever seen this young lady, especially within the last few days?"

The man studied the photo for a few seconds, then said, "No, I haven't. Not that I would, either. She doesn't look old enough to come in here. I don't serve minors, and I always check ID. As a matter of fact, I haven't seen yours yet."

Murton and Rosencrantz pulled out their badges.

"Well, at least you ain't Excise," the man said. "Those boys get a bug up their asses every now and again. About to drive me crazy, and I follow all the rules."

"Uh-huh," Murton said. "Is that security camera out back working and active?"

"It is," the man said. "Insurance requires I keep a record for at least thirty days."

"We're going to need to see the footage from three days ago," Rosencrantz said.

"Mind if I ask why?"

"The picture of the girl I just showed you? She's missing, and her phone is still actively pinging to this general location."

The man visibly swallowed. "Jeez, that's awful. I had no idea..."

"If you could just show us the security footage, sir," Murton said.

"Yes, of course. Follow me." The man locked the front door, then led them to a stockroom where a computer sat atop a small corner table. He sat down, brought up the security system's camera, then backed the footage up to the date in question. He showed Murton and Rosencrantz how to operate the controls, then went back out front. "Can't keep that front door locked too long."

"We're good," Murton said. They started playing the footage, faster and faster, covering the day that Kelly Price went missing. A few minutes later they saw a man in his mid to late thirties walking down the alley carrying a shopping bag. When he got to the recycling dumpster behind the liquor store, he reached into the sack, pulled out a purse, and threw it into the dumpster, before disappearing from the camera's view. Murton reversed the footage, getting the best shot of the man he could, then looked at Rosencrantz and said, "Go get the owner back in here."

A few minutes later the liquor store owner was back. "What's up? Find anything good?"

Murton pointed at the screen and said, "Ever see that guy before?"

The man laughed and said, "Yeah, he's in here about

three times a week. Name's Randy Something. He's a drunk and a bum."

"Any idea where we could find Randy Something?" Rosencrantz said.

The man scratched the top of his head. "Well, if he ain't in the county lockup on charges of drunk and disorderly, he's either at home or at work. Problem is, I don't know where either of those two places are."

"But he's been in the county drunk tank?" Murton said.

"It's his home away from home."

"Okay, can you email or text me a screenshot of that guy?"

"Sure. What's your number?"

Murton gave the man his cell phone number, then said, "We're going to go dig around in your dumpster for what I'm hoping is a few short minutes. Is there anything in there we need to be wary of?"

"Shouldn't be," the man said. "It's all recycle...broken down liquor boxes and the like."

"Got a broom we could borrow?" Rosencrantz said.

"I guess so. What do you need a broom for?"

Rosencrantz looked at Murton and said, "Clearly the man has never dumpster dove before."

———

MURTON BACKED HIS SQUAD CAR UP TO THE DUMPSTER, put on a pair of gloves, then climbed on top of the trunk and began rooting around the cardboard, looking for the purse. It took him about ten minutes, moving the boxes from side to side, but he eventually found what he was looking for. After a few unsuccessful attempts to hook the purse with the broom handle, Rosencrantz got tired of watching the struggle.

"You know, for a guy who lives with a pond in his backyard you're not very good at fishing. Let me see that broom."

Murton shrugged, handed the broom to Rosencrantz, who then tossed it aside and jumped into the dumpster. He grabbed the purse and climbed back out. "That's how you fish."

"It's also how you get Hepatitis," Murton said. When he looked inside the purse, it was completely empty, except for a cell phone.

When Rosencrantz dialed Kelly Price's number, the phone lit up. He looked at Murton and said, "Did that guy text you the picture?"

Murton checked his phone and saw that he had. "Yeah. Let's go back and talk with Ed…again."

---

WHEN THEY WALKED BACK INTO THE SHELBY COUNTY Sheriff's department, Betty looked up from her paperwork and said, "What is it with you gentlemen? I'm beginning to think we should assign you office space."

Rosencrantz smiled, looked at Murton, and said, "Hey,

did you hear that? We've risen to the level of gentlemen."

"It was a figure of speech," Betty said. "Let me guess. You're here to bother the sheriff again."

Murton and Rosencrantz just stared at her. Finally, Betty got up, went to Henderson's door, knocked once, and pushed open the door. "Mr. Wardrobe and his illiterate sidekick are back."

Henderson sighed, then said, "Betty..."

"What? It's an accurate statement." Then to Murton and Rosencrantz: "The sheriff will see you now."

They walked in and Murton got right to it. He pulled out his phone, held it up for Henderson to see, and said, "Know this guy?"

Henderson nodded in a weary way. "Do I ever. He's what we call a regular around here. Name's Randy Dodge. What's he done now?"

"Any idea where we can find him?" Rosencrantz said.

"Probably passed out at home," Henderson said. "I heard he got fired from his last job. Damned near killed a guy with a forklift."

"Get us his address?" Murton said.

"Sure, except you haven't told me why yet."

Murton squinted an eye at Henderson. "That picture I showed you? It came from a security camera at the back of a liquor store. We've got footage of Dodge tossing Kelly Price's purse into a dumpster."

Henderson's eyes widened a bit. "Oh boy, okay. C'mon, you can follow me to his place. I could get there in my sleep."

---

WHEN THEY GOT TO DODGE'S—A SINGLE-STORY rambler in desperate need of just about every imaginable repair—Henderson waited until Rosencrantz made his way around back, then he and Murton walked up to the front door and knocked. The wood on the door was rotted, and their knocks sounded like they were beating on a sponge.

Murton saw the blinds wiggle on the front window, then heard muffled footsteps running through the house. Henderson moved to kick the door, but Murton grabbed his arm to stop him. "Wait here. Rosie will get him."

Thirty seconds later, the front door opened, and Rosencrantz let Murton and Henderson in. Dodge was cuffed and sitting on a ratty sofa. His nose was bleeding, the blood crossing his lips and filling out the gaps in his beard. "What the fuck are you guys doing in my house? And what's with the cuffs? I ain't done nothing."

Rosencrantz walked out of the room, and Murton began to explain the situation to Dodge. "Randy, you're in some pretty big trouble right now. Heard you like to tie one on now and again."

"Ain't no law against that."

"Actually, there are quite a few laws against that, depending on what you're doing at the time. But we'll have that talk later. Right now I only have one question for you, and the answer you give me better be the truth."

"What?"

"Where is Kelly Price?"

"Who?" Dodge said.

Murton turned to Henderson and said, "Ed, you might want to wait outside for a few minutes."

"Murt..."

"I'm just looking out for you," Murton said. "You know...the election and all."

Henderson looked at nothing for a beat, then gave Murton a simple nod and walked out. Once he was gone, Murton turned his attention back to Dodge and said, "I lied before...about only asking once. So let's try again. Where is Kelly Price?"

"I don't know no Kelly Price, and that's the truth. I need some medical attention, man. I think your partner busted my nose."

Murton slapped Dodge in the face so hard he fell from the sofa. "We've got video footage of you tossing her purse into a dumpster behind the liquor store, asshole. We know it was her purse because her phone was still inside."

Rosencrantz walked back into the room. "Hey, look what I found." He held a woman's wallet out. He looked at Dodge, shook his head, and said, "Randy, Randy, Randy. If you don't know who Kelly Price is, how is it that you've got her wallet? It was sitting right on top of your nightstand." He opened the wallet, and Price's driver's license was right there, tucked behind a plastic insert. "There's no money in here, so I guess that means you already spent it. I try really hard not to judge others, but it's not looking too good for you right now, Randy. My partner here has a way of getting people to talk. It's usually not pretty, so I'd start to get on board with the program, if you know what I mean."

Dodge managed to get himself back on the sofa. "Okay, look. I gots my problems, and everyone knows all about it. Here's what happened: I found the purse, and I don't deny it. I took the money from the wallet because I needed it. What I didn't need was a purse or a phone, so I tossed those."

"Why'd you keep the wallet, Randy?" Murton said.

Dodge visibly swallowed. "The only reason I kept the wallet was because I was going to try to use her debit card, but then I seen on the news that the Price girl was missing. I didn't know what to do. Knew if I went to the cops they'd think I done it, but I didn't."

Murton smoothed an imaginary wrinkle from his shirt, looked at Dodge, and said, "So let me see if I've got this right. A teenage girl goes missing, and by your own account, you know about the situation. Then, you happen across some of her personal belongings and instead of notifying the proper authorities, you take the wallet, ditch the purse and phone, all so you can grab a six-pack. Want to know what we call that, Randy? We call that tampering with evidence. Evidence that could help us find this young woman."

"You got it backward, man. I didn't know the girl was missing until after I found her stuff. I didn't know it was evidence. I just thought, finders keepers. I needed a drink, is all."

Murton got right in his face. "What do you think Kelly Price needs right now?"

"I want a lawyer," Dodge said.

"That might be the smartest thing you've said yet," Rosencrantz said. "Here's why: In about an hour or so, the county's crime scene people and a few deputies are going to come out here and tear this place apart...right down to the goddamned sticks that are somehow still holding it together. If they find one single shred of evidence that Kelly Price has ever been here or in your vehicle...a single hair, a drop of blood, a fingerprint, anything, you'll be facing charges that'll make a night in the drunk tank seem like an all-inclusive stay at a vacation resort."

"Lawyer."

Murton and Rosencrantz looked at each other, then they each grabbed one of Dodge's arms and hauled him outside to where Henderson was waiting by his squad car.

"He wants a lawyer," Murton said.

Henderson put Dodge in the back of his squad, then pulled Murton and Rosencrantz aside. "He do it?"

Murton shook his head. "Probably not. He looked genuinely confused. You can charge him with tampering with evidence, and just to make sure, I'd get your crime scene people out here and do a proper search, but I think he's probably telling the truth."

"Sort of wish he wasn't," Henderson said.

Murton nodded, and said, "Me too."

# CHAPTER TWENTY-TWO

Becky finally got the tracking information from Kelly Price's phone out of the Verizon system and sent it to Murton and Rosencrantz. With that done, she dug into the Marion County Sheriff's Office records and began looking for the index of cases during the time Virgil's father, Mason, had been the sheriff. As she suspected, most of the files hadn't yet been digitized, and as a point of fact, she thought they probably never would be. But Virgil had been correct...the index itself was digitized, and after an hour or so, she was able to cull the indexed closed cases from the open and unsolved files. She printed the list, then walked it over to Virgil's office.

"It's quite a list," Becky said after she handed the pages to Virgil. "I wouldn't think there'd be so many."

Virgil picked up the sheets of paper—five pages in all

—and gave them a quick scan. "Well, it's a big department, and as sheriff at the time, my dad would be listed on each case. But, I think we can narrow it down. Do you have this on a spreadsheet?"

"Yeah. Why?"

Virgil took out a pen from his desk drawer, and said, "Come around here and look at something."

Becky walked behind the desk and looked over Virgil's shoulder. "What is it?"

Virgil ran his finger down the list on the first page, then stopped at one of the case file's index numbers. "See this one? It ends with the letters MCPD."

"Yeah, I noticed that all of the index numbers have some sort of letters at the end. I thought MCPD meant Marion County Police Department."

Virgil looked at Becky and gave her a kind, sad smile. "No, it means Missing Child Presumed Dead. Those are the case files I'm going to want to look through. Can you separate those out for me?"

Becky took the pages back and told him she would. "It'll only take about ten minutes."

"That's fine, Becks. Let me know when you've got it and I'll head over to the Marion County Sheriff's Office and start going through their archives."

———

MURTON AND ROSENCRANTZ WERE LOOKING AT THE tracking data from Kelly Price's phone. Becky had sent both the raw data and a map overlay to make the information easier to interpret.

"How do you want to handle this?" Rosencrantz asked.

Murton had the map pulled up on his iPad, looking at the various markers that showed where Price's phone had been on the day she went missing. "We know she left her dental appointment at 8:15. Her class wasn't scheduled to start until 9:45. According to this map, it looks like she stopped at McDonald's...the one right between Highway 44 and East Michigan Road. Let's head over there and see what we can see."

The traffic was light, and five minutes later they were at McDonald's. They walked inside and spoke with the manager, an overweight woman with fly-away hair, and tiny teeth. When she smiled at them, her gums looked like they needed to be trimmed back. "How may I help you, detectives?"

Murton showed the manager the picture of Kelly Price. "Have you seen this young woman?"

"Yes, I have."

"When?" Rosencrantz said.

"This morning."

Murton and Rosencrantz looked at each other, then back at the manager. "You're saying she was in here this morning?" Murton said.

The manager shook her head and turned a few different shades of red. "No, I'm sorry. I misspoke. I saw her picture on the morning news. She's the one that's missing, right?"

Rosencrantz nodded. "Yes ma'am. Let me rephrase the question my partner just asked. When was the last time you saw Ms. Price?"

"I've never actually seen her in here," the manager said. "But that doesn't mean she hasn't been here. Most of my interaction is with the employees in the back. I don't deal with the customers that often unless there's some sort of problem." Then she seemed to revise her own statement by saying, "Now that I think about it, I guess I have more interaction with the customers than I'd like. But anyway, I've never seen her. At least not that I recall."

"We'd like to take a look at your security footage from the day she went missing...both inside the restaurant and the drive-thru."

"Not a problem," the manager said. "Come around the counter. The system is in my office. And watch your step. The floor gets a little slick back here."

They followed the manager to the back of the building—she was right...the floor was slippery—and entered her office. "I hope you'll excuse the mess. Hardly anyone ever sees this part of the building except me and my assistants. Well, that and corporate when they come in for an inspection. We always know when that's happening though, so we've got time to clean up and—"

"Yes, ma'am," Rosencrantz said. "If we could just see the footage, please." He handed her a slip of paper with the specific date and time that matched the information Becky had given them.

The manager gave Rosencrantz a dry look and said, "I was just making conversation." Then without saying anything else, she brought up the camera that showed the drive-thru.

Ten seconds later, Murton said, "Freeze that. Right there." He looked at Rosencrantz and said, "There's our girl." The camera had caught a perfect shot of Kelly Price with a smile on her face as she handed her debit card to the cashier.

"Can you send us a picture of that?" Rosencrantz said.

"I'm afraid our system isn't set up that way," the manager said. "You could take a picture of the screen though."

Murton took out his phone and snapped a picture of Price, then asked the manager to let the footage roll. Two seconds later he again said, "Freeze that please." He took another picture of the back of Price's car, a late-model, red Nissan Ultima. He looked at the manager and said, "Thank you. You've been a big help."

The manager showed them her big gums and said, "Always happy to help law enforcement. Would either of you care for something to eat?"

"No, thank you," Rosencrantz said. "We just ate."

When they walked outside, Rosencrantz looked at Murton and said, "I don't think I'll ever eat at a McDonald's again. How does a place like that get past the health inspectors?"

Murton shrugged. "The fries are pretty good."

"Yeah, especially the ones with that 'just off the floor seasoning.'"

They were walking toward Murton's squad car when Rosencrantz grabbed him by the arm, pointed, and said, "Is it my imagination, or are we two of the luckiest bastards on the planet?"

Murton looked where Rosencrantz was pointing and saw a Big Lots store that essentially shared the same parking lot with McDonald's. Sitting at the edge of the lot was a red Nissan Ultima. They jogged over, staying a few feet away from the car. "Let's not touch anything," Murton said. "We might be able to get prints."

"Do the plates match?" Rosencrantz said.

Murton checked his phone. "Yeah, it's her car all right." Then he called Sheriff Henderson. "Ed, it's Murt. We've found Price's car at the Big Lots store next to McDonald's. Get your crime scene people headed this way."

Henderson said he would, and when Murton was finished with the call, Rosencrantz said, "You know what happened? She went through the drive-thru, then parked over here to eat. She might have even gone inside the department store."

"Hang tight, Rosie. I'm going to run back over and get my squad. I want to check the iPad again."

Murton went to his car and drove back over to where Rosencrantz stood, about ten feet away from Price's car. When he brought the map and tracking data back up, he noticed that Price's phone hadn't moved from where her car was currently parked for about ten minutes. Then it made an almost straight track to the liquor store where they'd been previously.

"This is clearly where she was taken," Murton said. He looked at the exterior of the Big Lots store and saw cameras mounted on both front corners. "I'm going to wait here for Ed and his crime scene techs. Run inside and see if those cameras caught anything, will you?"

Rosencrantz said he would, then added, "Pretty far away, man."

"Yeah, but it's their lot, so I'm hoping we'll get lucky."

And they almost did.

---

WITH HIS LIST IN HAND, VIRGIL DROVE OVER TO THE Marion County Sheriff's Office. He parked in the back and locked his gun in the truck before approaching the building. Once there, he pulled out his badge, pushed the intercom button, then looked up at the camera mounted above the door. When the door buzzed, he stepped inside and walked over to the interior door, and repeated the process again. This time a voice came through the intercom. "That you, Jonesy?"

Virgil knew most, but not all of the Marion County deputies, mostly from his time at the bar. But he couldn't tell who was speaking to him through the intercom. "In the flesh."

"Need to secure your weapon?" the voice said.

"Nope. Already locked it up in my truck."

The interior door buzzed, and Virgil pulled it open and walked into the booking area of the jail. When he saw the deputy, he smiled and said, "Haven't seen you in the bar lately, Jim."

Jim, the deputy, laughed at him. "That's because you're hardly ever there anymore. I, on the other hand, am in there so often Delroy is talking about making me a partner."

Virgil laughed right back. "Good luck with that. We don't need a fifth."

"I'll tell you what you do need if you're interested."

"What's that?"

"A financing plan. I'm about to go broke if I don't quit eating and drinking there all the time. Can't get the wife to cook for me anymore now that she's had a taste of Robert's cuisine. A guy like me ought to get a frequent eater's discount. Maybe you should have one of them punch cards or something."

Virgil put a serious look on his face and said, "Wish we could. But the margins are so thin in that business, we'd be busted."

"Nice try, Slick. I've seen the way you're packing them in." Then with absolutely no segue at all: "What's up?"

"Need to take a look in the archives. Got a list of cold ones I want to examine. Might need to sign some of it out, depending."

"You remember how to get down there?"

"By heart," Virgil said, as he turned to walk away.

"Speaking of hearts, I still miss your old man. For a lot of us old-timers, it hasn't been the same since he died."

*Hasn't been the same for me either, in ways you can't imagine,* Virgil thought. He turned back to Jim, and said, "I'll catch you on the way out, huh?"

---

SHERIFF HENDERSON'S CREW BEGAN WORKING THE CAR. Murton helped the sheriff set up some crime scene tape to keep the area clear. As they were finishing, Rosencrantz walked out of the store, his phone in hand. "You guys are going to want to see this."

"What have you got?" Murton said.

"Almost everything we need," Rosencrantz said. Then to the sheriff: "It's your call, of course, but you can go ahead and break off the search of Dodge's residence. It looks like his story is going to hold up."

"Show us," Murton said.

Rosencrantz brought the video up on his phone. It was slightly grainy and distant, but it clearly showed what happened. They all watched as Kelly Price pulled away from the drive-thru, then parked right where they'd located her vehicle. She sat in her car for about ten minutes—presumably eating—the video wasn't that good. But it was good enough to show her get out and walk toward the Big Lots' entrance. As soon as she was inside, a dark-colored panel van with a sliding door on the side parked next to her car. The door opened from the inside and a male figure crawled out backward, keeping his upper body inside the van. To a casual observer, he might have been searching for something in the van, or even changing a child's diaper. He was parked so close to Price's car, she wouldn't be able to open her own door without the man moving out of her way.

And that's exactly what happened. Five minutes later Price walked up to her vehicle, and she must have said something to the man because he climbed back into his van to make room. As soon as Price turned to unlock her door and get in her car, the man grabbed her by her hair with one hand, wrapped the elbow of his other arm around her throat, and yanked her inside the van. The move was so violent, Price dropped her purse and shopping bag, and they both slid about halfway underneath her own vehicle. The van's door slid shut, it rocked on its springs for a few seconds, then a few seconds after that it slowly drove out of the lot.

"The cameras are too far away," Rosencrantz said. "They didn't get a clear shot of the van's plates...not that it matters. You can tell they're covered in mud."

"With this black and white footage, we can't even tell what color the van is," Henderson said.

"We might be able to narrow it down, though," Murton said. "Becky has a program that can compare the shades of gray and give us some possibilities."

"How does that work?" Henderson said.

Murton looked around. "Have your crime scene people take high-res photos of Price's car, the McDonald's building, and all the car's in their lot. Once she has those, she can start to do a comparison model of all the various colors against the different shades of gray. That van looks like either a Chevy or GMC. A dealer will be able to tell us what year it is, and what colors were offered that year."

Henderson looked at Rosencrantz. "How does that footage clear Randy Dodge? For all we know, that was him in the van."

"I didn't say it cleared him," Rosencrantz said. "He clearly tampered with evidence, though given the fact that he didn't know what he had, that probably wouldn't hold up in court anyway."

Henderson still didn't understand. "Yeah, that part I get. What I don't get is how do we know it wasn't him in the van?"

"Because you haven't seen the rest of the video yet," Rosencrantz said. He brought up another portion of the video. "This is about ten minutes later." They watched as Dodge stumbled through the lot, walked past Price's car, did a classic double-take, then grabbed the shopping bag, stuffed the purse inside, then walked away.

Murton brought up the data tracking map on the iPad and compared the timestamps against the route. "Dodge didn't take her. Look, you can follow his route from here. He went straight to the liquor store. Didn't even bother taking the sidewalks or streets. He was cutting through backyards to get there as soon as he could."

Henderson shook his head. "I wonder where Kelly Price is."

Murton looked at Henderson and said, "Kelly Price is dead, Sheriff."

# CHAPTER TWENTY-THREE

Virgil went down to the basement of the Sheriff's Department, entered the file room, then began looking through the archived records from the years in question. The search wasn't as easy as he thought it might have been. Everything was there, but it was all out of order, mostly, he thought, because of the digitization process. Whoever was in charge of the process didn't put everything back in its proper place after they had finished.

He spent the rest of the afternoon finding, then gathering everything together. By the time he was finished, he had seven banker's boxes of case files—each case having its own box—all stacked neatly by the door. He found a two-wheel hand truck in the back corner of the room, stacked the boxes atop each other, and took the elevator back upstairs. Jim, the deputy was busy with a prisoner intake, so Virgil had to wait about ten minutes before he could sign all the necessary forms to remove the evidence from the building. With that done, he thanked Jim, loaded the boxes into his truck, and headed back to the MCU facility where he'd start the process of going through each file, pulling all the relevant information, and giving it to Becky, Wu, and Nicky. They'd enter it into the system, adding it to everything else they had so far. It seemed like a lot of work, especially given the potential for what it had to offer, but Virgil didn't want to leave any stone unturned. If they could find any connection at all between just one of Mason's old files, and the current ones they were working on, there might be a thread to pull on. And it had been Virgil's experience when that happened, things had a way of unraveling...usually for the best.

But not always.

THE LATE AFTERNOON RUSH HOUR TRAFFIC WAS BAD, and it took Virgil an hour to get back to the MCU. Chip Lawless, one of the MCU's crime scene techs was wandering around with nothing to do, so he helped Virgil carry the boxes up to his office. When Virgil told him what he was doing, Lawless said, "Looks like a lot of paper."

Virgil nodded. "It is. But I'm hoping there'll be something of value in here that can help us find whoever is taking these girls."

Lawless stopped and looked at his boss. "Is it just me, or is everyone being very careful not to use the term serial killer?"

"It's not you," Virgil said. "People hear the words serial killer and everyone starts to panic, the media goes nuts, and when that happens, the politicians start to get involved. We try to avoid it at all costs."

Lawless was interested. "Why?"

It was a good question, and Virgil said so. "The thing is, Chip, with the type of work you do, you're pretty isolated. You show up to the crime scene and everything is blocked off, no one gets in your way, and because you're an expert at what you do, there aren't too many people who can tell you how to do your job. Outside of that specific realm, it's a whole other ballgame. If the investigators are being chased around by the media when we're trying to do our jobs, the whole thing becomes a circus sideshow. They'll take any scrap of information they can get their hands on, turn it into nothing more than pure speculative sensationalism, and in doing so, they could tip off the killer or killers we're trying to catch. And the politicians are just as bad. Every single one of them thinks they know how to do my job better than I do because they've seen a Bruce Willis movie or watched a few episodes of Law and Order. The real world doesn't work that way."

"So whoever you're after isn't a serial killer?"

Virgil shook his head. "I didn't say that. In truth, he is. But the thing to remember is this: There are a lot of serial killers out there who never get caught. Most are travelers, going from place to place, killing for any number of reasons. They're careful, they don't take souvenirs—again, that's mostly a movie thing as well—and they spend their entire lives killing without getting caught. Unless they do something stupid, they often get away with it. And most of the time when they are caught, it's for a single murder. All the others go unsolved."

Lawless looked at the boxes of files. "And you think there might be something in these files from long ago that might lead you to whoever is taking these young girls?"

Virgil shrugged. "Never hurts to check."

"Seems like a long shot."

"That's why Jonesy hired me," Ross said. He'd just walked in the door, and overheard Lawless's statement. "Long shots are the ones that usually pay off." Then to Virgil, "Hey, Jonesy."

Virgil said hello, then asked Ross if he'd finished up with Sandy.

"Yep. Cool dropped her at your place. Nice landing pad, by the way."

"It should be, based on what it cost. Did you guys get to everyone?"

Ross nodded. "We did. I'll tell you something, even though you probably already know it, but your wife is pretty damned smart."

Virgil tipped a finger at him, and said, "I do know that. But tell me what you mean."

"It's the way she handled the investigators from the various counties. She had them eating out of the palm of her hand, and they didn't even know it. She knew exactly what questions to ask, and not only that, she knew what questions to stay away from. She also got every single one of them to agree to notify the parents of their child's whereabouts, with the exception of two of the girls, so the state doesn't have to take on that burden."

"Why'd she leave two of the girls out?"

Ross laughed in a sad sort of way. "Because it only took about five minutes to know that if those particular girls' whereabouts were made known to their parents, the girls would be brought right back to an abusive situation. The one in Mexico...the minor? She was one of them."

Lawless took the opportunity to excuse himself. "If there's nothing else, Jonesy?"

"No, that's it. Thanks for the help, Chip."

"You bet," Lawless said, then left the room.

Virgil turned back to Ross. "I'm surprised Sandy let the Mexico girl go."

"You wouldn't be if you heard what the investigators told us about her parents."

"That bad?"

"Yeah. But like I said, Sandy got the investigator to sign off on the fact that they are now aware of the girl's location, and if there's any pushback from the parents the county will take the heat, not the state."

Virgil wasn't exactly sure how he felt about that, so he

didn't say anything. Ross filled the vacuum with this: "So, I guess I'll see you in a few hours, huh?"

Virgil tipped his head to the side. A question.

"Sarah is already at your place. Sandy invited me over for dinner."

Virgil said, "Ah." Then, "Hell, you should have just stayed. You could have wet a line and entertained the fish for a while."

"I thought about it, but my car was at the airport, plus, I didn't know what anyone else was doing, so I thought I'd better check in."

"I appreciate it, Ross. But go ahead and take off. It looks like everyone else has anyway. I'm not going to dig into these files until tomorrow. If I start now, I won't be able to stop. So, I'll see you there."

Ross sort of snickered.

"What?" Virgil said.

"It won't be just me you'll see."

Virgil shook his head. "She did it again, didn't she?"

"What can I tell you, Jonesy? The woman told me she likes a full house. In addition to me and Sarah, Murt and Becky will be there, along with Robert, Delroy and Huma. I'm pretty sure she said Rosie and Carla were going to stop by, along with Nicky and Wu."

Virgil scratched at the back of his head. "Maybe I will stay here and work these files. There probably won't be any place for me to sit."

"Ah, put your party hat on and have some fun. Get away from all this business for one night. Besides, as we were landing, I saw a tent rental van in your backyard. Sandy called ahead and got a tent, tables and chairs...the works."

"Why is it I'm the last to know about all this?"

Ross smiled and said, "That, Boss, is a question you'll have to ask yourself. Let me know the answer if you ever figure it out." Then, as he was walking out the door: "Forget the files and go with the flow. It's not like whoever is snatching these girls is going to take another one tonight."

---

BY THE TIME VIRGIL GOT HOME, EVERYONE WAS already there...or so he thought. The tent was up, music was playing, Murton, Rosencrantz, and Ross were fishing with Jonas and Wyatt, while Huma, Sarah, and Shelby County's likely next sheriff, Carla Martin, were all fussing over Liv and Aayla. Robert was working the grill, and Delroy, along with Nicky and Wu were handing out drinks. Sandy was working the room—or in this case—the lawn, making sure everyone had what they needed.

Virgil walked over, grabbed his wife from behind, picked her up, and spun her in a circle. She giggled like a little girl, and when he put her down, she said, "I hope you don't mind. We need a little more fun in our lives."

"You're beautiful," Virgil said. "And no, I don't mind at all. Especially with the way you look right now. I am wondering why I'm always the last to hear about all this though."

Sandy was about to answer when they heard the beat of the state helicopter's rotor blades. Cool came in over the top of the house, turned into the wind, and gently set the craft down on the landing pad. Virgil glanced over at the pond and saw Murton had his arm on Jonas's shoulder, and Ross had Wyatt in his lap. Once Cool had the engine shut down and the tail rotor had stopped, the men let the boys go, and they ran toward the helicopter, shouting, "Uncle Mac's here!"

Cool hopped out and opened the door for his passengers. The governor climbed out, gave the boys a quick hug, then turned back to the chopper, reached inside, took Nichole's hand, and helped her down. Virgil and Sandy walked over and said hello.

The governor smiled, then said, "We heard something about a small gathering?"

Sandy smiled right back, looked Nichole in the eye, and said, "An entrance, huh?"

Nichole bit into the corner of her lower lip, glanced at Mac, then turned back to Sandy and said, "Be careful what you wish for."

---

JODIE CARTER, A SENIOR AT FRENCH LICK HIGH SCHOOL was going to do a little partying herself. She'd worked the whole thing out with her best friend, Emma Brady. Both girls worked evenings at the Dollar General store in French Lick, and while Emma wasn't currently seeing anyone, Jodie had a boyfriend she wanted to spend the night with. It was one thing to go park in the woods and do it in the back seat. It was a whole other thing to actually have a comfortable bed, a shower, and wake up in the morning with your boyfriend right next to you. What could be better?

The problem? Her parents.

But as a bright, if not somewhat sneaky young woman, with a little forethought, she got the whole thing worked out.

Their plan went like this: Jodie would tell her parents that she was going to spend the night with Emma, as they'd done all through high school. Her parents had rarely told her no, and ever since she'd been a senior, they had never refused. Their little girl was growing up. Emma, of course, would cover for Jodie by simply not saying anything to her parents. She'd go home after work, and hang out by herself. Maybe binge a little Netflix.

Jodie's boyfriend, Bobby Thompson—whose parents were out of town—had his place to himself. Bobby was under strict orders to not have any parties, but nothing was ever said about having his girlfriend over. In fact, the more Bobby thought about it, his dad had a mischievous look on his face before they left...almost as if he knew what would be going on. He'd also left a pack of condoms in plain sight on top of the master bedroom dresser.

Message delivered.

SINCE JODIE DIDN'T GET OFF WORK UNTIL NINE THAT evening, and wouldn't be arriving for a few hours at best, Bobby had some time to kill. His homework was done, he was tired of his video games, the house was empty, and in short, he had nothing to do until Jodie showed up. He was, in a word, bored.

That's when he decided to sneak a couple of brewskis from the garage refrigerator. He knew his dad didn't keep that close of an eye on how many beers were out there. The night was warm, so he drank a few beers, then decided he'd top off the bottles of beer with a few shots of the good stuff. When he opened the cabinet in his dad's office, he saw it was stocked like the local liquor store. There were bottles of vodka, whiskey, tequila, rum, gin, and every type of mixer anyone could ever ask for. Feeling good after the beers, Bobby got on the internet and looked up how to make a drink he'd heard of, but had never tried...a Long Island Iced Tea. One of his buddies had told him it tasted great and really kicked the party into high gear. So Bobby thought, why not?

He mixed all the ingredients together, topped it off with a splash of Pepsi—the recipe called for Coke—but Bobby said fuck it...a cola was a cola, and when he took a sip he couldn't believe how good it was. He could barely taste the liquor. One thing led to another, and with no food in his stomach, the Long Islands eventually hit him like a sledgehammer. He was a little over halfway through his third when the room began to spin. He shook it off, finished the drink, found his mom's stash of Oxy she'd kept after a root canal procedure a few months ago, and popped two of those. While he was waiting for the pills to kick in, he made one more drink, then sat down and tuned into Sports Center on ESPN. Half an hour later, he took another pill, then soon after, he passed out on the sofa. It was almost at the exact same time Don Whittle turned his van into the Dollar General lot and parked next to Jodie's car.

# CHAPTER TWENTY-FOUR

**R**oss and Rosencrantz were sitting under the tent at Virgil's. Dinner was over, they had their feet propped up on the table, and they were watching Delroy and Huma dance in the grass. Larry the Dog was sniffing around under the tables searching for leftover scraps. Rosencrantz gave the golden retriever a scratch on top of his head, then looked at his partner and said, "Hey, guess who I met today?"

"Who?"

"Sam Whittle. He's a famous author."

"I know who Whittle is," Ross said. "I've read all his novels. Though I have to admit, I'm a little surprised that you know who he is."

"Why would you think that?" Rosencrantz said.

"Because I didn't think you knew all your letters yet."

Rosencrantz bobbed his head. "Good one. Anyway, he seemed like a regular guy."

"As opposed to what? An irregular guy?"

Rosencrantz shrugged. "Ah, you know how it is with famous people. Sometimes they can be real jerks."

"You know who's the most famous guy I've ever met?" Ross said.

"Who?"

Ross pointed at the governor with his chin and said, "That guy standing right over there, doing his level best not to put his hand on Nichole's ass."

Rosencrantz laughed. "He's failing miserably. I've seen him do it three times in the last hour."

Carla snuck up behind Rosencrantz and said, "The only way you can see someone put their hand on someone else's ass is if you're looking at her ass, which you'd better not be."

Rosencrantz gave his girl a lopsided dopey grin. "Want to dance?"

Martin seemed to consider the question for a moment. "Are you going to grab my ass?"

"Of course," Rosencrantz said.

"Then let's go. I love this song."

Sarah sat down next to Ross, and a few minutes later, Virgil and Sandy walked into the tent, along with Murton and Becky. Ross looked at Virgil, and said, "What is it?"

"What's what?" Virgil said.

"You've got a peculiar look on your face."

"Do I?" Virgil said.

Murton looked at his brother and said, "Yeah, you sort of do. What's on your mind?"

Virgil looked away from everyone for a few seconds, then said, "I was thinking that last time we had a party like this, one of us didn't make it back."

Sandy took her husband's hand. "I think we'll all miss Ed for the rest of our lives, Virgil. Pam too. But even as awful as that day turned out, look what it's brought us. Wyatt has a brother he never would have had if things turned out differently. It's just like you and Murton."

Virgil nodded. "I guess so. Still, it's hard. Anyway, that's what I was thinking about...the party, and how Ed died to save Murt and Becky and me."

Murton clapped his brother on the back. "Well, the good news is this, Jones-man. We're all here, no one seems to be going anywhere, so there is no one to worry about."

Except Murton didn't know about Jodie Carter, and what she was experiencing at that very moment.

———

EMMA, WHO WAS THE ASSISTANT NIGHT MANAGER AT the Dollar General knew that Jodie was eager to leave so she could have as much time with Bobby as possible. "The store is empty, Jodie. We don't have one single customer. Steve is still stocking the shelves. Why don't you go ahead and take off?"

"Are you sure?" Jodie said. "I don't want to leave you here alone."

"I'm not alone. I just told you Steve is here stocking the shelves."

"What if you get a last-minute rush. It happens."

"I know it happens. I also know I can handle it. This isn't Walmart in the big city. It's Dollar General a half hour before closing time in French Lick. Go."

That was all the convincing Jodie needed. She took off her yellow smock and stuck it under the register. She was almost through the door when Emma said, "You better call me tomorrow morning and tell me all about it."

Jodie gave her friend a wicked smile and said, "Don't worry, I will as soon as I get home." And then she was gone.

Forever.

———

WHEN DON PARKED HIS VAN NEXT TO JODIE'S CAR, HE was glad he'd gotten there early, because Jodie was already on her way out. He quickly opened the van's sliding door from the inside, then hopped out and bent over like he might be looking for something inside the van. *If it worked before...*

———

JODIE WALKED OUT TO HER CAR, WHICH WAS PARKED along the side of the building. When she turned the corner, she saw a familiar vehicle parked next to her own. She saw a man bent over from the waist and looking inside his van. A small smile tugged at the corners of her mouth. *I'd know those knees anywhere,* she thought. As she got closer, she called out, "Hey Coach. Is that you?"

---

DON HEARD JODIE WALKING HIS WAY, AND WHEN SHE called out to him, he leaned back out of the van, smiled, and said, "Hi, Jodie. I was just about to run inside and grab a few things. You guys aren't closed yet, are you?" He closed the sliding door of his van right up to the latch, but left it cracked, like he didn't want her to see inside.

Jodie let her smile grow. "No, the store is still open, but I'm done for the night...sneaking out a little early. What do you have in there? It looks like you're trying to hide something from me."

Don waited until she was right next to the van. "I always suspected you were a sneaky one, though I have to admit, you've never snuck out on practice."

"And I never will," Jodie said. "So, what have you got in there?"

Don smiled at her. "Look, Jodie, I'll show you, but you've got to keep it a secret from the other girls. Think you can do that?"

"Sure."

Don gave her an amused look, one that was suggestive of Jodie's inability to keep a secret.

"C'mon, Coach. I won't tell a soul. I promise. What is it?"

Don smiled, stepped back from the van, and said, "Okay, see for yourself." He made a sweeping motion with his arm, an indication that Jodie should pull the door open.

Jodie turned toward the van, pulled open the door, and looked inside. The back of the van was completely empty. When she turned back around, Don didn't hesitate. He hit her with a massive uppercut to the jaw, and it sent her flying into the van. He jumped in after her, yanked the door shut, then hit her again, this time in the stomach to take the air out of her lungs. He quickly wrapped her hands and ankles with duct tape, then stuck a piece over her mouth. Then he climbed in the front, started the engine, and drove out of the lot.

---

HALF AN HOUR LATER AT CLOSING TIME, EMMA TOLD Steve the stock boy he could leave. Then she turned out the store's lights, set the security system, locked the front door, and walked out to her car. A smile tugged at the corners of her mouth when she thought about Jodie and Bobby. She knew they were going to have a great time, and she was glad to do her part and help make it happen for her friend.

As she turned her car around and drove past the far side of the building, her smile faded just a bit when she saw Jodie's car was still parked in the lot. She pulled up close to her friend's car, her smile now a full-blown frown, and wondered what the heck was going on. She put her car in park, got out, and looked inside the other vehicle. Nothing appeared to be out of order. The thought went through her head that maybe Jodie had simply left her car here, and Bobby had picked her up. But if that was the case, why hadn't she said anything?

Emma took out her phone and tried to call Jodie. After four rings, it clicked over to voicemail. She ended the call and sent her a text message, asking if she was okay. When no reply came back, she wasn't quite sure what to do next. Should she try Bobby? After a few seconds of self-debate, she did just that. But Bobby didn't answer his phone or respond to Emma's text message either. Emma thought that in all likelihood, Jodie and Bobby were going at it, their phones turned off, and nothing was wrong. But still, something didn't feel quite right.

She got back in her car and headed for Bobby's house, thinking she'd rather embarrass herself and make sure nothing was wrong, as opposed to finding out later that something had happened to her friend.

---

WHEN DON FINISHED WITH JODIE, HE THOUGHT HE might have felt a little bad about the whole thing, but as it happened, he felt nothing at all...except the afterglow that came from a good fight, and of course, the kill itself. He looked at Jodie's body on the ground for a few minutes, thinking about how good she looked, and how glad he was that she'd never have to experience the horrors of life that would surely come her way if she married the kind of man his own mother had.

After a few minutes of reflective thought about his mom, he picked up Jodie's body and carried her back to the edge of the clearing in the middle of the woods, where the old farmhouse used to be. He set her gently on the ground, then, with no small amount of effort, he opened the lid of the old cistern, picked Jodie back up, and let her slide from his arms and down into the bottom of the pit. There was a small splash as she joined the others, and somewhere in the back of Don's mind, the sound registered with him as applause.

When the stench overcame the pleasure of the applause-like sound, he pushed the lid back in place and hurried away. Time to get back to the casino. He needed to be seen having that after-dinner drink.

———

WHEN EMMA ARRIVED AT BOBBY'S HOUSE, SHE NOTICED most of the lights were on and she could see the flicker of the big screen TV through the front picture window. She walked up the steps, rang the bell, and waited. When there was no answer, she knocked on the door—hard—

and still got no response. When she tried the knob, the door opened right up.

She stuck her head inside and called out to Jodie. She could hear the TV in the background, but nothing else. When she stepped all the way inside and looked to her left, she saw Bobby on the sofa. It looked like he was sleeping. She ran that way and tried to wake him, but she knew immediately that there was something wrong. Bobby smelled like a distillery, and his breathing was shallow and irregular. She shouted for Jodie again, and still, nothing. She grabbed Bobby by his shoulders and shook him, yelling his name the whole time, but she couldn't get him to wake up.

She ran upstairs, took a quick peek in all the bedrooms and bathrooms. Jodie was nowhere to be found. When she went back downstairs she again tried to wake Bobby—this time with a slap to his face—but she still couldn't get him to regain consciousness. Panic had set in now, its grasp of her mental thought processes at odds with the calm, direct, and professional-sounding voice on the other end of the phone. "911. What is the nature of your emergency...?"

# CHAPTER TWENTY-FIVE

The party wound down. Cool flew the governor and Nichole back to the airport, where they'd go to wherever it was they were spending their secret time together. The kids were all in bed, as were Delroy and Huma. Nicky, Wu, and Robert had said their goodbyes, and Larry the Dog was passed out under one of the tables. Murton and Becky said goodnight and walked across the backyard, around the pond, and up to their house. Ross was helping Sandy clear some of the mess, carrying the plates and other dishes inside. That left Virgil and Sarah under the tent by themselves.

Virgil looked at his young female friend and said, "I'd like to share something with you."

Sarah tipped her head and smiled at Virgil. "What's that?"

"I couldn't have been more wrong about you and Ross. He's one of the finest young men I've ever had the pleasure of knowing and working with. When I see the way you guys look at each other, it reminds me of Murt and Becky...and me and Sandy. I hope everything is going well between the two of you."

Sarah looked at Virgil and said, "It's going so well that sometimes I'm afraid to believe it's real. Or I'm afraid that something might happen to him on the job. I'm not sure I'd be able to go through it all again."

"You can't live your life in fear, Sarah. It's a miserable existence."

Sarah looked away for a few seconds, then said, "Maybe I'm not saying it quite right. I'm not afraid, really. But I know his job can be a dangerous one, and after everything that happened with Gary, I sometimes have a little trouble falling asleep at night."

"Maybe you should talk to Bell."

"I half expected him to be here tonight," Sarah said. "But Cool told me he couldn't make it. I guess he had some sort of flight test he was prepping for."

"That sounds about right," Virgil said. "But listen, here's the thing: Every cop has a dangerous job, I won't lie to you, but Ross is smart, well-trained, very good at what he does, and he is extremely careful. I don't think you have anything to worry about."

"I never thought I had anything to worry about with Gary, either." Then before Virgil could respond, "Do you think I'll ever stop missing him? Gary?"

"I hope not," Virgil said. "I think as Liv grows up and becomes older, you'll be able to see Gary anytime you want. All you'll have to do is look into your daughter's eyes."

"I'm not betraying him, am I?"

"Of course not. If anything, you're honoring him by getting on with your life. You're taking care of yourself and the child the two of you had together. Do you think he'd want it any other way?"

"No...I'm sure of it. I'm also certain I wouldn't have been able to endure what I did without you and Sandy. That video you showed me? The one where Jonas became part of your family that night? It...changed me. It also helped me to understand that if you look at something with an open mind—not to mention an open heart— you'll see things you never thought possible."

Virgil could feel the shift in the conversation, like Sarah was trying to tell him something without coming right out and saying the words. He was about to say so, when she stood, gave him a brief hug, and said, "I think I'll go and help clean up. Give you a little time to yourself, so to speak." Then she turned and headed for the house.

Virgil watched her go, then turned and looked at his father's cross. Mason stood there, waiting. When Virgil turned back and looked at Sarah, she was on the back deck, smiling at him. She nodded once, then went inside the house.

MASON LOOKED AT HIS SON, AND SAID, "SARAH'S A FINE young lady, isn't she?"

"She sure is," Virgil said. "Was she able to see you?"

Mason shrugged. "I'm not really sure. I think she sensed my presence more than anything. I can tell you this, though: What she said is true. She wouldn't have made it after Gary was murdered if you and Sandy hadn't been by her side. It would have been a mistake to let her go after the case was over."

Virgil squinted an eye at his father. "What exactly are we talking about here?"

"Same thing as before, Virg. Mistakes. Mine in particular."

"You never did say what those mistakes were," Virgil said.

"No, I didn't. There's only so much I can say, Son. I've told you that before."

Virgil thought about that for a minute, then said, "Am I making some sort of mistake?"

"Not necessarily. Though you may come to view it that way."

"View what?" Virgil said.

Mason let out a little chuckle. "Nice try." Then, as serious as Virgil had ever seen his father, "You've got work to do. That feeling you had earlier in the evening? The one where you said last time you had a party like this, one of you didn't make it back? You weren't entirely wrong."

Virgil visibly swallowed. "Are you telling me that one of us is in danger?"

"I'm telling you that there is pure evil in the world, Virg. It's not always easy to see. You've got to look for it. My mistake was I didn't look hard enough. My excuse? I was worried about you and Murton fighting in the war, and your mother dying of cancer. I should have looked harder, but I didn't. I turned in my badge and let someone else take over."

"I'm already looking through your old files," Virgil said.

"It won't do you any good tonight. He's already taken another."

Virgil walked right up to his father and got in his face. "Who is it? Tell me, and I'll either put him away or put him in the ground."

Mason put a hand on his son's shoulder. "You have to understand, it's not that I don't want to. I can't, Virg. I don't make the rules any more than you do."

Virgil was getting angry. "I find that all a little hard to believe."

Mason shook his head. "I think maybe a better way to say it is you find it hard to understand. There's a difference." Virgil was about to respond, but his father wasn't done. "You've got all the answers, Son. All you need to do is put the individual pieces together."

"I don't feel like I have any of the pieces," Virgil said. "I feel like I'm running blind."

"Your own statement is a clue in itself."

"What? That I'm running blind?"

Mason ignored his son's question and asked one himself. "How many counties are there in this state?"

Virgil shook his head. What was this, some sort of political science quiz? "Ninety-two, Dad. You know that."

"Indeed I do," Mason said. "So, go sit under that tent and think about that for a few minutes. When you figure it out, wake your brother, and get to work. Tonight."

———

VIRGIL DID WHAT HIS FATHER ASKED OF HIM, THOUGH he had to admit, he didn't see how it would do much good. He went back under the tent, sat down, and started thinking about the individual counties. As a former trooper, Virgil knew the names of every county in the state and had long ago committed them to memory. He went through them in his head alphabetically, trying to understand his father's cryptic message.

A mild breeze was rippling the tent's upper flap where the decorative lights had been hung earlier in the day. The lights were similar to the old-fashioned multicolored Christmas tree bulbs that hardly anyone used since the advent of LEDs. He wasn't really staring at the lights, but he was looking at them when the wind picked up and he heard a slight popping noise. Then one by one the lights started to go out until only a few remained illuminated.

Virgil got up and pulled the plug from the extension cord and the rest of the lights went dark. The last thing he needed was an electrical fire because of a short in the line. He sat back down and finished thinking about the counties, but eventually gave up, his own frustration overpowering his analytical thought process. Disgusted with himself and his inability to figure anything out, he stood and headed for the house.

He made it all the way to the back deck before his subconscious finally kicked into overdrive and thumped him on his frontal lobe. The thought stopped him dead in his tracks. Was the answer that simple? Had he been overthinking it the entire time? He ran back down to the tent, grabbed the extension cord, and plugged the lights back in. The blue, yellow, red, and green lights refused to illuminate. The only ones that lit up were orange. Virgil took out his phone and made a call.

"I was almost asleep," Becky said, the tone in her voice full of irritability.

"Sorry, Becks," Virgil said. "Need your skills, and I need them right now."

"Why am I not surprised? About the right now part, I mean."

"You can yell at me later. Get into the system and tell me what's happening in Orange County...at this very moment."

Becky let out a sigh, told Virgil to hang on, and went to her computer. Virgil could hear her typing away, and when she finally came back with a response, she'd lost the attitude of someone who'd been roused from bed by their boss, brother-in-law or not. "How did you know?"

"It doesn't matter," Virgil said. "Tell me."

"They're putting a search team together right now. Jodie Carter, female, seventeen years old, senior at the high school in French Lick. Left her job a little before nine this evening and hasn't been heard from since."

"Wake Murt and tell him to bring his squad car."

"He's already getting dressed. He says five minutes. You're not flying down?"

Virgil had thought about that while waiting for the information from Becky. It was not quite an hour and a half drive from Virgil's house down to Orange County. With lights and siren they could make it in an hour if the traffic cooperated. By the time Cool got to the airport, got the helicopter ready, then picked them up, they could be there, so it was a wash. "Nope, but we'll be running hard down the interstate. Notify the troopers and the other counties that we'll be coming through."

"You got it, Jonesy. You guys be careful."

Virgil told her they would, then ran inside to tell Sandy he was going.

# CHAPTER TWENTY-SIX

When Murton turned into Virgil's driveway, he pulled right up to the front door, got out of his squad car, and took the passenger seat. He knew Virgil would want to drive, and in truth, Murton knew his brother was better at the wheel than he was. He'd seen it any number of times.

Virgil ran out the door, jumped into the driver's seat, and had the car rolling before his door was closed. He took it easy on the gravel road—sliding into the ditch only a mile from home wouldn't be good for anyone—but when he hit the highway, he turned on the flashers and floored the accelerator.

They spoke little of the ongoing incident during the drive. There simply wasn't much of an opportunity. Virgil was concentrating hard on the road ahead, as was Murton, calling out the dangers and potential threats as they drove. *'Two on the right...got one coming up the on-ramp, slow mover in the left lane a quarter-mile ahead, motorcycle on the right, watch your closure rate...'* Like that, all the way there. It was ninety-eight miles from Virgil's front door to their destination.

They made it in fifty-seven minutes.

---

VIRGIL TOOK THEM STRAIGHT TO THE ORANGE COUNTY Sheriff's office, located in Paoli, Indiana. The building was squat, with red bricks, low windows, and a gray metal roof. Even though it was dark outside, Murton thought the place looked like it might have been converted from a funeral home. When he said as much to Virgil, the reply he got back made him wish he'd kept his thoughts to himself.

"Let's hope that's not a harbinger of things to come," Virgil said.

They got out of Murton's squad car, their badges visible hanging from chains around their necks. When Virgil pushed the buzzer to gain access to the building, a red light winked at them from above. Both men looked up, and when they did, the lock on the door clicked, and Murton pulled it open. Once inside the building, they found a single female deputy out of her element, trying to contain a situation that looked like it was going from bad to worse. Two adult men were arguing with each other, while a young teenaged girl sat on a visitor's bench, her face lined with tears. For a brief instant, Virgil thought the girl might be Jodie Carter, and that they'd wasted a trip down to Orange County. But as he listened to the argument between the men, he quickly learned his thoughts were nothing more than wishful thinking.

The female deputy slapped her palm—hard—on the reception counter, then told everyone to shut up. When she looked at Virgil and Murton, she said, "Are you the detectives from the state? I was informed by a woman named Becky Wheeler that you were on the way here."

"That's us," Murton said. "I'm Murton Wheeler. Becky is my wife, and an operational member of the Major Crimes Unit." He tipped his head at his brother and said, "This is my partner and lead Detective of the MCU, Virgil Jones."

The deputy dipped her chin...a single tight nod, and said, "I'm a reserve deputy with the department. My name is Tracy Dunn. Everyone else from our department, including the sheriff, is out searching the county right now, looking for Jodie Carter."

Jodie Carter's father, Eugene, took a step forward and pointed at the other man. When he spoke, his voice was full of rage and panic. "They wouldn't have to be out looking for my daughter at all if that asshole knew how to properly raise his little bitch sitting right over there on the bench."

Emma Brady's father, Lee, stepped up, and said, "Call my daughter a name like that again and see what happens. You'll be eating out of a feeding tube for the next six weeks."

Virgil and Murton got between the two men and pushed them away from each other. Once they had them separated, Virgil said, "Everybody take it easy. That's not a request. I know you're all frightened, but name-calling and arguing aren't going to help anyone. I'm asking you to act like adults. If you can't do that, we'll be interviewing you in an interrogation room, handcuffed to the table. Now, I want someone to tell my partner and myself exactly what happened."

Emma Brady stood from where she was seated, wiped her eyes with the sleeve of her shirt, and said, "Mr. Carter is right—though he didn't have to call me a bitch. This is my fault. I lied to cover for Jodie. She wanted to spend the night with her boyfriend."

"What's the boyfriend's name?" Virgil said.

"Bobby Thompson," Emma said. "His parents are out of town and he had the place to himself. Jodie told Mr. and Mrs. Carter that she was going to spend the night with me, but she was really going to go over to Bobby's house. All I was supposed to do was go home after work and keep my mouth shut. But when I left the store—Jodie and I both work at Dollar General in French Lick—I noticed that her car was still parked on the side lot, even though she left a half hour before I did."

"What did you do when you saw her car was still at the store?" Virgil said.

"I'll tell you what she should have done," Eugene Carter said. "She should have acted like an adult and—"

Murton walked over to Mr. Carter, grabbed his arm,

and spoke quietly into his ear. "I'm only going to say this once, sir, so I suggest you listen carefully. I know you're upset. I know you're scared. I would be too. But you're not helping us, and more importantly, you're not helping your daughter. Say one more word to anyone without being asked to speak, and I'll lock you up and deal with you later. Have I made myself clear?"

Carter tried to pull his arm free, but when he did, he discovered that Murton had no intention of letting go. The end result was Carter's struggle only pulled him closer to Murton.

"I asked you a question, sir. Have I made myself clear?"

"You have," Carter said. He spoke through his teeth.

"Good," Murton said. "Now go sit on that bench and cool out. We'll speak again in a few minutes."

Carter did what he was told, and Murton turned back to the conversation. Emma glanced at Carter, then her own father, and finally Virgil. "I'm sorry. What was your question?"

"I asked what you did when you saw Jodie's car was still at the store," Virgil said.

Emma closed her eyes as she replayed the events in her mind. "I got out of my own car and looked around to see if...if...I don't know...I guess to make sure everything was okay. I think I was looking for Jodie, or her keys or her purse or something like that, though I wasn't really thinking those things at the time."

"What were you thinking?" Murton said.

Emma looked at Murton, and said, "I guess I was simply wondering why her car was still parked at the store even though she'd been gone for over half an hour. I thought maybe Bobby had picked her up or something."

"Did you try to call, or text your friend?" Virgil said.

"I did. I also tried to call and text Bobby, but neither of them answered. Then, even though I didn't want to intrude, I thought I'd better go over to Bobby's house to make sure everything was okay. When I got there, I discovered it wasn't. Nothing was okay. Nothing at all." Emma began to cry again, and her father put his arm around his daughter and pulled her close.

Tracy Dunn, the reserve deputy looked at Virgil and Murton, and said, "The 911 call came in at 9:23 pm. Miss Carter's boyfriend, Bobby Thompson, was unconscious and non-responsive. He's at the IU Health hospital here in Paoli right now."

"What's his current condition?" Murton said.

Then, as if the mere asking of the question could connect the cosmic strings that held the universe in check, the phone behind the counter rang. Deputy Dunn answered, listened for a few minutes, said, 'thank you,' then gently set the receiver back in place. "That was the hospital," she said. "Bobby Dunn died ten minutes ago from a combination drug and alcohol overdose. They want someone to make the notification." She was looking at Virgil and Murton when she spoke her eyes pleading in a way that needed little, if any explanation.

Emma pulled away from her father, ran outside, and

screamed. Eugene Carter glanced at Murton, then looked at Emma's father, and said, "I'm sorry, Lee. I shouldn't have said those things about your girl. She's a fine young woman, and Jodie has never had a better friend." When he looked at Murton, he said, "I know you told me not to speak, but I don't care. My daughter is missing. I'll spend the rest of my life to find her if that's what it takes." Then he walked out the door without another word.

---

VIRGIL AND MURTON TOOK A FEW MINUTES TO LET Dunn bring them up to speed on the search efforts thus far, then got the sheriff's cell phone number. When they went outside they found Lee Brady sitting on the front steps of the sheriff's office, trying to comfort his daughter. Virgil looked at Brady and said, "If you don't have any objections, sir, my partner and I would like Emma to come with us."

"Where?"

"Back to her place of employment, for one. We'd like to retrace her steps from the time she left work until she arrived here. We'll drop her at your house when we're finished."

"I don't see what good that can do for Jodie," Brady said. "And it sure as hell isn't going to help Bobby, is it?"

"No, sir, it won't help Bobby at all," Murton said. "But with respect, it sounds as though he made his own choices." He was looking at Virgil when he spoke.

Emma looked at her father and said, "It's okay, Dad. I want to help."

"What about the search for Jodie?" Brady said.

"We'll do what we can to help in that regard," Virgil said. "But the truth of the matter is this: We don't know the county or its residents the way the sheriff and his deputies do. Our efforts would be better spent investigating Jodie's abduction instead of taking part in a general search operation."

Brady looked at his daughter. "Are you up for this, honey?"

Emma seemed to have pulled herself together during the conversation. She nodded at her father and said, "I am. I'll do whatever I can to help."

"What should I do?" Brady said. "Believe it or not, Eugene Carter and I are friends. At least we were. Now? Who knows? But it feels like I should be doing something."

"I think the best thing you can do right now is go home," Virgil said. "Let us do what we do. Your daughter will be safe with us, and we'll have her back at your place in two hours or less. Why are you looking at me like that, sir?"

Lee Brady ran his fingers through his hair, then said, "Because my daughter's life-long best friend was abducted only hours ago. No one knows who took her. I don't mean to offend you, or your partner, but could I please take a closer look at your IDs?"

AFTER ADDRESSING LEE BRADY'S CONCERNS AND convincing him his daughter was safe, Virgil and Murton drove Emma back to the Dollar General in French Lick. The first thing they did after they arrived was take a close look at Jodie's vehicle and the surrounding area. "Did you touch her car at all when you noticed it was still here?" Virgil said.

Emma shook her head. "No, but if you're thinking about fingerprints, or whatever, you'd find mine all over anyway. I'm in her car as often as she is in mine."

Virgil and Murton took out flashlights, got down on their hands and knees, and looked under the car and very carefully around its immediate area. They found absolutely nothing of evidentiary value. Murton turned to Emma and said, "Does the store have security cameras?"

"Yes, but only for the front entrance...and the inside, of course. But not out here on the side of the building."

"How about we take a look?" Virgil said. "Maybe we'll catch something."

They all walked around to the front of the building, and Emma unlocked the door. Once they were inside, she relocked the door and led them to the back of the store where the manager's office was located. She brought up the security system and was about to run the video back when she paused.

"What is it?" Virgil said.

"The system runs twenty-four hours a day. That means

it's going right now. It's some sort of insurance thing, I guess."

"That's not uncommon," Murton said.

"I know," Emma said. "But if I stop it to run it back, then there will be a gap in the coverage. If something happens while we're looking at the video, I'm responsible."

Virgil had to smile to himself, and the innocence of a young teenage girl not wanting to get in trouble. "Except that's what the system is for, Emma. If you can't ever shut it down to look at what it might have captured, what good does it do to have it at all?"

Despite the situation, Emma shook her head and laughed at herself. Then, even though it wasn't necessary, she added, "Duh," then pressed the button on the keyboard.

"Run it back to just before Jodie left," Murton said.

Emma did as Murton asked, and they watched a split screen that showed the front entrance and parking lot, as well as the checkout lanes inside. "There's me and Jodie right there," Emma said. "I told her she could leave early because I knew she was eager to meet up with Bobby. See...she took off her smock, tossed it under the checkout lane, then headed for the door. But the camera only shows the front lot."

"Can't even see the street," Murton said.

Virgil shook his head. "Okay, it was worth a shot, but this isn't going to get us anywhere. Let's head over to Bobby's house."

"What good is that going to do?" Emma said. "As far as anyone knows, she never even made it there."

Murton jumped in before Virgil had a chance to answer Emma's question, and said, "What's Jodie's phone number? Bobby's too."

Emma told Murton the numbers, and as soon as he had them, he called Becky. "Can you get to work on a couple of phone numbers?"

"Yeah. You guys okay?"

"We're good," Murton said. Then he quickly explained the situation, gave Becky the numbers, and said, "We need a last known location on the Carter phone. That's the first number I gave you. We need account information on the second. Fast as you can, Becks."

After Murton ended the call with Becky, Emma looked at Virgil and said, "You didn't answer my question. If Jodie never made it to Bobby's house, how does that help us find her?"

"That's not why we're going, sweetheart," Murton said.

"Then why?" Emma asked.

"Because we need to find a way to get in touch with Bobby's parents."

# CHAPTER TWENTY-SEVEN

When Virgil and Murton and Emma Brady arrived at the Thompson residence, they saw an Orange County Sheriff's deputy sitting in an unmarked squad car at the front of the house. Virgil walked over and introduced himself, then informed the deputy why they were there. "Is the house still unlocked?"

"As far as I know," the deputy said. He looked tired, like he might have been pulled out of bed to help with the search. "I was asked to wait here in case the Carter girl shows up. Why are you looking at me like that, Detective?"

"Because in all likelihood, the Carter girl has been abducted. She won't be showing up here. Your efforts would be better spent helping with the search."

"Take it up with the sheriff. I just do what I'm told,

especially when I was supposed to go off-duty three hours ago."

"Have you spoken with any of the neighbors?" Murton said.

"Only to tell them to go home and mind their business. After they pulled the Thompson boy out of here, you'd have thought the circus had come to town."

Virgil looked at Murton and said, "I'm going to take Emma through the house real quick. You know what to do."

Murton nodded once, then as Virgil and Emma went through the front door, he turned back to the deputy and said, "We're trying to locate Bobby Thompson's parents. Any idea where they might be?"

The deputy shook his head. "I've never met them. They could be anywhere, for all I know."

Murton didn't respond. Instead, he jogged over to his car, turned his flashers on, and burped the siren a few times. Then he ran back over to the deputy and said, "Light it up."

"What the hell for? We'll wake half the neighborhood."

"That's the point. I want everyone out on their porches or in their front yards. C'mon now, hit the lights and get on the horn. I need to talk to some people."

The deputy shook his head, like maybe the state cop who was ordering him around had lost his marbles. But he did what Murton asked, and a few minutes later the circus was back in town.

VIRGIL AND EMMA WERE LOOKING THROUGH BOBBY'S house, checking for anything they could find that might help them locate the Thompsons. When Emma heard the sirens, she looked at Virgil and said, "What's going on?"

"We might need the neighbors' help. If we can't find anything in here, maybe one of them will know where Bobby's parents are right now."

They spent a quick five minutes checking the obvious places for information...a note stuck to the refrigerator, a destination brochure in the home office, a printed itinerary...anything. But in the end, they found nothing that indicated where Bobby's parents might be.

"You're sure Jodie didn't tell you where they were going?" Virgil said.

"I'm positive," Emma said. "I don't think she knew. Even if she did, it's not really something we would have talked about. The fact that they were going to be gone was all that mattered to Bobby and Jodie."

Outside, the sirens suddenly went silent. Emma looked at Virgil and said, "Why did they stop?"

"Probably because it worked," Virgil said, the hollow tone of his voice an expression of what waited for two parents who didn't yet know they'd lost their only son.

EXCEPT IT DIDN'T WORK. OUTSIDE, VIRGIL ASKED Emma to wait by the car, then he ran over to Murton, who was standing in the street, speaking with a group of neighbors who had gathered around him. He caught the tail end of Murton's questions.

"Any idea at all where they might be? Even a guess would be welcome at this point. Someplace they've gone before, perhaps."

Everyone shook their heads, and an elderly gentleman spoke for the group. "We mostly keep to ourselves around here. The Thompsons are nice folks, but they just didn't interact with any of us that much. They're friendly and all, but not friends, if you understand what I'm saying."

Murton's phone buzzed at him, and when he checked the screen, he turned and walked away from the neighbors. "Give me something good."

"I wish I could," Becky said. "The last known location of Jodie Carter's phone pinged off a tower just west of French Lick...probably not more than two miles from where you are right now. Then it dropped off the grid. I'm guessing the battery got pulled. I couldn't even get an exact location."

"What about the Thompson phone?"

"Yeah, I've got the account pulled up right now. I've got both the parents' numbers and their location. First names are Jake and Ellen. They're both currently hooked into the Wifi system at the Fourwinds Lakeside Inn & Marina on Lake Monroe." After Becky relayed the information to her husband, she said, "It's on your way back. Are you guys going to make the notification?"

"Yeah, I guess so. Better us than someone with limited information."

"Be gentle, Murton Wheeler. You're about to tell two people something that will change their lives forever."

And Murton thought, *It wouldn't be the first time.*

———

VIRGIL AND MURTON DROPPED EMMA AT HOME, gathering as much information from her as they could along the way. Murton took notes as Virgil drove, and by the time they reached the Brady residence, they had a decent portrait of another young teenager who, like Lisa Tate from Kokomo, and Kelly Price from Shelbyville, had been kidnapped and in all likelihood was now dead.

Once Emma was safely inside, Murton took over driving, and they headed back north. Along the way, Virgil called the Orange County Sheriff, introduced himself, and told him they'd handle the parental notification regarding Bobby Thompson. "We know where his parents are, and we'll be going right by there anyway."

The sheriff, a man named Wes Harper, sounded both tired and relieved. "I appreciate your help, Detective. We're doing everything we can to find the Carter girl, but with nothing to go on and no witnesses, it's darn near impossible to even hold out hope. We're driving around looking for her on the street, and you and I both know how much good that's doing anyone."

"Keep after it, Sheriff," Virgil said. "At this point it's all you can do."

"I've been watching your bulletins on the task force. Never thought my county would be a part of it. Think you'll get to the bottom of all this?"

"I know we will, Wes. It's just a matter of time. Our entire unit is working this thing from top to bottom."

"Let me know if there's anything else we can do," the sheriff said. Then, before Virgil could answer, the sheriff continued with something else. "It's sort of odd that you and I are talking right now."

"Why's that?" Virgil said.

"I was going to get in touch with you anyway and ask for your help on another matter, mainly because our county investigator couldn't find his own reflection in a house of mirrors."

"That's what our unit is for, Sheriff, but unless it's urgent, the case we're working on right now has to take priority."

"I understand. It can wait. Just wanted to give you a heads up that I might be ringing your bell. Do you know Ed Henderson, up in Shelby County?"

"Of course," Virgil said, suddenly interested. Kelly Price had gone missing from Henderson's county. "Does Ed have something on Kelly Price?"

"No, no. I'm sorry. It doesn't have anything to do with the missing girls. He called me about a family squabble a friend of his is involved with, right here in my county."

"What sort of squabble?" Virgil said, his interest waning almost as quickly as it had peaked.

"Money, mostly. Anyway, we've got one dead, one missing, and two brothers—one is famous, by the way—fighting about everything under the sun. The famous one wants to dig up the dead one. Thinks his brother and his missing sister killed their own father."

No matter the events of the night, or the case he was currently working, Virgil had to suppress a laugh, because he could tell the sheriff was serious. "Sounds more like a mystery novel than a matter for the state's MCU."

"Funny you should say that," the sheriff said.

"Why's that?"

"Because the famous one is a novelist. Guy named Sam Whittle."

"Never heard of him," Virgil said. Then, eager to wrap up the call, Virgil said, "Listen, Sheriff, when we're finished with this case, if you haven't figured it out, let me know. We might be able to help."

"Will do. Catch this bastard taking these girls, will you?"

"Count on it," Virgil said.

After Virgil ended the call, Murton glanced at his brother and said, "What was all that? Something about Kelly Price?"

Virgil shook his head. "No. Sounds like a family feud. You ever hear of a guy named Sam Whittle?"

"Yeah. Famous author. Lives in French Lick. I saw him when Rosie and I were in Ed's office."

Virgil nodded. "Sounds like the father died, and the family is fighting over the money."

Murton, lost in his thoughts of what they were going to tell the Thompsons, didn't put much thought into it. "Yeah, that's pretty much what Ed told me. It'll eventually blow over...probably in court."

———

IT WAS A LITTLE PAST TWO IN THE MORNING WHEN Murton parked his squad car near the front entrance of the Fourwinds Lakeside Inn & Marina. He killed the engine, looked at Virgil, and said, "Sometimes I think I'd rather have Ross snipe me than do what we're about to do."

Virgil knew how Murton felt. He'd done his share of family notifications over the years when he'd been a trooper, and it was without question, one of the most difficult parts of the job. When they walked inside the lobby, they found a priest sitting near the reception desk, a bible resting on his lap. His hair was slightly askew and as white as his collar. He had sleep lines etched along the side of his face.

Virgil looked at Murton, and said, "Becky." It wasn't a question.

Murton nodded. "She knows how to do her job, doesn't she?"

Virgil and Murton walked over to the priest and introduced themselves. The priest shook hands with them both, and said, "I'm Father Charles Box, from St. Agnes Catholic Church. I got here as quick as I could. I'm afraid I don't know the Thompsons, or even if they are of the catholic faith, but we are all God's children, are we not?"

"I suppose so," Virgil said. "Have you informed the desk clerk why you're here?"

"No, I have not," Box said. "The young woman who contacted me...Miss Wheeler, told me the nature of the situation and asked that I wait for you gentlemen." Then he turned to Murton, and said, "Wheeler. Any relation?"

"My wife," Murton said.

"She sounds like quite the young lady," Box said.

Murton gave the priest a sad grin. "That she is, Padre." Then, "Have you ever done this before?"

"Sadly, yes," Box said. "It's never easy, especially in the middle of the night. The last thing any parent wants to do is answer the door at three in the morning and see two police officers and a member of the clergy. Words aren't often necessary."

Virgil walked over to the reception desk and spoke quietly with the night manager, explained their presence, then told him what he wanted. The manager gave him the suite number, along with directions to where the room was located, and said he'd be ready for Virgil's call.

Virgil thanked him, turned to Murton and Box, and said, "Let's go."

---

WHEN THEY GOT TO THE ROOM, VIRGIL TOOK OUT HIS phone and called the front desk of the hotel. When the manager answered, he simply said, "Make the call."

A few seconds later, as they stood in the hallway, Virgil and Murton and Box could hear the phone ringing inside the Thompson's room. It rang six times before it stopped.

---

THE SOUND OF THE PHONE WOKE ELLEN THOMPSON first, who nudged her husband awake, and said, "Phone."

Jake had a bit of trouble clearing his head, trying to figure out why their room phone was ringing in the middle of the night. He grabbed the receiver, said, "Hello," then listened.

"Mr. Thompson, this is the front desk calling. I'm terribly sorry to wake you sir, but there are some gentlemen waiting outside your room. They need to speak with you right away. I wasn't informed why. I'm so sorry." Then he hung up.

Jake, still half asleep, looked at his wife, and said, "Prank call, I think."

"What kind of prank call?"

"Someone who said they were calling from the front desk. Says there are some gentlemen here to see us."

"Then why aren't they knocking?" Ellen said. "What time is it, anyway?"

WHEN THE PHONE STOPPED RINGING, VIRGIL PUT HIS ear to the door and heard the muffled conversation between the Thompsons, though he couldn't hear exactly what was being said. That's when he leaned back and knocked quietly on the door.

Thirty seconds went by, and Virgil was just about to knock again when the door opened. Jake and Ellen Thompson stood there, both wrapped in robes, their faces sleepy and masked with confusion. They looked at Virgil and Murton, who had their badges clearly visible. When they saw Father Box, he took a half step forward. He opened his mouth to speak, but as he'd told Murton only moments ago in the lobby of the hotel, in that exact moment, words simply weren't necessary.

Ellen Thompson said exactly three words, each the same, save their intensity. Her first reaction was a question, one so basic she didn't realize her voice was calm and without concern, as if she might be daydreaming. "Bobby?"

The second time she said his name, she looked up and down the hall, her voice now loud and panicked, *"Bobby?"*

The third time she said his name, she screamed it in horror, a final realization that the men standing in the doorway weren't part of a daydream, but a mother's worst nightmare. When she collapsed into her husband's arms, he looked at Virgil and Murton and Box. His eyes were watering and his jaw quivered with such intensity his teeth were clacking together like a jackhammer.

# CHAPTER TWENTY-EIGHT

Virgil and Murton were back home by five in the morning. They each managed to get about three hours of sleep before showing up at the MCU headquarters just before nine. They gave all the information they'd gathered on Jodie Carter's abduction to Becky, who entered the fresh data into the system.

An hour later, the entire investigative team, along with Nicky and Wu was gathered in the conference room. "I still have to go through the old case files I dug out of the archives," Virgil said. "If there is anything valuable in those reports, we should have enough information to connect Lisa Tate, Kelly Price, and Jodie Carter together somehow. That has to be our sole focus right now. Whoever is taking these girls is accelerating. There must be a connection we're not seeing. I want every single scrap of information on this table, and we're going to sit here until we figure it out."

Becky pointed at the binders in the center of the table. "It's all right there, Jonesy. I added Carter's information this morning. None of the girls knew each other, none of the people who have been interviewed knew the other girls—which is logical because Tate was from Kokomo, Price was from Shelbyville, and Carter was from French Lick."

"I know where everyone was from," Virgil said. He snapped it at her. When he saw the look on Becky's face, he immediately apologized. "I'm sorry, Becks. I didn't mean to bite at you. I'm just exhausted."

Becky waved him off. "I understand. Don't worry about it. I'm simply saying these are three of the most typical teenage girls you'd ever see, and there isn't anything that connects them."

"Except there is," Murton said. "We just aren't seeing it."

Becky separated the Tate, Price, and Carter binders from the rest of the stack. Ross and Rosencrantz set the others aside, while Nicky and Wu worked at the computers. "Wu make visual for big screen."

While Nicky and Wu worked the computer, putting everything together to view on the large-screen monitor, Virgil turned to Becky and said, "That was a beautiful thing you did last night...having the priest at the hotel."

"I thought it might make things go a little easier," Becky said.

"It did," Murton said. "It wasn't easy, but as it turns

out, the Thompsons are Catholic, and Father Box was a huge help. If he hadn't shown up, we might still be there."

They talked it back and forth for a while...the difficulties of the job and the notification process. "It's something they don't teach you at the academy, that's for sure," Virgil said.

"Maybe they should," Murton said.

"Here's everything we have on these three girls," Nicky said. He hit a series of keystrokes and the large monitor at the end of the room lit up. Everyone turned their chairs, and Nicky and Wu began by putting up three separate pictures of each girl.

"First is Miss Tate, of Kokomo," Wu said. "Missing over three weeks now. Age seventeen. She is an only child who lived at home with her parents, her grades were very good, she volunteered, was involved in athletics, and held a part-time job."

"Next is Price," Nicky said. "Almost identical in every way, the exception being where she lived. She was an only child, a senior at Shelbyville high school with good grades, she was also involved in athletics, and she volunteered at the cultural center."

"And finally, the latest, Jodie Carter," Becky said. "Resident of French Lick, an only child, a senior in high school, also involved in sports, and had a job with her best friend working at the local Dollar General."

Everyone looked at the screen for a few minutes, and the three beautiful young faces staring back at them.

Finally, Virgil turned and faced Becky. "Did you ever get a definitive color on that van?"

"Yes. And believe it or not, it's gray."

"Okay, at least that's something. And we are one hundred percent positive that none of the people we interviewed about each young woman knew or had any connection with the interviewees of the other girls?"

Nicky, Wu, and Becky all nodded. "We are certain, Jonesy," Nicky said. "We have been through the data every possible way. There is no connection at all. The information on Miss Carter is a little thin because the only people interviewed were the ones you spoke with last night. But no matter, even if you were to conduct more interviews, I believe the results would be the same."

Virgil stood from his chair and walked closer to the screen. He stared at the girls, the list of names of everyone who'd been questioned and cleared, the locations of where the girls went missing, and all the other relevant facts regarding each case. When he turned around, he looked at no one in particular, and said, "You know what? Maybe we're looking at this the wrong way."

"What do you mean?" Murton said.

"We've been looking for something that connects the girls together, but almost everything about them is practically identical. We may as well be looking at their yearbook pictures and lists of accomplishments. That isn't going to get us anywhere."

"What are you suggesting?" Nicky said.

"I'm suggesting we need to do what Ross and Rosen-crantz did with Lisa Tate, and what Murton and Rosie did with Kelly Price. We need to reconstruct their lives."

"That didn't seem to get us very far," Rosencrantz said.

"That's because you didn't do what I'm talking about," Virgil said. "I know you took a thorough look initially, but we've got to go back further. We need to find a way to look at their individual lives over the past twelve months, not just around the time they went missing."

"That's going to take a lot of leg work," Rosencrantz said.

"Maybe not," Virgil said. "In fact, I think it could be done from this room. What do all these girls have in common?"

Becky shrugged. "Everything, Jonesy. It's all right there on the screen."

"Except I'm betting there's something else, and it's the one thing we've all overlooked."

"What's that?" Rosencrantz said.

"Social media. When was the last time you ever knew a teenager who wasn't on Facebook, or Twitter, or whatev-er?" He turned to Nicky and Wu, and said, "I'm going to ask you to do something, and if it ever comes up, I'll deny it until the day I die."

Nicky gave Virgil a wicked little grin. "You don't have to ask, because I know what you want. We've already looked at each girl's profile. To go deeper and extract the type of data you're looking for will take at least a week, but we can do it."

"I don't want to sound like the idiot in the room," Ross said, but—"

"Too late," Rosencrantz said.

Virgil gave them both a look and said, "Guys, please."

Wu looked at Ross and said, "Virgil would like us to hack into the social media sites, examine the girls' profiles, and find out who, if anyone has been stalking them prior to their abduction."

"And if we can figure that out," Nicky said, "we should be able to pin down an IP address of the perpetrator."

"Exactly," Virgil said. "And if you can figure out who, I'm positive that you'll find he stopped stalking them after they were taken."

"Wu hate to say it, but Nicky is right. It will be at least a full week...maybe more before we could have any meaningful data."

"Then get started right away." He turned to Becky and said, "Can you help with this?"

Becky was mildly offended. She was about to say so, but Wu beat her to the punch. "She opened a secure socket layer and bounced a packet through Ukraine one time. Nicky and I watch her do it. The more people we have working on this the quicker it will go."

Virgil held up his hands. "Okay, sorry. Just asking. And listen, don't be offended by my next question, but the social media sites won't be able to trace this back to us, will they?"

Becky and Wu and Nicky all looked at each other. Then Wu, sounding exactly like an Asian Valley girl, said, "Like, oh my God…"

———————

Ross looked at Virgil, and said, "While the computer whizzes are doing their thing, what are me and Rosie supposed to do?"

Virgil gave him a fake grin. "The same thing Murt and I are going to be doing. Follow me."

Everyone was following Virgil as he walked into his office, and once there, he stopped so quickly that they all practically bumped into each other. "Your brake lights aren't working," Rosencrantz said.

"What is it?" Murton said.

Virgil spun in a circle, then pointed. "The files I dug out of the archives. They were all stacked right over there next to my desk. But now they're gone." He turned to Murton. "Did Becky take them?"

Murton shook his head. "I doubt it. I'm sure she would have said something. Let me run back and ask her, just to make sure."

Thirty seconds later he was back. "She not only didn't take them, she said she never saw them in your office."

Virgil scratched the back of his head. "What the hell?"

"You've been running on empty for a few days now," Rosencrantz said. "Are you sure you put them in here?"

"Of course I'm sure," Virgil said. "Ross saw them."

Ross was nodding. "He's right. They were here." Then he let a smile form on his lips. "I bet I know where they are." He took out his phone and sent a quick text.

---

TWO MINUTES LATER LAWLESS WALKED INTO VIRGIL'S office holding a banker's box. He looked completely exhausted. He set the box on Virgil's desk, glanced at Ross, and said, "I was just about to bring this up to you guys." Then to Virgil: "I've been up all night. After you left yesterday, I didn't have anything to do, or anywhere to be, so I thought I'd take a preliminary look at the old files. The rest of them are still down in the lab."

Virgil looked at the box on his desk. "Did you find anything?"

Lawless's eyes were bloodshot and resting at half-mast. He yawned, then rubbed his face with both hands. "Yeah, I'm pretty sure I did." He removed the lid from the box and pulled out a single sheet of paper. "These are my notes from one of the old cases. The original notes are still right here in the box, but I wanted to summarize everything."

"Tell us," Virgil said.

"I will, but I've got to sit down. If I don't, I'm going to fall over."

Everyone grabbed a chair, and they arranged themselves in a little semicircle. Lawless took his notes and walked them through his discovery. He looked at Virgil, and said, "The last MCPD case your father worked as sheriff of Marion County was back in 1990."

"That's right," Virgil said. "It was just before he retired."

"We were still in sand-land," Murton said.

Virgil nodded. "I remember him telling me he was going to retire so he could take care of Mom. That's when we found out how sick she was."

"He was personally involved in a missing child case when he retired," Lawless said. "The new sheriff took over, but the case eventually went cold. The victim disappeared during a cross-country meet at one of the Marion County parks."

Virgil's eyes widened, then he turned and looked at nothing for a few seconds, his mind suddenly racing. What were the words his father had used? He was examining his past mistakes and running down some clues? Then he remembered the girl at the park down in Jamaica...the one who'd asked him for an apple, then disappeared, leaving a single shoe in the middle of the path.

Lawless cleared his throat, then went on with his report. "Anyway, as I said, the case went cold, and the only evidence ever recovered was—"

"A running shoe," Virgil said. He looked right at Lawless, and said, "Was the victim's name Mary Adams?"

Lawless visibly swallowed, then said, "Yes. And you're right about the shoe. How did you know?"

Virgil ignored the question and ran down to the conference room.

# CHAPTER TWENTY-NINE

Virgil burst into the room so fast he scared the hell out of Becky. She spun her chair around, and said, "What's going on? Is the building on fire, or something?"

Oddly enough, Virgil took her question seriously. "No. Everything is fine." Then he pointed at the screen, and said, "Listen, I don't know that much about what you guys do with the computers and all that, but I've got a hard connection between these girls, and one of my dad's old cases. Her name was Mary Adams, and it was one of the last things he was working on before he retired."

"Didn't he retire back in the 90s when you and Murt were still in the Army?" Becky said.

Virgil was nodding rapidly. "Yes, yes, but the girl went missing from a cross-country meet right here in Marion County. Those three girls on the screen were athletes. We know for a fact that they all ran cross-country. It was right there in front of us the whole time."

Becky was skeptical. "Was she also a good student, a single child, and worked at a part-time job? Because if that's the case, it's really not new information."

"I'm getting ready to look at the entire file in a few minutes, so I don't have those answers, Becks. But I do have a strong gut feeling that if you pulled up the information from all the other girls, you'll find at least some of them were runners too."

"We can certainly do that, Jonesy," Becky said. "But I don't think the victim from your dad's case will help us that much."

Virgil suddenly felt a little deflated. "Why not?"

"Two reasons: Kids back then didn't have cell phones like they do now, and, we're trying to find out who's been taking them based off of their social media accounts. Facebook and Twitter weren't born yet. MySpace wasn't even around back then."

"It doesn't matter, Becks. I'm simply saying keep doing what you're doing, but do it with an eye toward the one thing that connects my dad's old case with the more recent ones, and that's cross-country runners. That's how we'll find this guy."

Nicky and Wu were listening in, and Nicky agreed with Virgil. "He's right, Becky. At the very least, it will narrow our search parameters enough that we won't be looking at a week or more to get the data. We could have it in a couple of days. Maybe less."

Virgil pointed a finger at Nicky and said, "Do it."

———

VIRGIL RAN BACK TO HIS OFFICE, AND WHEN HE GOT there, he found everyone was gone. So too was the banker's box that contained the Mary Adams case file. He made his way down to the lab, where he found Lawless and the rest of his team all peering at a running shoe that sat on one of the tech's workbenches.

He squeezed in, and said, "Is that the shoe?"

"Is it ever," Murton said.

"How does it help us?" Virgil said.

"If you'd have stuck around for a minute, you'd already know," Ross said.

"He's right," Rosencrantz said. "You missed the best news of all."

"Well, not to sound too impatient about it, but as the leader of the MCU, how about someone bring me up to speed?"

"I don't think you can say, 'not to sound too impatient about it,' then sound totally impatient about it," Rosencrantz said.

Virgil jerked his thumb at Ross, and said, "You've been hanging out with this one too much. Now spill it, will you?"

"We've got DNA," Lawless said. "There was a single spot of blood on the laces. I was able to get enough for a sample. If you can find your killer, we'll be able to get a match."

Virgil clapped him on the back. "That's great work, Chip. Really great. Listen, you look like you're about to drop. Go home and get some sleep."

Lawless looked so relieved Virgil thought he was about to be hugged. "Thank you," Lawless said. Then he left the lab without saying another word.

Virgil grabbed the Adams case files and they all headed back to his office.

---

Virgil looked at Ross and Rosencrantz, and said, "Go back to the conference room and start going through the files where any of the other missing girls were cross-country runners. When you've got those separated, I want you to do three things. First, start putting a timeline together of when their last meet was, and compare that with the date of their abduction."

Ross was taking notes as Virgil spoke. "What else?"

"Get the names of their coaches, because we'll want to talk to each of them. I know some of these cases go pretty far back, so the coaches might not remember much, but it's worth a shot."

"And then?" Rosencrantz said.

"Once you've got that list put together, we'll divide it up, and start doing the legwork...again. Murt and I are going to go through the Mary Adams file, and then we'll

hit the coaching staff of all the schools. They know something, I'm sure of it, even if they don't know they know."

———————

VIRGIL AND MURTON BEGAN GOING THROUGH THE
Adams case notes. Most of it was typed up, but the file
also contained notebook pages that Virgil recognized as
his father's handwriting. A number of black and white
photographs showed the general area where the meet was
held, the trail where Mary's shoe was discovered, then a
few close-ups of the shoe itself, with an evidence marker
sitting next to it.

"According to these notes, the coach for the Ben Davis
team back then was a woman named Susan Banner,"
Murton said.

Virgil brought up Google and got the phone number
for the Ben Davis school. When he called and asked for
Susan Banner, the woman who answered the phone
informed him that she'd retired years ago. Virgil thanked
her, then hung up. He pressed the intercom button on his
desk phone and said, "Hey, Becks?"

Becky's voice came right back. "Yup."

"Can you get me an address and phone number for a
woman named Susan Banner? Last known place of
employment was Ben Davis High School."

"When do you need it? Wait, never mind. I already
know the answer. Give me five minutes."

While they were waiting, Virgil looked through the

case notes, and said, "You know what I'm not seeing here?"

"What's that?"

"The name of the other team, and the name of their coach. Why didn't Dad include it in his report?"

"Didn't you tell me that he said he was examining his past mistakes, or something like that?"

Virgil nodded. "Yeah, I did. I'm wondering if this was one of them."

A few minutes later the intercom buzzed, and Becky's voice came through the speaker. "Jonesy? You guys still in there?"

"Yeah, Becks. What do you have?"

"I just sent you a text with Susan Banner's phone number and address. Looks like she retired to Madison, Indiana...not the county, the town down by the Ohio River."

"Okay, thanks. Murton and I will probably be gone for the rest of the day. Tell Ross and Rosencrantz to keep digging. They know what we're looking for."

"You got it, Jonesy. Send Murton in before you leave so I can give him a smooch."

Murton gave his brother a wink, then got up and left the room. Virgil took out his phone and called Cool. "Hey, Motherfucker, we need to aviate. And to demonstrate my gratitude for your participation in said aviating, I'm willing to come to the airport this time."

"You must be at the MCU, huh?" Cool said.

"Yeah."

"When and where, Boss?"

"Madison, Indiana," Virgil said.

"Madison County up north, or the town by the river?"

"The town. We'll need a rental car waiting at the airport down there. How soon can you be ready to go?"

"Half hour okay?"

"Perfect," Virgil said.

---

THIRTY MINUTES LATER VIRGIL AND MURTON TURNED into the Million-Air parking lot, went inside, and found Cool and Bell waiting for them.

Virgil tipped his head, then said, "Hey, Bell. Didn't know you'd be joining us."

"I've got a flight test coming up, and I need the practice. Hey, Murt."

Murton said hello, then Virgil glanced at Cool before turning to Bell. "When you say practice…"

Bell waved him off. "I'm working on my instrument rating. I've already passed the written test, but the flight test is coming up pretty soon, so I've got to be ready for that. Don't worry…for you guys, it will be a regular flight."

"What do you mean when you say, 'for you guys?'" Virgil said.

"You worry too much, Jonesy," Cool said. "Are we going or not?"

"Maybe we should drive," Virgil said. "The weather looks a little iffy."

Bell shook his head. "It's not iffy, as you say. It's cloudy. That's why I'm going along. I need to fly in the clouds using only the instruments, as opposed to looking out the window."

"What's wrong with looking out the window?" Virgil said.

Murton shook his head, opened the door, and climbed inside the helicopter. "Stop being such a control freak and hop in, will you? It's not like you know how to fly the damned thing."

Virgil took a seat next to Murton, and said, "Yeah, but that time when we were heading into Freedom, I pushed on one of the levers and saved us."

Murton frowned at him. "That's one way of looking at it."

Virgil shrugged. "Whatever. I'm just going with what Cool told me."

Murton laughed. "I seem to remember you saying something like, 'So, I'm a pilot now,' and Cool saying, 'sure, keeping thinking that.'" Then, before Virgil could respond, Murton continued with, "I am one hundred percent certain he was being facetious."

"Facetious, huh?" Virgil said. "What did you do, sign up for a word of the day course, or something?"

"I know my words," Murton said.

"Then why didn't you use jocose instead? That's Latin from 'jocus,' which is where the word 'joke' originally came from."

Like that...all the way down to Madison.

THE RENTAL CAR WAS WAITING WHEN THEY ARRIVED and Virgil told Cool and Bell that they'd probably be back in an hour or two.

Twenty minutes later, after two wrong turns and a little confusion with the nav system that kept trying to reroute them around some road construction detours, they finally arrived at Susan Banner's house, only to discover she wasn't home.

Murton looked at Virgil and said, "I'm not trying to be too critical here, but maybe you should have called before we left." Then to drive home his point, he added, "No jocose."

But Virgil, who was sometimes as lucky as he was good, pointed to the car that was turning into the drive, and said, "Who says I didn't? I called while you were smooching Becky goodbye. We're just a little early."

Susan Banner parked her car, got out, and walked over to Virgil and Murton. "Hello, gentlemen. Are you the state detectives?"

"Yes, we are," Virgil said. "I'm Detective Virgil Jones, and this is my partner, Murton Wheeler. As I said on the phone, we have some questions for you regarding the disappearance of Mary Adams. May we come in?"

Banner unlocked the door, led them inside, and they all took a seat in the living room. "I could make coffee if you'd like," she said. Banner was a severe-looking woman who appeared to be in her mid to late sixties. She had short gray hair, and wore a comfortable-looking tracksuit. There was an edge in her voice when she spoke, one that seemed to be habitual rather than intentional.

"Thank you, but that won't be necessary," Virgil said.

"I hope you'll excuse me for saying so, but it's about time somebody took up Mary's case again. After all these years I'm surprised anyone has bothered."

"We're looking into Mary's disappearance as part of a larger investigation," Murton said.

Banner crossed her arms, and said, "So in other words, if someone else hadn't gone missing, Mary's case would still be gathering dust."

Virgil leaned forward and put his elbows on his thighs. "I won't lie to you, Mrs. Banner...you're probably right. It's the nature of the beast in law enforcement sometimes. Cases go cold. No one likes it, especially the cops who can't capture the person or persons responsible for the crime. But every once in a while, new information comes to light, and when it does, we follow up on it to the best of our abilities. That's why we're here today."

"So, how can I help?" Banner said.

"Take us back to the day Mary disappeared," Murton said. "Tell us exactly what you remember. Even the smallest of details could be significant..."

# CHAPTER THIRTY

Banner took them back, and spent thirty minutes going through her version of events. Virgil and Murton both took notes, asked clarifying questions, and prompted her to explore different parts of her memories the day Mary Adams went missing.

When she was finished, almost as an afterthought, she tipped her head just so, looked directly at Virgil, and said, "I know it's a rather common name...Jones, but if I'm not mistaken, the Marion County Sheriff at the time was named Jones. He was there that day. Do I have that right?"

Virgil nodded at her. "Yes, you do."

"Any relation?" Banner said.

"My father."

"Well, I'm certain he'll be pleased to know that you're looking into this situation."

Virgil looked away for a split second, and Banner caught it.

"I'm sorry," she said. "Has he passed?"

"Yes, ma'am, he has," Virgil said. "But I believe that your statement is true. He will be pleased."

There was a brief moment of awkward silence, then Virgil said, "All of the information you've given us today will be a tremendous help." Then he lied a little, as if the feelings of a dead man had to be protected. "One of the things that happen in cases like this is that over time, information can sometimes get misplaced."

"Such as?" Banner said.

"You mentioned that the opposing team that day was from French Lick. Do you happen to know who the coach was at that time?"

"Of course. His team has taken the state title a number of times. He was fresh out of college when he took over as the coach. If I'm not mistaken, he's also a guidance counselor at the school as well. His name is Don Whittle."

---

THEY THANKED BANNER FOR HER TIME, THEN GOT BACK in the car and headed toward the airport. On the way, Virgil called Cool and told him they needed to stop in French Lick on the way back. He asked to have another car waiting. Cool told him he'd take care of it, and ended the call.

Murton called Becky and asked for Don Whittle's address. Ten minutes later, he got the text, and it listed Whittle's address.

"It's quite a coincidence, don't you think?" Virgil said. "The fact that the name Whittle keeps coming up in one way or another."

Murton nodded. "I do. Maybe we should talk to Sheriff Harper before we talk to Whittle."

"My thoughts exactly," Virgil said.

---

NINETY MINUTES LATER, VIRGIL AND MURTON WERE sitting in Sheriff Wes Harper's office. Virgil got right to the point. "The first thing I'd like to know is if you have any leads at all regarding the disappearance of Jodie Carter."

Harper shook his head. "Not a damn thing. Feels like she got plucked right off the planet."

Virgil didn't have a response to that, but he did spend a few seconds thinking about it. The sheriff let him, then finally said, "I appreciate your help with the notification regarding the Thompson boy. I know those things aren't easy. How'd it go?"

"About like you might imagine," Murton said.

The sheriff looked at nothing for a moment, then said, "You didn't come all the way down here to ask about my progress with the Carter girl. You could have done that with a phone call."

"You're right," Murton said. "We didn't."

"What is it, then?"

Virgil looked at Harper and said, "Yesterday you said that you were going to get in touch with me to ask for help on another matter."

"That's right," Harper said. "Although I can't believe that you're going to take the time to get involved with a family squabble when you've got all these girls missing."

"We're not," Virgil said. "Not exactly."

Harper pinched an eye shut, and said, "What exactly are we talking about here?"

Murton squinted right back at the sheriff, and said, "The fact that we don't like coincidences."

"What's the connection between the Whittle family feud and the missing girls?" Harper said.

Virgil turned his palms up. "There might not be one, but we're running down clues on a particular case, and apparently Don Whittle was a witness. We'd like to speak with him about it."

Harper checked his watch. "He'd be over at the school. Class hasn't let out yet. You want me to come with you?"

Virgil shook his head. "I appreciate the offer, Wes, but that won't be necessary. We simply want to ask him about what he saw—if anything—on the day one of the victims went missing."

"Fair enough, then," Harper said. "Let me know if you find anything out."

"Will do," Virgil said, and then they were gone.

When Virgil and Murton arrived at the high school, classes were just getting out. They sat in their rental car for a moment, then Murton looked at Virgil, and said, "How do you want to play this?"

Virgil turned the corners of his mouth down, then said, "I think we should play it straight. We're interviewing a witness. Nothing more. I don't want to get side-tracked with a family estate problem that in all likelihood doesn't have anything to do with us."

They walked into the building and went to the administrative offices, identified themselves, and asked where they could find Don Whittle's office.

The woman behind the desk said, "Is this about Jodie Carter?"

Murton gave her a big smile, but there was no joy in his eyes. "In a manner of speaking. We're helping Sheriff Harper with his investigation."

The woman told them where Whittle's office was located, then said, "He should be in there. I know he's canceled practice...given everything that's happened with Jodie."

Virgil thanked her, and they turned to walk out of the office, but she wasn't quite done with them. "Detectives?"

Virgil and Murton both stopped and turned back. They looked at her without speaking.

The woman looked around to make sure no one was listening, then she motioned Virgil and Murton over to the counter. When they were close, she leaned in, lowered her voice, and said, "Please don't tell anyone I said this, but there is something off regarding Mr. Whittle."

Virgil raised his eyebrows. "Off, how?"

"I'm not exactly sure I could put my finger on it. It's more of a feeling than anything. The same kind of feeling you get when you're walking down the street and see someone who you know isn't quite right. Does that make sense?"

"It does," Murton said. "We call it listening to our gut."

She pointed a finger at him and said, "Yes, that. I'll tell you something else. He's a habitual liar. Everyone knows it, and very few people trust him."

"What does he lie about?" Virgil said.

The woman shook her head, then said, "That's what's so weird about him. He lies even when it's not necessary. He could be five minutes late for office hours and make up some dramatic story about how he got held up by a major funeral procession going through town. That's not just an example. He actually used that once."

Murton leaned in a little closer, and said, "How do you know that wasn't the case?"

"Because my husband is the caretaker out at the cemetery."

Virgil and Murton looked at each other, thanked her again, then headed for Whittle's office.

Whittle was sitting at his desk, doing some sort of paperwork when Virgil and Murton walked in. He put a question on his face, then said, "May I help you, gentlemen?"

"Don Whittle?" Murton said.

"Yes."

"I'm Detective Wheeler, with the state's Major Crimes Unit. This is my partner and boss, Detective Virgil Jones. We'd like a few minutes of your time."

Whittle dropped his chin for a moment, then looked up and said, "Jodie. Please tell me you've found her and that she's safe."

"May we sit down, sir?" Murton said.

"Of course. But Jodie?"

Virgil and Murton took the two chairs that fronted Whittle's desk, sat, then stared at Whittle until he broke eye contact. As soon as he did, Virgil said, "Mr. Whittle—"

"Please, call me Don, or Coach. Mr. Whittle was my father." He let out a little chuckle the way everyone does when that line gets used.

Murton gave Whittle a sympathetic nod. "I understand you lost your father not long ago. You have our condolences."

Whittle looked away for a moment, and wiped the corner of his eye with the side of his thumb. "Thank you. It was a shock to us all. He was old, but still very strong and healthy. Our entire family is extremely close, and now that both our parents are gone...well, I'm almost ashamed to say so, but it's managed to bring us all closer together in ways I wouldn't have thought possible."

"Then you should count yourself among the fortunate ones," Murton said. "Most times, it tends to go the other way."

"I'm aware," Whittle said. "As the school's guidance counselor, I see it from time to time. Tell me, how can I help with Jodie? I've spoken with the sheriff a half dozen times so far, and his department doesn't seem to have any leads whatsoever. The entire team is worried sick about her."

"I'm sure they are," Virgil said. "But there really isn't anything you can do. We'll figure it out. In the meantime though, we are here on another matter."

Whittle tipped his head and let his face form a question. "What sort of matter?"

"A number of years ago a young girl just like Jodie went missing during a cross-country meet up near Indianapolis," Murton said.

Whittle snapped his fingers, then said, "Yes, I remember. Our team was visiting that day. The match was canceled. The young lady...um, let me see...Mary something, if I'm not mistaken?"

"That's right, Coach," Virgil said. "We were hoping you could walk us through that afternoon and give us your thoughts. Anything you can tell us could be significant, whether you realize it or not."

Whittle tipped his chair back and closed his eyes in thought. After a few seconds, he began to replay the events of that day. Virgil and Murton both took notes as he went through his story, but they didn't interrupt or ask any questions as he spoke.

When he was finished with his version of events, he looked at Virgil and Murton, and said, "If you don't mind my asking—and believe me, I understand that every case like this deserves to be solved—why are you focusing on one that is so old, instead of spending more time looking for Jodie Carter?"

"I don't mind at all," Virgil said. "The truth is you're right. Every case like this does deserve to be solved. Our entire unit is looking into all the cases of missing girls—both the cold ones and the most recent—trying to find the commonalities...anything that ties them together in any way."

Whittle couldn't help himself. "I hope you're not suggesting that because I happened to be present during Mary's abduction—"

Virgil waved him off. "Not at all, Coach. We're simply interviewing everyone we can. We have other detectives who are doing the same thing with coaches from other schools." Then he slapped his thighs and stood from his chair. "You've been a big help, Don. We'll add your statement to our case file and keep interviewing other witnesses. If anything breaks, we'll be sure to let you know."

"I appreciate it," Whittle said. "Do you think...well, does Jodie have a chance? Is she still out there?"

"She's out there, Coach," Murton said. "The only question left is whether she's dead or alive."

As they were about to step out of the office, Virgil suddenly stopped, turned back, and said, "You know, this is going to seem weird, but with everything that's been happening, it only just now occurred to me. Are you related to the famous author, Sam Whittle?"

Don let a huge smile form on his face. "I sure am. He's my older brother, and I love him with my whole heart. I don't know how I would have made it through Dad's death if it weren't for him. He's not only my brother, he's my best friend. I don't think I've ever been more proud of anyone in my entire life."

"Sounds like you're a couple of lucky guys," Virgil said. "Do you have any other family?"

Whittle nodded. "Yes, a sister. Karen. She's vacationing out in Vegas right now. I spoke with her just yesterday. She's staying at the Bellagio, and by all accounts is having the time of her life. Anyway, you'll let me know if anything turns up with Jodie Carter?"

"We will," Murton said. Then, "It's sort of weird when you think about it..."

"What's weird?" Whittle said.

Murton let his face go blank. "The fact that all these missing girls are cross-country runners. There has got to be a connection buried in there somewhere. But don't worry, we'll eventually figure it out."

VIRGIL AND MURTON WALKED OUTSIDE, CLIMBED INTO their rental car, and drove out of the visitor lot. Murton was at the wheel, and he made a quick turn around the block and parked along a side street that had a good view of the faculty parking lot. Virgil looked at his brother, a tight smile forming at the corners of his mouth. "Do you think it was a good idea to bump him like that, right there as we were leaving?"

Murton smiled right back. "Sauce for the goose, Jonesman." He pointed out the front window of the car. "Here he comes." Then: "Look at that. He drives a gray van."

"Sit tight for a minute. I don't want him to see us."

"You don't want to follow him?" Murton said.

"Not yet. We've got his address. If he's our guy—and I've got a feeling he just might be—it's time to let him cook for a bit."

Once Whittle was out of sight, Murton said, "Where to?"

"Back to Harper's office. I've got a few more questions for the sheriff."

# CHAPTER THIRTY-ONE

With school out for the day and practice canceled, Don Whittle was at his cabin doing two things. He was trying to decide if the cops showing up at the school today was nothing more than a coincidence, or were they really looking at him. On one hand, they seemed like they were simply gathering basic information. But on the other—cops being cops—they might have been playing him. He'd been so careful over the years, but had he been careful enough? Had he taken risks? Yes. But most of the serious risks were years ago when he was just getting started. Over time, he'd learned how to mitigate the dangers to himself. Now he wondered if taking one of his own might have been a mistake. Did he draw the cops closer by being too clever? He simply didn't know.

What he did know was this: That fucking Jodie Carter had always turned his crank, and he'd have taken her eventually. And not only that, his urges were growing. When he first started taking the girls, he'd only take one per year. But now it felt like he couldn't go more than a few days...a week tops, without taking another.

He sat down in front of his laptop and brought up the social media profiles of a girl he'd been eyeing for a while now. He had all the information he needed to take her, even though it was too soon. He had to find a way to control his urges, at least until the cops went away.

He looked at the girl on the screen and thought, *But still, if I was careful enough...*

---

WHEN VIRGIL AND MURTON ARRIVED BACK AT THE Orange County Sheriff's office, Harper asked them how it went. Instead of answering right away, Virgil said, "Tell me again, in detail, what you said on the phone about the Whittles."

They all sat down, and Harper said, "Dick Whittle died a number of months ago. He did well for himself over the years, and rumor has it that he was worth quite a few million. I know it's not right to speak poorly of the dead, but he was also a mean son of a bitch who pretty much hated everyone he came into contact with, including his wife before him, his own children, and probably even himself. Anyway, the oldest boy...the author, Sam, called Ed Henderson over in Shelby County. Apparently they were college roommates back in the day, and

Sam expressed his concerns about what was happening with his siblings after the old man died."

"They were fighting about the money?" Virgil said.

"Yeah, and it wasn't just finger-pointing," Harper said. "Sam says Don pulled a gun on him, stuck it in his ear, and said if he ever saw him again, he'd kill him."

"Do you believe him?" Murton said. "Sam?"

"I do, mostly because he admitted that he instigated the argument by throwing a punch that knocked his brother on his ass. Sam swears that Don, along with their sister, Karen, killed the old man for his money."

"Any proof of that?" Virgil said.

"To answer your question, no. But let me ask you this: You ever listen to your gut?"

"Always," Virgil said.

"Me too," Harper said. "In short, I believe him. He told me that he thinks Don and Karen killed the old man, and then Don killed Karen."

"He may be right," Virgil said. "To answer your original question, Don Whittle was lying through his teeth when we spoke with him."

"In what way?" Harper said.

Murton let out a snort. "Mostly by opening his mouth. If he said anything truthful, it was purely by accident. He said things like he loved his brother with his whole heart, and he wouldn't have made it through their father's death if it wasn't for Sam and his support. Said he's never been more proud of anyone. He also said he's spoken with you a half dozen times about Jodie Carter. Any truth to that?"

"Absolutely none," Harper said, his face turning redder by the second. "You think he's the one who's been taking these young girls?"

"Too soon to tell," Virgil said. "But it's leaning that way. We've got our people doing some deep research, so we'll know more by this time tomorrow."

"I ought to go out there right now and lock his ass up," Harper said.

Virgil shook his head. "Please don't do that, Sheriff. It could compromise everything we're doing. If it's him, we'll know soon enough, but for now, leave him be."

Harper said he would, then asked, "Do you think Don and Karen could have killed their own father?"

Murton looked the sheriff in the eye. "Like I said, we don't like coincidences."

"Neither do I," Harper said. "Patricide? Good lord. So what's our next move?"

Virgil looked at Harper, and said, "We're going to have a little talk with Sam Whittle. Depending on what he says, and our assessment of his statement, we might want to do a little end-run on Don Whittle."

"What kind of end-run?" Harper said.

Murton winked at Harper, and said, "One thing at a time, Sheriff. How long would it take to get Sam Whittle in here?"

"If he knows you guys are here? About twenty minutes."

"Make the call," Virgil said.

SAM WHITTLE BEAT HARPER'S ESTIMATION OF HIS arrival time by five minutes. He walked in, introduced himself to Virgil and Murton, then got right to the point. "I'm telling you in no uncertain terms that my brother and sister killed my father."

Harper motioned for everyone to sit down, then Virgil looked at Sam and said, "What makes you so sure?"

Sam shook his head. "Don. I've known him my entire life, Detective. He lies, cheats, and manipulates at every turn."

"That doesn't automatically make him a murderer," Murton said.

"No, it doesn't," Sam said. "But that night I punched him out? He admitted it to me. He didn't get the entire sentence out before Karen shut him up, but he said enough."

Virgil looked at Sam, and said, "Speaking of Karen, he says she's vacationing out in Vegas. Staying at the Bellagio."

"Then he was flat-out lying to your face. He came to my house—this was after he threatened to kill me—and told me that Karen was missing." Sam pointed a finger at Virgil and said, "He killed her. He's trying to clean up his own mess. There's no way Karen would vacation in Vegas...ever."

"Why's that?" Murton said.

"Because she works in the casino at the French Lick

Resort. That's like a coal miner taking two weeks off and spending it at the rock quarry."

"Maybe she went there because it's familiar territory, so to speak," Virgil said.

Sam shook his head. "She hates casinos. The only reason she works in one is because the money is good. Besides, I spoke with her boss, and he says she hasn't been in at all. They've already replaced her. So Vegas? Forget it. I'm telling you, she wouldn't go there, not in a million years."

"There's one way to find out," Murton said. "Excuse me for just a moment." He stepped out of the sheriff's office and made a call.

---

VIRGIL AND HARPER SPENT A FEW MORE MINUTES listening to Sam's story. He was calm, rational, and in the end, very convincing. When Murton walked back in, he sat down, looked at everyone, and said, "If Karen is staying anywhere in Vegas, she's doing it under an assumed name, which is all but impossible these days."

"How do you know that?" Sam said.

"Because I had our researcher check."

Now it was Sam's turn to be skeptical. "That seemed pretty fast. There are a lot of places to stay out there."

Murton tipped his head back and forth. "We have, mmm, certain abilities when it comes to checking these types of things. The bottom line is this: I believe your statement about her not being out there."

Virgil touched Sam lightly on the forearm. "I'm going to ask you something, and I hope it doesn't upset you."

"What?" Sam said.

"If we got an order of exhumation for your father, would that bother you?"

Sam let out a little chuckle. "No. In fact, it's something that I've wanted done all along. As far as I'm concerned, my father died under suspicious circumstances, an autopsy was never done, and unless we bring him back up, we'll never get the truth. Not from Don, that's for damned sure."

"Are you married, Sam?" Virgil said.

"I am. My wife, Danika, is staying with her sister in Chicago. After Don threatened to kill me, we thought he might try to come after her as well, so I persuaded Danni to get out of town for a while."

"May I have your cell number, please?" Virgil said.

Sam recited the number and Virgil entered it into his phone. That done, he looked at Sam and said, "I'd like you to join your wife if at all possible."

"It's possible," Sam said. "But do you mind if I ask why?"

"Because I think you're right. We're going to rattle your brother's cage a little, and we don't want you to get caught up in any of it."

"I can take care of myself," Sam said.

"I'm sure you can, sir," Murton said. "But it's one less thing for us to worry about."

Sam didn't like it, but he eventually agreed. "You'll keep me updated?"

"That's why I wanted your number," Virgil said.

---

AFTER SAM WHITTLE LEFT THE SHERIFF'S OFFICE, Virgil turned to Harper and said, "Do you have a judge in this county who'll sign an order of exhumation based on our written statement?"

Harper actually laughed. "I've got a judge who'll sign a ham sandwich with a squeeze bottle of mustard if you want." Then, "In case that isn't clear enough for you, swear out a statement, and they'll pull Dick Whittle out of the ground by this time tomorrow, I guarantee it."

---

VIRGIL AND MURTON MADE A QUICK RUN BACK TO THE school to speak with the same woman they'd met earlier. Fortunately, they got there just as she was leaving. They ended up talking to her in the parking lot.

Virgil looked at her and said, "Mrs. uh...sorry, I don't think we ever got your name."

She gave Virgil a friendly smile and said, "Ryder. Beth Ryder."

"Okay...sorry. Listen, Mrs. Ryder, you said your

husband is the caretaker out at the local cemetery, is that right?"

"Yes."

"I'd like to ask a favor. I want to make it perfectly clear that you're under no obligation whatsoever to participate or cooperate with us regarding what I'm about to ask. Do you understand?"

"Of course," Ryder said. "What is it?"

"I'll need your word that you'll keep this under your hat until tomorrow."

"I can do that."

"The cemetery is going to do an exhumation tomorrow," Virgil said. "I assume your husband would play a part in that?"

"Yes, he absolutely would. It doesn't happen often, but when it does, it's part of his job."

"I also assume that if he knows about it in advance, that would be something the two of you might talk about."

"Sure," Ryder said. "We talk about our jobs all the time."

"Okay, good," Virgil said. "Here's what I want you to do." When Virgil told her the rest of it, she smiled, and said, "It sounds sort of sneaky. I like it."

"So you'll do it?"

"I won't be in any danger, will I?" Ryder said.

Virgil shook his head. "Not at all. Even though I don't think it's necessary, we'll have someone very close by. You'll be perfectly safe."

"Talk to you tomorrow then," Ryder said.

---

MURTON DROVE THEM OUT TO THE FRENCH LICK Resort, where they booked five rooms. "Cora isn't going to like the bill."

"Then I'll pay for it myself," Virgil said. Once they were settled into their respective rooms, Murton knocked on Virgil's door. When Virgil opened up, he was already on the phone with Cool.

"Listen, Rich, I need you to head back up to Indy and get Ross and Rosencrantz back here as quick as you can. They don't know you're coming yet, but I'm going to speak with them as soon as we're done. Don't worry about duty hours or any of that because I've got you a room at the French Lick Resort. So get back, grab Ross and Rosencrantz, and the three of you head over here." Virgil gave him his room number, then ended the call.

Next, he asked Murton to call Becky and have her get two rental cars lined up. As Murton was doing that, Virgil called Rosencrantz. "Rosie, Cool is on his way back to pick up you and Ross. Grab your go-bags and get to the airport. In fact, before you do that, go into Murt's office, and mine, and grab our bags as well."

"You got it, Jonesy. You on to somebody?"

"It's likely. I'm sixty percent there. Maybe seventy. But I want you guys down here. We're going to put a twenty-four-hour watch on someone. Where are you and Ross at regarding the other coaches?"

"We've spoken with most of them over the phone. There are a few we haven't been able to locate yet."

"Any useful information?"

"Yeah, I think so, but I'll let you decide."

"Meaning?" Virgil said.

"Is the guy you're sixty to seventy percent on named Don Whittle?" Rosencrantz said.

"Yeah, and now I'm at ninety-five percent. Grab the bags and get down here, quick as you can. Meet us at the Orange County Sheriff's office in Paoli."

# CHAPTER THIRTY-TWO

While Virgil and Murton were waiting for Ross and Rosencrantz to arrive, they decided to do a casual pass of Don Whittle's house. Whittle lived in Prospect, which turned out to be nothing more than a smattering of houses on a few quiet streets near the intersection of Highways 150 and 56. Virgil found Whittle's street, then drove at a normal speed past his residence, which was a small ranch-style home that appeared neatly kept.

"Gonna be tough to set up here without being spotted," Murton said.

"Maybe," Virgil said. Then he pointed to his left. "We might be able to use that. Grab a picture of the sign."

Murton took a quick picture of the sign, and then Virgil rolled through the intersection and they headed east, back to Paoli.

MURTON BROUGHT UP THE PICTURE OF THE SIGN, handed his phone to Sheriff Harper, and said, "Do you know this guy?" The picture showed a For Rent sign, complete with a realtor's face and name, along with a phone number.

Harper chuckled and said, "Do I ever. He's one of our reserve deputies. Does a little real estate on the side, among other things."

"Think he'd let us set up inside?"

"Let's find out," Harper said. He grabbed the phone and made a quick call. "Yeah, Kenny, it's me. Can you get down to the station, right quick? Yeah? Okay." Harper ended the call, looked at Virgil and Murton, and said, "He'll be here in ten minutes."

"Why didn't you just ask him over the phone?" Murton said.

Harper tipped his head, looked away for a moment, then said, "Well, you sort of gotta know Kenny before I can answer that."

KENNY, IT TURNED OUT, WAS A BIT OF A DEAL-MAKER. When Virgil explained what they were doing and asked if they could set up in the house, Kenny looked at him and said, "I don't think there's any monetary reason in the world why we couldn't work something out. How long do you need it for?"

Virgil shrugged. "I'm not sure. Probably no more than a couple of days. Three or four, tops."

Kenny pushed out his lower lip, then rubbed his chin with his thumb and forefinger. "I guess I could see my way clear to letting the state use it for, oh, I don't know...how's five hundred a night with a three-night minimum sound?"

Murton, who'd seen Virgil's negotiation skills first-hand, dropped his chin to his chest, and thought, *Oh boy. Here we go.*

Virgil couldn't quite believe what he'd just heard. "Five a night with a guarantee of fifteen? I'll tell you what that sounds like. It sounds like a fucking rip—"

Murton stepped forward, put his hand on his brother's arm, and said, "Virgil?"

Virgil turned, looked at Murton, and said, "What? The guy's a county deputy and he's trying to rip us off." Then he turned back to Kenny, and said, "I'll give you—"

Murton had to intercede again. "Virgil!" Then to Kenny: "How about we step outside for a minute and figure this out?"

Kenny shrugged, said, "Sure," and walked outside with Murton.

Harper looked at Virgil, and said, "What was that all about?"

Virgil shook his head and didn't answer. Five minutes later Murton and Kenny were back inside. "We're all set,"

Murton said. "We've got the place for as long as we need it, free of charge." He winked at Virgil and tossed him the keys to the house.

Virgil looked at Murton, and said, "How'd you swing that?"

Kenny looked at Virgil, shook his head in a sad sort of way, let out a little chuckle, then left.

The sheriff looked at Virgil, then Murton. "Would one of you please tell me what the hell that was all about?"

Murton grinned, jerked a thumb at his brother, and said, "This one here? He's what you might call negotiation-challenged. We were working a case one time, and he tried to park his truck in a valet spot..."

———

VIRGIL DIDN'T WANT TO HEAR IT. HE LET MURTON AND Harper trade stories while he went outside and called Sandy. He told her what was happening with the case, what they had planned, and that with a little luck, he'd be home in a day or two.

"Promise me you'll be careful, Virgil Jones."

"I will. I always am. The boys doing okay?"

"They're fine. They'll miss you. I'll miss you."

"Don't worry, I'll be back before you know it." They spent a few more minutes getting caught up on all things marriage-related when Virgil saw Ross and Rosencrantz turn into the parking lot. He told Sandy he loved her, and that he had to go. When he walked back inside with Ross and Rosencrantz, Harper looked right at Virgil, laughed out loud, and said, "Forty bucks, huh? It's a good thing your brother was here. Kenny would have taken you to the cleaners."

———

VIRGIL LET EVERYONE HAVE THEIR LAUGH, THEN THEY all went into the sheriff's conference room and got down to business. Virgil looked at Rosencrantz, and said, "Tell me how you got to Don Whittle."

"Exactly the way you thought we would, although we didn't yet know it was him. When we matched up the missing girls who fit the profile and contacted their coaches, it became pretty obvious he was our guy because every girl who went missing had previously participated in a meet against Whittle's team."

"I'll tell you something," Ross said, "it almost got by us. It would have if it weren't for Nicky and Wu."

"In what way?" Virgil said.

"The timelines I just spoke of?" Rosencrantz said. "They weren't exactly matching up with many of the earlier girls. Sometimes more than a month would go by before anyone went missing."

"How did Nicky and Wu put it together?" Virgil said.

"How else?" Ross said. "They're computer geeks. They were working the list based on social media profiles, while Rosie and I were working on the earlier cases. Eventually, it became clear that prior to social media, it took Whittle longer to track down the girls. He probably had to stalk them the old-fashioned way."

"How many young ladies are we talking about here?" Harper asked.

"Nearly thirty," Ross said.

Harper rubbed his face with both hands, then said, "Dear God. Do you mean to tell me that I've had a monster living in this county right under my nose the whole time?"

"It looks that way, Wes," Virgil said. "But not for much longer. We're going to put a twenty-four-hour watch on Don Whittle. Ross and Rosencrantz, I want you guys to take the first shift." He slid them the keys to the rented house, then gave them Whittle's address. "The rental is two houses down, on the other side of the street. You'll see the sign. Go now, and keep a constant watch on his house. We're not sure if he's there now or not."

"I've got a blocked line," Harper said. "Why don't we call his house and find out?"

Virgil tipped a finger at the sheriff. "Good idea." He pulled up the information Becky had given him, then relayed Whittle's home number to the sheriff. When Harper made the call, no one answered.

"He might be outside," Harper said. "But he's not answering. He does have a bit of a gambling problem, from what I've heard, so he might be at the casino."

Virgil looked at Ross and Rosencrantz and said, "Murt and I will keep an eye out at the resort, but we'll have to be careful because he's seen us."

Ross and Rosencrantz stood to leave, then Ross said, "If he's seen you guys, maybe we should split the shifts the other way."

"That's not a bad thought," Murton said. "The problem is, Virgil and I have been running almost non-stop. We need the rest before tomorrow."

Virgil nodded. "Murt's right. Besides, we won't be looking for him at the casino. I'll get with their chief of security and let his team keep an eye out with their cameras. All we're going to do is grab something to eat, and get some sleep."

"What if he's there, and sees you?" Harper said.

Virgil turned his palms up. "What if he is? He knows we're in town helping with the Jodie Carter case. The resort is a logical place to stay. I don't think it matters. After tomorrow it might, but it won't make any difference tonight. Ross, Rosie, go. Murt and I will switch out with you at the school tomorrow morning. You guys take him there and we'll already be in place and waiting."

━━━━━

AND THAT'S EXACTLY WHAT THEY DID. AT SIX-THIRTY the next morning, Virgil and Murton parked near the same intersection as before, one that gave them a clear view of the faculty parking lot. Twenty minutes later they took a call from Ross who let them know that Whittle was headed their way.

"Hang back quite a bit," Virgil said. "I don't want him to see you."

"Not the first time we've worked a tail, Boss-man. Rosie has four cars between him and us."

"Okay, just be careful. What's your ETA?"

"Unless he stops for coffee or something, you'll see us roll past in about ten minutes."

"Good enough. Once he's in the lot, go ahead and get some sleep. There are room keys waiting for you at the resort."

"What time does the show start?" Ross said.

"Right when school gets out. That's 2:45. He should be out on the track by three. I'll want both of you in place before he gets out there...so let's say in the bleachers at 2:30, just to play it safe. Remember, all you have to do is make sure he doesn't hurt the woman who'll be speaking to him. Her name is Beth Ryder. It's highly unlikely that anything will go wrong, but I promised her she'd be protected when she drops the bomb on him. After he leaves, Murt and I will take it from there. You guys can hang at the resort until it's time to go back to the rental and put him to bed. Understood?"

"Got it," Ross said, and then he was gone.

---

VIRGIL AND MURTON SPENT THE ENTIRE SCHOOL DAY watching Whittle's van, making sure he didn't leave, even though it wasn't likely that he would. Virgil kept in contact with Harper and his end of the operation, and when it was time, told him to get started.

When Ross and Rosencrantz turned into the lot and headed for the bleachers, they looked like a couple of dads ready to watch their girls practice on the track. A few minutes later, the bell rang and school let out for the day.

And twenty minutes after that, once Whittle was on the track with the girls, Virgil called Ryder and told her to go.

———

BETH RYDER TOOK THE CALL FROM VIRGIL, THEN walked out of the building and headed for the track at the back of the school. She tried to remain calm, but discovered it wasn't as easy as she imagined it might be. Yesterday the thought of helping the police seemed exciting and daring. Now it seemed stupid and dangerous. What was she, some sort of undercover agent? No, she was a school secretary, mostly in charge of student attendance. *What the hell was I thinking?* she asked herself as she crossed the lot.

She noticed two men she'd never seen before sitting in the bleachers, laughing and having a good time. Were they her protection? The answer to her question came as one of the men pulled out his phone and answered a call. Then both men turned, looked at her, nodded once, and moved all the way down to the first row.

And that gave Beth Ryder the confidence she needed. She called out to Whittle. "Coach? Coach, could I speak with you for a moment?"

Whittle turned, an odd look on his face. He blew his whistle and told the girls to start running warm-up laps. Then he walked over to Ryder, and said, "What is it, Beth? You know I don't like my practices interrupted."

"I'm terribly sorry, Coach, but I thought you should know. My husband just called me. He said he did so as a matter of courtesy and respect because we work together, so I'd appreciate it if you kept where the information came from to yourself."

Whittle looked at her, and said, "What information?"

"The sheriff, along with the county medical examiner are both out at the cemetery right now. They have a court order to exhume your father's remains."

Whittle's face turned pale, then he gave Ryder a look that scared her, one she'd not seen before. "Tell the girls practice is canceled, and that I have a family emergency." Then, without another word, he ran toward his van.

# CHAPTER THIRTY-THREE

As soon as Virgil and Murton saw Ryder headed toward the field, Virgil called Ross, and said, "That's her. Keep her safe. We're headed to the cemetery. We want to get there before Whittle does."

"We got it covered here, Boss-man. Go."

Virgil dropped the car in gear and they drove from the high school over to the cemetery, which was only a few miles away.

"Better keep your foot on it," Murton said. "We don't want him to beat us there."

Virgil increased his speed, but he had to be careful as they were in a rental car. Five minutes later they turned in, and Murton pointed over to the left. "There they are."

"Looks like they've got him up already," Virgil said. He parked their car next to the coroner's van, then both men got out and stood next to the sheriff.

Harper looked at them and said, "Is Whittle on the

way? Never mind, here he comes. I hope he loses his cool."

"That's the plan," Murton said. "If we can lock him up, we'll be able to get his DNA."

Whittle pulled up so fast, for a moment it looked like he was going to plow right through the gravesite. Everyone jumped back, but Whittle managed to get his van stopped just shy of Virgil and Murton's rental car.

When he got out of his van his face was red and his hands were balled into fists. He walked right up to Harper, his feet stomping the ground like a child. "What the fuck is going on here? Why are you people digging up my father's remains?"

Harper held out his hands, and said, "Take it easy, Don. We've got a court order giving us the authority to exhume your father's body."

Whittle was so mad he was vibrating. "Authority? Authority? Whose fucking authority?" Then, before Harper could answer, he turned his wrath on Virgil and Murton. "And why the fuck are you two here? You should be out looking for Jodie Carter."

Virgil walked over and got right in Whittle's face. "That's exactly what we're doing, Don. But we're also capable of doing more than one thing at a time."

"What the hell is that supposed to mean?" Whittle said. "What does my father have to do with Jodie Carter's abduction?"

Virgil gave Whittle an evil grin. "Probably nothing. In

fact, I'm all but sure of it since he's been dead for a number of months."

"Then why are you digging him up?"

"Because we have reason to believe that his death may not have been from natural causes. In case that's a little foggy for you, try this instead: We believe your father was murdered."

Whittle's jaw quivered as he spoke. "Murdered? You're out of your mind. He was old and sick. Who put you on to this?"

Murton let out a little chuckle. "Well, it sure wasn't your sister, Karen. She's out in Vegas right now. Isn't that what you told us?"

Whittle was starting to get confused. "Uh, yeah, she's staying at the Bellagio."

"Except she isn't, Don," Virgil said. "We checked. As a point of fact, she isn't anywhere near Vegas. And by the way, we had a little talk with your brother, Sam. That song and dance you tried to sell to me and my partner? You were lying the entire time."

"The fuck I was. Everything I told you was the truth."

Murton laughed again. "What about the part where you stuck a gun in his ear and threatened to kill him? I don't remember you mentioning that when we spoke. I guess you were too busy telling us how much the two of you love each other."

Virgil reached out and grabbed Whittle's arm to get his attention. "Funny way of showing it, Don...pulling a gun on your own brother."

"Fuck you," Whittle said. He jerked his arm free, and when he did, his elbow caught Murton in the center of his chest.

Murton, who was a decent actor, doubled over in faked pain and dropped to one knee. As soon as that happened, Virgil tackled Whittle to the ground, put him in handcuffs, and said, "That's assault on a police officer. You're under arrest." He read him his rights, then turned him over to the sheriff.

Harper walked Whittle to his squad car and locked him in the back seat, then rejoined Virgil and Murton. "You realize he'll probably bond out by this time tomorrow."

Murton brushed the dirt from his pant leg, then said, "Doesn't matter to us, Wes."

Virgil nodded. "He's right, Sheriff. All we needed was to get him out of the way for a few hours. He can bond out tonight, for all we care." Then, "Better get that judge back on the phone."

Harper looked a question at Virgil. "Why?"

"Because we want to do a little sneak and peek over at Don's house. Gonna need the judge to sign another ham sandwich."

Harper looked at Virgil and Murton, and said, "Is this the way you state boys always operate? Wait, never mind. I'm not sure I want to know. Swing by the station when you're done with the coroner. I'll have your warrant waiting."

DICK WHITTLE'S CASKET WAS LOADED INTO THE coroner's van, and Virgil and Murton followed it all the way back to the hospital in Paoli. Once they had Whittle inside, Virgil asked the coroner how long the autopsy would take.

"I can start this afternoon, but if there aren't any visible signs of trauma—which there probably won't be, otherwise the funeral home would have said so—I won't have any chemistry back for a few days."

"Quick as you can," Virgil said. "If there aren't any visible signs of trauma, what sort of chemistry will you be looking at?"

The coroner pursed his lips, and said, "Any sort of poisoning. Anti-freeze, arsenic, that sort of thing. It's a rather comprehensive list. That's why it takes so long."

"Doesn't the fact that the body has been embalmed create a problem?" Murton said.

The coroner nodded. "It does make things more difficult. There can be quite a few false positives. But the good news is this: Since an autopsy wasn't performed, his organs will still be intact. I'll be able to get quite a lot of good information from the liver itself."

"Tell me more about the arsenic," Virgil said.

"That's always what we look for first in cases like these. The telltale signs remain with the body for years. Hair and fingernail samples will indicate if that was the cause of death."

"And that takes how long?" Virgil said.

"A few days."

"Could you get us hair and fingernail samples now? I'd like our crime scene techs to look at them."

The coroner slipped out of his lab coat and began putting on scrubs, along with a heavy apron. "Of course. But you might want to wait out in the hall. When I crack this casket, it won't be pretty." Then he grabbed a face mask with a respirator and slipped it over his head.

When Virgil and Murton saw that, they took the coroner's advice and waited out in the hall.

---

WHILE THEY WERE WAITING, VIRGIL TOOK OUT HIS phone and called Cool. "Where are you?"

"Sitting at the Blackjack table spending my retirement. What was I thinking?"

"Well, I'm here to save you."

"You mean you're going to pay me back?" Cool said.

Virgil laughed. "Hardly. But I am going to get you away from the table. Get to the airport and get the helicopter ready. Murt and I will be there shortly. I've got some samples that we need to get back to our lab. Chip or Mimi will be waiting for you up in Indy when you land."

"Roger that," Cool said. "You want me back down here after I drop the samples?"

"I'm not sure yet," Virgil said. "Hang tight up there and I'll let you know."

Cool said he would, and Virgil ended the call. Then he got in touch with Mimi and told her what was happening. "I'll need to know—as quick as possible—if you find anything."

Mimi, her voice full of whiskey, said, "I'll get started as soon as the samples arrive."

Virgil smiled into the phone, and said, "Perfect. You're the best, Meems."

"Like I didn't already know that."

———

THE CORONER GAVE VIRGIL AND MURTON THE SAMPLES in a small plastic container, then made them sign about a dozen forms before he let them leave. They drove out to the airport, handed the samples to Cool, then headed back to the sheriff's office to get their warrant.

———

VIRGIL PULLED HARPER ASIDE, AND SAID, "DID YOU GET copies of Whittle's keys?"

Harper reached into his desk drawer and shook the keys from an envelope. "Right here. Cost me ten bucks down at the hardware. I've got a couple of my people going through the van right now, but I have to tell you, it looks cleaner than a gnat's ass after a thunderstorm."

"That's a new one," Murton said.

"You didn't tell Whittle what we're doing, did you?"

Harper gave Virgil a look that didn't require an answer.

"Okay, okay," Virgil said. "Just making sure we're on the same page. Where is he right now?"

"Down in lockup, speaking with his lawyer," Harper said.

"Is the lawyer any good?" Murton said.

"Good enough. The first thing he did was shove a piece of paper at me that stated in no uncertain terms would a DNA sample be given. The second thing he did was tell me that he'd have Whittle out within the hour."

"Think he will?" Virgil said.

Harper nodded. "Probably, since the same judge who signed your ham sandwich will hear Whittle's motion to dismiss. I'd get a move on, I were you."

"Call me when he's out," Virgil said. Then he and Murton ran out the door.

---

VIRGIL AND MURTON MADE IT TO WHITTLE'S HOUSE AS fast as they could. They parked in the driveway, then went to the back of the house. It took Virgil three tries before he found the right key, but once he did, they were in. "Remember, we're looking for anything regarding the missing girls, photos, or—"

"Jonesy?" Murton said.

"Yeah?"

Murton snapped on a pair of latex gloves, and said,

"I've done this before. I'll take the bedroom. You can have the office if he has one."

He did. The house was small, with only two bedrooms and a single bathroom. The office was located in the second bedroom. Virgil began quickly rifling through the files stored in a desk drawer, while Murton took the master bedroom. They spent over an hour going through the entire house, but in the end, they didn't find one single piece of evidence that would implicate Whittle in any of the girls' abductions. Nor did they find any sort of poison, liquid or otherwise.

"I think it's a bust," Murton said.

Virgil was about to agree when his phone buzzed at him. He looked at Murton, and said, "Harper." When he answered, the sheriff said, "If you're still inside, it's time to go. I'd say you've got five minutes, tops."

Virgil said, "Thanks, Wes," then hung up. He looked at Murton, and said, "Time to roll out."

"Give me thirty seconds," Murton said. He ran down the hall to the bathroom, took a plastic bag out of his pocket, grabbed Whittle's hairbrush and pulled as many hairs free as possible before stuffing them inside the bag. Then he headed for the back door, where Virgil was waiting.

"What'd you get?"

"DNA samples. If they match the shoe from Mason's case, we've got him."

## CHAPTER THIRTY-FOUR

Virgil and Murton got out of Whittle's house, locked the back door, then quickly drove over to the rental house down the street. They turned into the driveway just as Whittle was getting out of his van.

It was that close.

---

WHITTLE GOT OUT OF THE VAN AND JUST HAPPENED TO glance down the street at the rental. The front door was closing as he watched, but there was no mistaking the rental car in the driveway. It was the same one at the cemetery. The same one the state cops were driving. He looked away in case they were watching him at that very moment, then went inside his own house.

He went to the fridge and grabbed a beer, then sat

down on his living room sofa, which gave him a decent view of the rental. He was watching the watchers when he noticed something odd. Everything seemed a little off somehow. Like all of his things had been moved, then put back in their original place. The chair was slightly askew, the curtains were open a tad more than they had been. He went into the kitchen and noticed a cupboard not quite closed all the way. When he checked his office, some of his personal files seemed to be out of order, and the clothing in his closet wasn't hanging the way it usually did.

They'd been in his house, Don was sure of it. Had they placed listening devices? He'd have to check. He looked under every lamp, behind every picture, under all the tables and chairs, but he didn't find anything. *Maybe I'm being paranoid,* he thought. *But why search my house? There'd be nothing to find.* He'd made sure of that long ago.

*Now what?* Don thought. If they were closing in on him, it was either take the money and run or find a way to distract the cops and get them focused on something else. He had to think...

---

VIRGIL AND MURTON DASHED INTO THE RENTAL, BUT they knew Whittle probably saw them. "We should have just kept going," Murton said. "There are already two cars in the garage, and now we've got one in the driveway. We might as well put up a flashing sign that says Surveillance Team Inside."

Virgil shrugged. "It's not that big of a deal. In fact, if he did notice us or the car, I think it works to our advantage."

"How's that?" Ross asked. He and Rosencrantz had returned to the rental after Whittle left the school.

"Simple," Virgil said. "If he knows he's being watched, it increases the pressure. Murt and I left just enough clues at his house to let him know we'd been through."

"If he's smart enough to notice," Rosencrantz said.

"I think he is," Virgil said. "If he's been getting away with taking all these girls, he's no dummy."

Ross was skeptical. "Except now that he knows we're watching him, what if all he does is stay loose, and go about his routine? Then we won't have anything."

"Yeah, we will," Virgil said. "Cool is taking samples up to the MCU lab right now from Dick Whittle's body. If we can prove that he was poisoned, and if Sam Whittle's story holds up, at the very least, we'll have him on that."

"And if it turns out he died of natural causes?" Rosencrantz said.

Murton grinned. "I almost hope he did because we've got hair samples out of Don's house we can compare with the DNA that Chip found on Mary Adams's shoe. If those match up, he'll either be put away for life or get the needle."

Virgil shook his head, and Murton caught it. "What?"

"I wasn't thinking. I should have had Cool wait. He could have taken both samples back to our lab."

"Want me to run them up?" Ross said. "It's not that far. I could be back by tonight."

"No, I'll do it," Virgil said. "It was my mistake, so I'll make the run." He looked at both Ross and Rosencrantz, and said, "Besides, Whittle still hasn't seen your faces, and I'd like to keep it that way for as long as possible. That means you two are going to be here for a while."

"Works for me," Rosencrantz said. "The resort is too noisy anyway."

Virgil turned to Murton and said, "After I leave, take one of the rental cars and go get some food for Ross and Rosencrantz. After that, head back to the resort, and I'll meet up with you there tomorrow morning."

"You're not coming back tonight?"

"I doubt it. I'll want to see what Chip and Mimi come up with regarding the DNA."

Rosencrantz looked at Murton, and said, "Don't worry about the food. We stopped on the way over and stocked up. We're good." Then to Virgil: "You think the DNA will come back that quick?"

Virgil nodded. "Chip told me he and Mimi have been using a new rapid testing method, and they're getting great results. If we get a match tonight, I'll be back in the morning, we'll hook Don up, and all of us will be home by this time tomorrow."

Unfortunately, not all of that happened, and Virgil was about to learn that his thoughts of the past were still there, waiting to haunt him.

KENNY WOLFE, THE RESERVE DEPUTY, NOT ONLY DID A little real estate on the side, he also worked part-time as a security guard for the resort's casino. That meant he had access to the cameras, and that meant he'd been helping Don cheat at the poker tables, and keeping the pit bosses off his back. The problem was, Don wasn't paying his fair share back to Kenny, which now amounted to over fifty grand. When Kenny heard that the state cops were watching Don Whittle, he did the only thing he could think to do if he was ever going to get his money. He made a deal with the devil.

---

AT THE SAME TIME VIRGIL WAS DRIVING BACK TO INDY, and Murton was resting comfortably at the resort with nothing to do until the following morning, Kenny made a call to Whittle's cell phone. When Whittle checked the screen and saw who it was, he answered by saying, "Give me thirty seconds," then ended the call. When he looked out the front window, the rental car was gone.

He still wasn't sure if the cops had listening devices in his house, so he stepped outside to the back patio, and called Kenny. "What?"

"You've got trouble, man. The cops are all over you, both at your house and the casino."

"No shit. I've already seen them at the house. The

same house that has your picture on the sign in the front yard. Thanks for the heads up, asshole."

"What do you think I'm doing now?" Kenny said. "It's the first chance I've had."

"What else do you know?" Whittle said.

"They've got a warrant to search your house. I think they did it while you were locked up."

"I already know that, too. You're not giving me much help here, Kenny."

"Yeah, says the guy who owes me fifty large."

"Don't worry, I've got a plan," Whittle said.

"If your plan is to run, you better pay me first."

"I'm not running. Running only gets you caught."

"So what's your plan?"

"You know the street behind my place...one block over?"

"Yeah?"

"Park in front of the yellow house. The woman who lives there is about two hundred years old and blind as a bat. You can cut through her backyard and get to mine without being seen. Here's what I want you to bring..."

---

KENNY DID WHAT WHITTLE ASKED, AND AN HOUR later, he and Don were sitting in the backyard speaking quietly. "Here's what we're going to do," Whittle said. "Tonight, after dark, I'm going to slip out the back—the same way you came in—and grab an Uber over to the casino. Then, while I'm on camera gambling at the resort and being seen by as many people as possible, you're going to go over to the rental and take out the cops who are watching me."

Kenny shook his head. "I can't do that. I've got no business being there."

"Yes, you do. It's your rental. You have every right to go there. Tell the cops you wanted to check in and make sure everything is all right with the water heater, or whatever. Or take them a pizza or something. Anyway, once you're inside, kill them both, then get the hell out and drive away. You're a cop, so they won't suspect anything."

"I'm a reserve deputy. That's not exactly the same thing."

"Whatever. Wear your uniform. It'll be a piece of cake, and I'll be at the casino with a rock-solid alibi. That means they'll start looking for someone else instead of me."

"Man, I don't know," Kenny said. "What if they start looking at me?"

"Why would they? No one knows our arrangement."

"Yeah, that's another problem," Kenny said. "Our arrangement isn't exactly paying off the way you said it would."

"Do your part tonight and it'll pay off big time."

"I've heard that one before."

"Then how about this?" Whittle said. He reached down and grabbed a bag sitting close to his feet and handed it to Kenny.

"What's this?"

"Open it and see for yourself," Whittle said.

When Kenny opened the bag and saw the stacks of cash, his eyes got wide. "How much?"

"The fifty I owe you, plus another hundred. You in or not?"

---

VIRGIL TURNED INTO THE MCU PARKING LOT, WENT inside with the hair samples from Whittle's house, and found Chip and Mimi working away in the lab. "What have you got?"

Mimi looked at Virgil, and said, "Absolute proof that Dick Whittle was murdered. The arsenic is in both his hair and fingernails. The levels are extremely high. My guess is that someone was giving him this stuff over a long period of time."

"Wouldn't he have known it?" Virgil said.

"Not unless he saw them do it. There's no smell or taste, which is why it's one of the first things they test for in poisoning cases. Any idea who did it?"

Virgil nodded. "Yeah, we've got a line on a guy." He pulled the plastic baggie out of his pocket and said, "If you can match this with the blood spot Chip found on the running shoe, we'll have him for sure. Can you run that rapid test you guys are always bragging about?"

"Sure," Chip said. "Still going to take about three hours, though."

"That's fine. I'm going home for the night. Need to see the family. Call me the minute you have the results. If there's a match, I'll have Murt and the rest of the crew lock him up tonight."

Mimi took the bag, peered at it closely for a few seconds, and said, "We've got plenty of follicles here, so the testing should go well. Go home, Jonesy. I'll call you the minute we know anything."

Virgil thanked Mimi and Chip, then headed for home.

# CHAPTER THIRTY-FIVE

W hen Virgil arrived at his house, he was surprised to find the state helicopter sitting on the pad in his backyard. When he walked out onto the deck, he found Sandy, Becky, Sarah, Cool, Mac and Nichole, along with Nicky and Wu, all sitting at the large picnic table eating burgers and fries. "It looks like I missed dinner," Virgil said.

Sandy stood and gave her husband a hug and a kiss. "Don't worry, we've still got plenty. Huma is inside feeding the kids. Let me grab you something."

Virgil thanked her, then turned to the governor. "Mac. Good to see you. What's going on?"

The governor tipped his head at Nicky and Wu, and said, "Those two are breaking my heart by leaving tomorrow."

"How does that break your heart?" Virgil said.

Nichole smiled. "Because they're taking me with them."

Virgil raised his chin, and said, "Ah." Then, "So you guys have wrapped everything up?"

"We have," Nicky said. "There really isn't anything else for us to do. The data all points to your man, Don Whittle, so with that in hand, you shouldn't have any trouble nailing him to the wall."

Virgil nodded. "We've got a watch on him right now, and Chip and Mimi are doing some DNA testing that should come back tonight. If it's a match, then we'll have Whittle locked up tight. After that, it's just a matter of getting him to tell us where the bodies are buried."

The governor shook his head. "Nasty business...these serial killers." He looked around the table. "I'm grateful for your work, all of you." Then, just to be polite, he looked at Virgil and said, "Now that you're home, Jonesy, perhaps we should all be on our way."

"Ah, stay a while, if you can, Mac. All of you. It's a beautiful night, I'll bring you up to speed on the case, and we can wait for the test results."

"Miss Sandy did say something about pie," Wu said. "I would enjoy a slice."

Nicky just shook his head.

The governor looked at Cool, and said, "Rich, you good?"

"I'm at your disposal, Mac."

So they stayed for a while. And it changed everything.

----

An hour later, Whittle was at the casino, gambling away, buying drinks for everyone at the tables, and just like before, leaving a paper trail of credit card receipts everywhere he went. Every now and again he'd look directly at one of the security cameras to make sure they had perfect, time-stamped pictures of him. It took everything he had not to smile. The plan, coming together. *Fuck a bunch of state cops,* he thought. And that did make him smile.

----

Kenny Wolfe didn't have any problem killing. In fact, just like Whittle, he longed for it. The fact that it would be state cops? Even better. He'd wanted to be a cop all his life, but the closest he ever got was being a reserve deputy for the county, and even they wouldn't take him full time. There was always an excuse. If it wasn't this, it was that. No money in the budget, we're scaling back as it is, maybe in a year or two...

Like that. *A year or two my ass.* So instead of being a full-time officer of the law, he was reduced to traffic duty a couple of times a year if he was needed. They wouldn't even let him carry a gun. Did it matter that he spent hours and hours at the range, practicing until he could outshoot just about anyone he'd ever met? Answer: No.

The real estate gig didn't pay worth a damn, and the security job at the casino was a joke.

Those were the thoughts going through Kenny's mind, ramping him up, as he parked in the alley behind the rental house the cops were using. He straightened the tie on his uniform, grabbed the pizza box, checked his gun—a GLOCK 19, complete with an AAC Ti-Rant suppressor—then got out and bumped his car door closed with his hip. He walked around the corner, up the driveway, and rang the bell. Then he pulled his gun and held it under the pizza box, out of sight.

Time to rock and roll.

———

ROSENCRANTZ WAS AT THE WINDOW WHEN OUT OF THE corner of his eye, he saw the deputy coming up the driveway. He turned his attention from Whittle's house and took a hard look at the man. When he glanced at the rental sign in the yard, he noticed the reserve deputy was the same guy. That, together with the uniform, put Rosencrantz at ease. He called out to Ross. "Looks like one of the locals brought us a pizza."

Ross came around the corner, just as the doorbell rang. "That's a little weird, don't you think?"

Rosencrantz shook his head. "Naw. Whittle knows we're watching him. Plus, this guy owns the joint. Get the door, will you? I'd rather have take-out pizza than any of that other crap we bought."

Ross was, as Virgil had told Sarah, very good, and very careful. He pulled his sidearm from its holster, held it out of sight behind his back, then opened the door.

Kenny looked at Ross, smiled, and said, "Courtesy of Orange County's finest." Then he shot Ross twice in the chest.

At the sound of the gunfire, Rosencrantz rolled off the chair and pulled his weapon free, but Kenny was already moving. He'd slammed the door shut, spun around the corner, and took two more quick shots at Rosencrantz, hitting him in the leg and the side of his stomach. He fired one more time, but missed, then said, fuck it, and ran out through the back of the house and into the alley. He jumped in his car and forced himself to drive as slow as possible. When he was a mile away, he parked and waited ten minutes.

No sirens.

No sign of life.

No more state cops.

———

MURTON, WHO WAS BORED OUT OF HIS GOURD, DECIDED to take a little run at the poker tables in the casino. He wasn't much of a gambler, but he knew how to play, and promised himself he wouldn't spend more than fifty dollars, no matter what. He walked inside, spent a few minutes watching the various tables, then found the game he was looking for. He was just about to sit down when he happened to glance to his left. Don Whittle was headed his way.

Murton turned away, not wanting Whittle to see his face. Once Whittle had passed, Murton looked around for Ross and Rosencrantz, but didn't see them anywhere. If Whittle was here, they should be as well. At the very least, they should have called him. He took out his phone and tried Rosencrantz, but didn't get an answer. When he tried Ross, the result was the same. He kept his eye on Whittle at a distance, then took out his badge, and looked straight into a security camera. Thirty seconds later a security guard was standing next to him.

"May I help you, Officer?"

"Yeah, I'm Detective Murton Wheeler with the state's Major Crimes Unit. Do you know who Don Whittle is?"

The security guard laughed quietly. "Do I ever. Is he causing problems again?"

"I'm not sure, but we've got him under surveillance. He's five tables down on the right. See him?"

The guard casually turned and looked. "Yeah, I do."

"Can you get someone to run your video back—right now—and tell me how long he's been here?"

"You bet." The guard took out his phone and made a call. Less than two minutes later they had their answer. "Video shows he's been here for hours."

Murton raked his bottom lip with his teeth. "I can't reach the guys who should be watching him. That means I have to go." He gave the guard his phone number, and said, "If he leaves, call me."

The guard said he would, and Murton, who was starting to get a bad feeling, ran out of the casino, jumped in his car, and headed for the rental house. He kept trying Ross and Rosencrantz along the way, but he never did get an answer.

---

WHITTLE SAW THE COP BUT PRETENDED LIKE HE DIDN'T. He walked right past, and sat down at one of the Blackjack tables, angling his chair slightly as he did, giving him a decent view of the cop without being obvious. He watched as the cop held his badge up to the security camera, and then saw the guard approach. The two men spoke for a minute or so, and then the cop ran from the room. Whittle smiled because his alibi was set, and it was the cop himself who'd make it happen.

---

IT WAS ONLY TWO MILES FROM THE CASINO TO Prospect, and Murton covered the distance in less than ninety seconds. He ran to the front door, threw it open, and when he saw his friends and partners on the floor, both of them in their own separate puddles of blood, he stopped for a full second and had to hold onto the door frame to keep from falling over. Then his training kicked in.

As desperate as he was to help his friends, he had to

clear the house first. He drew his Sig P226 and ran room to room, ready to fire at anything that moved. When he discovered no one else was in the house, he ran back and dialed 911. He identified himself, told the dispatcher he had two officers down, gave his location, then dropped his phone and got to work.

Rosencrantz was bleeding from his leg and his side. Both wounds were through and through, and neither was pumping, which Murton hoped meant no major arterial damage. He pulled out his knife and sliced Rosencrantz's shirt free, then used it to wrap his stomach as tight as he dared. Then he cut his pant leg and used that, along with his own belt as a tourniquet for the leg wound. That done, he turned his attention to Ross.

He ripped Ross's shirt free, and when he saw the wounds, he lost all hope. But Murton wasn't a quitter and he never lost his drive. He began doing chest compressions and rescue breathing, the whole time with tears streaming down his face. Ross wasn't breathing on his own, and his lips and face were starting to turn blue. In the distance, Murton heard the first sounds of sirens, and though he wouldn't later remember, the thought going through his head at the moment was, *too far away...too far away*.

---

EVERYONE WAS STILL SITTING OUTSIDE ENJOYING THE evening when Virgil's phone buzzed. Virgil put the phone on speaker, held up a hand to quiet the conversation, then said, "What have you got, Mimi?"

"It's a perfect match, Jonesy."

"You're sure?"

"One hundred percent. DNA doesn't lie. You've got your proof. Now go get your man."

The governor leaned close to Nichole, and said, "My goodness, that woman does have a voice, doesn't she?"

Nichole smiled, reached over, and pinched the governor on his tit.

"Count on it, Mimi. Great work. Tell Chip I said thanks as well. Listen, do me a favor and call Orange County and let them know we'll be bringing Whittle in." Then, "Hey I gotta go. Murton's calling."

The phone was still on speaker when Virgil hit the button to switch calls. "Hey Murt, good news, we've—"

"Virgil, don't speak. Listen to me. Listen, listen, listen." Murton's voice was hoarse, filled with grief and despair, and something else Virgil had never heard from his brother before. Fear. "It's Ross and Rosencrantz, man. Somebody got to them at the house. They're both in surgery at the hospital in Paoli right now. Rosie took one in the leg and one in the side. Ross..." Murton had to collect himself before he could say the words. "Ross took two in the chest, man. It's bad. They don't think he's going to make it."

Virgil looked at Sarah, who stood up so fast she almost fell. She covered her ears with her hands as if she could stop Murton's words from entering her brain. She turned and began backing up until she bumped into the house. Then Sandy was there at her side, and as Cool ran toward the helicopter, Virgil was screaming into the phone. "We're coming, Murt, we're coming right now."

Becky grabbed Sarah, looked at Sandy, and said, "Let me." Then they started toward the helicopter.

Sarah glanced at the house and said, "Liv."

Sandy said, "I've got her. Go." Then to Virgil: "Take care of your brother."

Virgil's mouth was so dry he couldn't speak. He nodded once, and ran, following Becky and Sarah into the helicopter. Once they were on board, Sarah grabbed a headset, pulled the microphone close to her lips, squeezed Cool's arm, and said, "How long?"

# CHAPTER THIRTY-SIX

When Whittle saw the cop run from the casino, he knew Kenny had come through for him. But the fact that casino security was still watching him was unsettling. What had the cop said to the guard? Maybe it was time to go. He took out his phone and called for an Uber, then walked outside to wait.

The guard watched him go, then dialed Murton's number. When he didn't get an answer, he left a short message, then hung up.

WHITTLE'S PHONE BUZZED WHEN HE WAS ABOUT halfway home. When he answered, Kenny spoke quickly and quietly. "Listen to me. Don't speak. I'm at the station right now. They've got your DNA from one of the girls.

Half the cops in the state are looking for you right now."
Then, *click.*

Whittle stared at his phone in disbelief. After a few seconds, he leaned forward, and said, "Could you drop me at a different location? It's only a mile or so from the original destination."

The Uber driver, a nice young lady who was eager to please, said, "Of course. What's the address?"

"I'm afraid there isn't one. At least not yet. I've got a place that's still under construction and they haven't assigned an actual street number yet. If you take a left at the light, I'll guide you in from there..."

---

THE CHOPPER RACED THROUGH THE NIGHT SKY, ITS passengers quiet. The only person who spoke the entire way down was Sarah. She sat forward in her seat with her elbows on her knees, her hands balled into fists and pressed against her forehead. She kept repeating one word, over and over. It was her daughter's name, except it wasn't. Not exactly.

---

WHITTLE LEANED FORWARD FROM THE BACKSEAT AND pointed over to the right. "There's the drive, right next to that telephone pole. The cabin is quite a ways back. If you'll turn into the drive, I'll walk from here."

The driver said that was fine, and turned where Whittle told her. She put the car in park, which automatically unlocked the doors. As soon as she did, Whittle reached up and snapped her neck. He unbuckled her belt, pulled her into the back, then got in the driver's seat and headed into the woods, safe, and out of sight.

---

Cool took them in hot, and Virgil had the door open the second they touched down on the hospital's landing pad. They ran inside through the emergency department entrance and found two state troopers, and about half the Orange County cops, including the sheriff all standing around. Virgil went straight toward Harper and said, "Tell me what you know. Give me everything you've got, right now. What the hell happened?" He knew he was pressing too hard, but he couldn't help it.

"Take it easy, Jonesy," Harper said.

"Fuck easy. Two of my men are down. What's their condition? Get me someone who knows something. Where the hell is Murton?"

Murton, who'd heard the helicopter come in, came around the corner and said, "I'm right here."

Virgil spun around, and when he saw Murton, it helped calm him, even though his brother's shirt and face and hands were covered with blood. "Murt…"

Murton held up a wait-a-minute finger, gave Becky a quick hug, and then went straight to Sarah. He grabbed her by her arms, then looked right into her eyes, and said, "He's still alive. They've got three docs working on him right now. He lost a lot of blood, but they're pumping it in as fast as he'll take it."

"Please tell me he's going to be okay," Sarah said. "I can't lose him. I can't go through this again. I won't go through this again."

"I can't do that, sweetheart," Murton said. "I don't know if he's going to be okay or not. But I can tell you this: That man of yours is a fighter. I didn't think he was even going to make it to the hospital, much less into surgery, but he did, and he's in there right now, fighting for his life...fighting for you."

"How bad was he hit?"

Murton looked away for a moment before answering. "One of the surgical nurses has been keeping me updated. One round punctured his right lung before exiting through the back of his shoulder. The other shattered his left clavicle, and a bone fragment pierced his aorta. They had to crack his chest to get to the fragment, and he's being kept alive right now by mechanical ventilation, and a cardiopulmonary bypass machine. If they can get the bone fragment out and get his heart restarted, he's got a chance. That's all I know."

Sarah seemed to gather herself together, the facts—dire as they were—helped steady her. The words she spoke next proved to everyone who was present just what kind of woman she really was, and how lucky they were to have her in their lives. "What about Rosie?"

A single tear escaped the corner of Murton's eye, and when he spoke, the words he used seemed cruel somehow, as if good news maybe wasn't good at all, even though it was. "He's already in recovery. He's going to be okay."

---

WHITTLE DUMPED THE DRIVER'S BODY AND HER PHONE down the cistern, then moved the car behind the cabin, out of sight. If he had to run, he'd need the wheels. Right now, he needed to think. Kenny told him they'd matched his DNA to one of the victims. How was that possible? Every single victim was at the bottom of the cistern. Had he left evidence behind somehow? And did it even matter? If they had it, they had it. He took out his phone and tried to call Kenny, but got no answer.

He was going to need his help and began to wonder how much that was going to cost him.

---

THEY ALL WENT UP TO THE SURGICAL WAITING ROOM and tried to get comfortable. Virgil pulled Harper aside and said, "We have absolute proof that Don Whittle is our guy. I'd like you, and a couple of your men to come with me to his house. If he's there, we'll take him right now. If he's not, we'll wait him out."

"We can do that," Harper said. "You think he's the one who shot your men?"

"He must be," Virgil said. "He knew we were at that house. He somehow managed to ambush two men who are very well trained and extremely good at what they do."

Murton stepped over and said, "It wasn't Whittle."

At the sound of Murton's words, Virgil turned his head so fast he heard his neck click. "What? How can that be?"

"I don't know, Jonesy. All I know is it wasn't him. That's how I found Ross and Rosencrantz. I was getting bored just sitting around my room, so I went down to the casino. Whittle was there, walking around like he didn't have a care in the world. I asked one of the security guys to run the tape back, and it showed he'd been there most of the night. When I heard that, I knew something was off. I ran back to the rental house, and that's when I found Ross and Rosencrantz. Since they were still alive when I got there, it couldn't have been Whittle."

Virgil didn't want to hear that. "That means he's working with someone."

"And we have no idea who it is," Harper said.

"Not yet," Virgil said. "But one thing at a time. Let's get out to Whittle's. If we can grab him, we'll figure out who the other guy is if I have to beat it out of him." Then he turned to Murton. "You coming?"

Murton shook his head. "I'm staying right here until we know something about Ross and Rosencrantz."

Virgil understood and didn't argue. He had enough manpower with Harper's men. "Call me if you hear anything at all."

Murton said he would. But he was lying on more than one count, even though he didn't know it at the time.

---

Becky had the good sense to call Rosencrantz's girlfriend, Carla Martin. She explained the situation and made it perfectly clear that Rosencrantz was going to be okay. "They told us a few minutes ago that he's already awake. Murton is in talking to him right now."

Carla said she'd get there as quick as possible, and hung up.

---

When Murton walked into the recovery room, Rosencrantz looked smaller somehow. His voice was weak and shallow, but the words he used told Murton everything he needed to know.

"You're sure?" Murton said. "You've got to be one hundred percent on this one, Rosie."

"Positive...Get prints...pizza box...Kenny was shooter. One...hundred...percent."

"I'll take care of it. Rest easy. You're going to be okay." Murton turned to leave, but Rosencrantz wasn't done, no matter how weak he was.

"What...about...Ross?"

Murton's jaw quivered when he answered. "They're still working on him."

"One...hundred...percent. Kenny."

---

MURTON WALKED BACK INTO THE SURGICAL WAITING room, touched eyes with Becky, then walked out into the hall. Thirty seconds later she was by his side.

"I need your help," Murton said.

Becky didn't hesitate. "Name it."

"Two things. One, I'm going to leave. I know who the shooter is, and I'm going to go get him. If anyone asks, I went back to the resort to change clothes."

"Got it. What else?"

Murton pulled out his phone and brought up the picture of the rental sign that featured Kenny's face and phone number. "Call Nicky or Wu and have them get me an address for this guy."

"I spoke with Sandy a little while ago," Becky said. "They haven't left yet, so they can use my setup at our house if that's okay with you."

"That's fine. Get them over there right now. I need the intel as fast as they can get it."

"You'll have it in about fifteen minutes. I guarantee it."

"Love you, Becks."

"I love you too. Watch your back, baby."

"Always," Murton said. Then he kissed his wife and walked down the hall, and out the door.

MURTON HAD THE ADDRESS TWELVE MINUTES LATER. HE punched the address into the nav unit in his rental car, and ten minutes after that he made a slow pass of Kenny's house. The curtains were closed, but he saw movement from the backlighting. He parked his car around the corner, then crept behind the house, his gun held low at his side. When he tried the door handle, he was surprised to find it unlocked. He cracked the door as quietly as he could and heard the sounds of a ball game on the TV in the front room.

He waited a few seconds to make sure Kenny hadn't heard the door open, then he brought up his gun, walked straight through the kitchen and into the front room.

Kenny heard someone coming and stood from his chair, but Murton was on him like a tiger. He pistol-whipped him across his brow, then bent down and pressed the barrel of his gun into Kenny's forehead.

Kenny's eyes were wide with fear. When he spoke, he was surprised by the sound of his own voice, which seemed two octaves higher than normal. "What the fuck, man? What are you doing?"

Murton pressed the gun harder into Kenny's forehead and said, "Negotiating."

AFTER HE HAD KENNY RESTRAINED, MURTON SEARCHED him for weapons but didn't find any. Kenny, ever the deal-maker, was trying to figure out how the cop knew he'd done the shooting, and how to get out of it. He looked at Murton, and said, "Listen, how about we make a deal. Things got a little out of hand, I'll give you that, okay, but maybe we can work something out."

"Don't worry," Murton said. "We'll get everything sorted out. That's why I said we were negotiating."

Kenny felt himself relax a fraction. Maybe they could make a deal. "What did you have in mind?"

"First, I've got a question," Murton said. "Your answer decides how much we're going to negotiate."

"What's your question?"

"Where is Don Whittle?"

"What if I don't know? What happens then?"

"Then we negotiate," Murton said. "Here's how it works." He pulled the hammer back on his Sig and stuck the barrel into Kenny's mouth. "I'll either kill you quick by blowing your brisket against the wall, or..." He pulled the gun out of Kenny's mouth, de-cocked it, and put it in its holster.

"Or what?" Kenny said.

Murton reached down, pulled a wicked-looking blade from his boot, and said, "Or I'll kill you as slowly as possible with this. Tell me where Whittle is, and I might let you live."

Kenny visibly swallowed, and said, "He's got a cabin in the woods not far from here. No one knows about it. I think it's listed under his father's name. I can take you there, but if I do, you've got to let me go. I'm sorry for what I did, but he threatened to kill me if I didn't help him out."

"Uh-huh," Murton said. "Where's your phone?"

"Right over there on the table."

Murton stepped backward and grabbed the phone. "Passcode?"

Kenny's face reddened slightly. "One two three four."

"Clever." Murton punched in the code and it showed two missed calls from a contact listed as 'Whit.' "It looks like good old Don has been trying to reach you, Kenny. Time to call him back. Let's put him on speaker." Murton dialed, and right before he pressed the Send button, he pulled his gun, cocked it, and pressed it into Kenny's groin. "I've had the trigger on this thing reworked. It's got the lightest pull imaginable. It'll hurt like hell, but it won't kill you. Say one wrong word, and I'll finish with the knife."

Then he pressed the button.

# CHAPTER THIRTY-SEVEN

Virgil, Harper, and two deputies went to Whittle's house and tore the place apart. Whittle wasn't there, and they found nothing that would indicate where he might be. Harper instructed the deputies to remain behind, stay alert, and keep an eye on the place. Then he and Virgil walked down to the rental house to check in with the Orange County crime scene crew.

As they made the walk, Virgil looked at Harper, and said, "How good is your crew?"

"They get the job done. Prints, DNA, scenario analysis...that sort of thing. They don't get much practice though, I can tell you that."

"I've got a couple of people we could bring in if you think we'll need them."

The sheriff bobbed his head in a way that might have

meant yes, or no. Virgil wasn't sure. Finally, Harper said, "Let's see what they've got, then I'll let you know."

---

WHEN WHITTLE'S PHONE RANG, HE PULLED IT FROM HIS pocket, checked the screen, then said, "Where the hell are you? I've been trying to reach you."

"I'm at home," Kenny said. "I just got here. My phone died while I was out pretending to look for you. I hope you've got a plan because they've got you cold, man. They said they've got DNA."

"I'm not sure I believe that," Whittle said. "You've seen my work. I've been very careful."

"Well, they got it somehow," Kenny said. "Right now, I don't think it matters how or where. You've got to split, whether you want to or not."

"No shit. I've already put that together. I need your help."

"After what I did, it's going to cost you."

"Don't worry," Whittle said. "I'll take care of you. But we've got to do this tonight."

"What do you need?"

"I've got a car, but I need good plates."

"What kind of car?"

"It's a Chevy Malibu. There are only about a billion of the damned things out there, so get out to the resort, swap out a few, and bring me two clean plates to the cabin. Got it?"

"Yeah, yeah, I got it," Kenny said. "It's gonna be a minute, though."

"Quick as you can, man. I'm running tonight."

———

KENNY LOOKED AT MURTON, AND SAID, "HOW WAS that?"

Murton pulled the gun away from Kenny's groin, and said, "Good enough for now. Where's your car?"

"In the garage. Why?"

"Because we've got work to do."

———

VIRGIL AND HARPER WALKED UP TO THE FRONT DOOR of the rental but didn't go inside. They didn't want to contaminate the crime scene any more than it already had been. One of the techs came over, nodded at Virgil, then looked at Harper and said, "Sheriff."

"What have you got for us?" Harper said.

The tech looked at Virgil and said, "I understand these were your men."

"That's right," Virgil said. "Anything you can give us right now? Anything at all?"

The tech nodded. "We thought the pizza box was odd. If your guys were running surveillance out of here, why order pizza delivery? Plus, it looks like there's plenty of food in the fridge. Anyway, we're running prints from the box against the state database to try and get a quick hit."

"How long will that take?" Virgil said.

"With two state cops shot? About another thirty minutes. The request went right to the top of the list."

Harper looked at Virgil. "Might as well wait here."

Virgil nodded. "I'm going to call the hospital. See if there's any news."

---

MURTON TOOK KENNY OUT TO HIS GARAGE, THEN released one of his handcuffs, wrapped it around the leg of the workbench, then reattached it to his wrist. With Kenny now safe and secure, Murton got to work. He turned on the overhead lights, looked around for a few minutes, then walked over to Kenny and said, "I need a sledgehammer."

"What for?"

"Don't ask questions, Kenny. Questions aren't your friend right now. Where is your sledgehammer?"

"I don't have one."

"That's unfortunate," Murton said in an almost whimsical fashion. "Let me ask you this: What's your golf handicap?"

"I'm between a ten and a twelve, depending."

Murton pushed out his lower lip. "Impressive, though you're probably lying. Where do you keep your clubs?"

"In the trunk."

Murton walked over to the car—a big, older model Chevy Caprice—reached inside, and popped the trunk. Then he pulled out Kenny's bag of clubs, and when he did, he saw the gun with the suppressor still attached. He pulled a pair of gloves from his pocket, put them on, then picked up the gun and pointed it at Kenny. "Is this the gun you used on my friends? Don't lie to me."

Kenny nodded without speaking.

"Well, not to worry," Murton said. "It may come in handy." He set the gun on the workbench—out of Kenny's reach—then went back to the golf bag. He checked the clubs and discovered a 2-iron. He pulled it from the bag and said, "A 2-iron, huh? Maybe you weren't lying about your handicap."

"I wasn't. What are you doing with my golf clubs?"

Murton took the 2-iron and swung it at Kenny, hitting him in the leg. He pulled his swing at the last second, so the blow wasn't that bad, but still, Kenny cried out in shock. "I told you before, Kenny, questions are not your friend right now. You better close your eyes for this next part. It could be dangerous."

Kenny didn't know what the cop was going to do, but he closed his eyes. Then Murton got to work. He took the 2-iron and completely smashed out the back window of Kenny's car. Once the glass was out, he ran the shaft of the club back and forth around the perimeter of the window area, removing any smaller pieces that were wedged into the rubber seal. Then he tossed the club aside, grabbed Kenny's gun, and said, "I guess we better get a move on. Don's waiting."

---

AFTER VIRGIL CALLED THE HOSPITAL TO CHECK ON ROSS and Rosencrantz, he called Sandy to keep her up to date. With that done, he tried Murton but didn't get an answer. He was about to call Becky to ask where Murton was when the crime scene tech came out of the house and called out to the sheriff. Virgil walked that way.

Harper looked at the tech, and said, "What have you got?"

"Something you're not going to want to hear. The prints on the pizza box came back. They belong to Kenny Wolfe."

Harper looked at the tech for a moment before speaking. "You're saying that Kenny was the shooter? I can't believe that. He's a reserve deputy."

Virgil stepped forward. "What about the shell casings?"

The tech nodded. "That's what cinched it. The prints on the box are identical to the shell casings we recovered. Nice clear thumbprints from pressing the rounds into the magazine."

Harper ran his fingers through his hair. "Christ Almighty. One of my own people did this? I'll kill that son of a bitch myself." Then to Virgil: "Let's go. Kenny's place is about five minutes from here."

They ran toward the sheriff's squad car, jumped in, and took off.

———

KENNY DROVE WITH HIS HANDS CUFFED TOGETHER IN front of himself, while Murton sat in the back seat with Kenny's gun pointed at the back of the man's head. "One false move and you'll die by your own gun, Ken. How much further?"

"We're almost there. The drive is just ahead. The cabin sits pretty far back."

"When you turn into the drive, I want you to stop and put the car in park. Understand?"

"Yes, but…" Kenny caught himself and didn't finish his thought.

"See, you're learning," Murton said. "You were going to ask why, weren't you? It's okay, you can answer."

"Yeah, I was. But it doesn't matter now. We're here." Kenny turned into the drive and did what Murton asked.

"Now put your hands behind your head and grab the headrest," Murton said.

Kenny reached back and did what Murton said.

"Now stay right there," Murton said. "If you move, you die." When Murton was sure Kenny was going to cooperate, he got on his hands and knees in the seat, then slid out the back window and rested his body on the trunk of the car. He kept one hand wrapped around the seatbelt, and in the other, he held Kenny's gun. "Turn your high beams on and leave them on."

Kenny flipped the lights on bright, then said, "Now what?"

"I'll let that one slide because it's a valid question," Murton said. "I want you to drive straight up to the cabin, nice and slow. When we get there, turn the ignition off, and toss the keys in the back seat. Leave the lights on, and do not get out of the car. If you don't do exactly as I say, you won't be the last one to die tonight, Kenny. You'll be the first. Now drive."

───────

WHEN VIRGIL AND HARPER TURNED THROUGH THE intersection that would take them to Kenny's house, Virgil noticed Murton's rental car parked around the corner. He looked at Harper but didn't say anything because Harper seemed to take no notice of the car. When they turned in the drive, Harper said, "You want the front or the back?"

"I'll take the back. Give me thirty seconds before you hit the door." Virgil jumped out and ran to the rear of the house. When he got there, he noticed the door was hanging wide open. He pulled his gun, went inside, clearing each room as he went. He was just entering the front of the house when Harper kicked the door in.

"Let's check the bedrooms," Virgil said. "But I think we're clear. The back door was hanging open."

They made a quick run through the house and discovered no one was there. "Garage?" Harper said.

Virgil nodded and they carefully made their way into the garage. When they were inside, they found nothing except an overturned bag of golf clubs, and a bunch of broken glass. Harper looked around, and said, "What the hell?"

Virgil looked around, and thought, *"Oh, Murt, what are you doing?"*

---

KENNY DROVE UP TO THE CABIN, NICE AND SLOW, exactly as Murton had told him. He put the car in park, turned the ignition off, and tossed the keys in the back seat. He left the lights on.

Murton slid from the back of the trunk and was standing directly behind the car. When he spoke, his voice was barely audible. "Do not get out of the car. Do not speak. Not one single word, no matter what. Nod if you understand."

Kenny nodded.

"Good," Murton said. "Now tap the horn. Just a polite little toot-toot to let Whittle know we're here."

Kenny honked the horn, and Murton slid low, almost all the way to the ground.

---

VIRGIL WAS AT A LOSS. HE DIDN'T KNOW WHERE Whittle was, he didn't know where Kenny was, and he didn't know where Murton was, or what he was doing, though he had a pretty good guess. Murton had somehow found out that Kenny was the shooter, and he was going to lead him to Whittle. But where would that be? Then he had a thought. He turned to the sheriff, and said, "Looks like a bust for now. Mind giving me a lift back to Whittle's house? My car is still there."

Harper nodded, and said, "Sure."

Ten minutes later Virgil got out of Harper's car, and said, "I'm going to run back over to the hospital and check on my guys. I'll be in touch."

Once the sheriff was gone, Virgil got into his car, took out his phone, and made a call, praying that it would be answered.

And it was.

---

WHITTLE WAS PACKING UP HIS GOLD, THE BEARER bonds, and all the cash he had when he heard the horn honk. He looked out the window and wondered why Kenny wasn't getting out of his vehicle. He grabbed his pistol, tucked it into the back of his jeans, and walked outside. "Hey, Kenny...did you get the plates?"

---

MURTON STAYED DOWN LOW BEHIND THE TRUNK. When Whittle approached the driver's side of the car, he looked in and saw Kenny sitting there, his hands cuffed and resting in his lap.

Murton stood from behind the car, Kenny's gun pointed right at his head. "Hi, Coach. How's it going? No, no, no. Don't do that. That'd be a huge mistake on your part. Keep your hands where I can see them."

"What the hell are you doing on my private property?" Whittle said. "You've got no right to be here."

"Wrong, asshole. I've got every right." Murton had moved from behind the car and stood right in front of Whittle, no more than five feet away. "On your knees, right now, or I'll put you there myself."

Somewhere in the back of Whittle's mind, he always knew this day would come. In fact, he was surprised it had taken so long. He wouldn't let anyone put him in jail, or even worse, on display as the monster he knew he was. It wouldn't have taken much for his life to turn out differently, but those were the thoughts of fools...dullards who tricked themselves into believing their place in the world wasn't already preordained and set in stone. He dropped his hands and reached behind his back.

Murton shot him twice in the chest, then once in the forehead when he was down. Then he opened the car door and pulled Kenny out. "What does he do with the bodies?"

"There's a cistern behind the cabin at the edge of the woods."

"Show me." He pushed Kenny toward the cabin.

---

"Sam, it's Virgil Jones."

"Hello, Detective. Have you made any progress on—"

"Sam, I'm sorry to drop all this on you at once, but please just listen. I need your help, and I need it right now. You were right. Your father was murdered. Your brother is on the run, but he was spotted earlier this evening. We think he's close, but we can't find him. He's not at his house, and the Orange County cops said he's not at your sister's either. Tell me one place where he'd go to hide and get out of sight."

"Have you checked his cabin?"

"What cabin?" Virgil said. "I don't know about a cabin."

"He's got a cabin in the woods not more than five minutes from his house," Sam said.

Virgil dropped the car in gear and started driving. "Tell me where, right now."

"It's right outside of Prospect, northeast of Highway 56..."

---

When they got to the cistern, Murton cuffed Kenny's hands behind his back, then told him to sit on the ground. When he slid the heavy lid aside, the stench of the rotting corpses filled the air. He turned away, gagged, then replaced the lid. He looked at Kenny and said, "Get up."

Kenny rolled onto his side and pushed himself upright. When they were back at the front of the cabin, Murton took Whittle's gun from his waistband, then told Kenny to get on his knees.

"Hey, c'mon now, man. I thought we had a deal."

"We do. And I'm keeping up my end of it. You weren't the first to die, were you? On your knees."

"Fuck you," Kenny said.

"Yeah, fuck me," Murton said. "Like I haven't heard that one before." Then he shot Kenny twice in the stomach with Whittle's gun. Once he was down, Murton removed the cuffs, leaned in close, and said, "It'll take a few minutes for you to bleed out. Enjoy the ride, asshole. Those were my friends you gunned down."

Then he fired Kenny's gun into the woods until the slide locked open, before dropping it next to him in the dirt. Next, he took Whittle's gun, placed it in the dead man's hands, and fired two shots into the side of the car.

With that done, he took his gloves off, put them in his pocket, and sat down in the dirt.

Virgil turned in thirty seconds later.

# EPILOGUE

Beth Ryder's husband, the caretaker of the cemetery, knew that a police officer's funeral was often packed with cops from around the state, and in many instances, from jurisdictions all across the country. It wasn't just to say goodbye to a fellow officer, but a way to honor their life and the service given to those who trust and depend upon them to protect, serve and keep them safe. It was a sight he'd witnessed twice while working for the cemetery, one he hoped never to experience again.

Fortunately, he didn't have to because when the casket was lowered into the ground for Reserve Deputy Kenny Wolfe, there were only three people present...all of them cemetery workers, simply doing their job.

IT TOOK THE STATE POLICE CRIME SCENE TECHNICIANS five days to get all the bodies out of the cistern. It took another three weeks to make all the identifications. Twenty-eight girls were brought up, along with Karen Whittle. Two of the girls were never identified.

———

THE ORANGE COUNTY CRIME SCENE TECHS FOUND three bottles of arsenic at Karen Whittle's house.

Dick Whittle was unceremoniously re-buried.

Don and Karen Whittle were both cremated. When no one claimed their remains, the county coroner put them in the trash.

———

AS THE ONLY LIVING RELATIVE OF DON WHITTLE, SAM was eventually awarded everything that remained of his father's estate, and his siblings' estates as well. All told, it amounted to almost four million dollars. Sam and Danni split the money twenty-six ways and had their lawyer make anonymous donations to the parents of the victims.

———

ROSS SPENT TWO WEEKS IN INTENSIVE CARE, AND another week and a half in a private room at the hospital before he was released. Sarah rarely left his side. With hard work and plenty of physical therapy, the doctors told him he could be back to work in twelve to sixteen weeks.

Rosencrantz's injuries, while severe, weren't nearly as bad as Ross's, and he was released after a week. He went straight to Shelby County and hobbled around on crutches with Carla Martin by his side, thus ensuring her victorious election to the office of sheriff. Once she was sworn in, she immediately hired Ed Henderson as under-sheriff, who, by all accounts, was both thrilled, and relieved.

———

SHERIFF HARPER GAVE VIRGIL AND MURTON PLENTY OF time to get their paperwork turned in, which everyone knew was cop-speak for 'get your stories straight.' They did just that, and the county prosecutor who knew a smokescreen when he smelled one, wanted no part in the matter. He handed the paperwork off to the judge, who looked at it, decided that the prosecutor was a wimp, everything was in order, and signed off on the whole thing. He happened to be eating a ham sandwich at the time, and a little spot of mustard dripped onto the form.

———

ONCE THEY WERE IN THE CLEAR, MURTON AND VIRGIL drove up to Kokomo and went to the Tate residence. When they knocked on the door, John Tate, Lisa's father, answered. "Detectives, thank you so much for what you and your men did...for my family and the others. I understand your fellow officers are going to make full recoveries."

"They've got a tough road ahead," Virgil said. "But, yes, they're going to be all right."

"Would you like to come in?"

Murton looked directly at John, and said, "Thank you, but that's not necessary. This won't take long. I wanted you to know that the sensationalized stories you read in the paper and see on the evening news regarding the deaths of Don Whittle and Kenny Wolfe aren't entirely accurate. In truth, they're not even factual."

"So you did what I asked?" John said.

"I'm afraid that's all we can say about the matter, sir," Virgil said.

Murton turned and looked at his brother. "No, it isn't." Then he looked John Tate in the eye and said, "I'm sorry about your daughter. I can't change any of that. I wish I could, except life doesn't work that way. But know this, sir: When I make a promise like the one I made to you, I keep it. I hope you find some measure of comfort in that."

"I do," Tate said. "And I completely understand what you're telling me, Detective. Thanks to you, there is a little less evil in the world today."

*Is that right?* Murton said to himself.

"What was that?"

Murton looked away when he spoke. "I said, that's

right." Then he turned and walked back to the car without another word.

Tate turned to Virgil, and said, "The day both of you came here to my house…I never should have said the things I did. I'm sorry."

"I don't believe a grieving father has to account for every single thing he says or does."

"Maybe not," Tate said. "But I put a weight on your brother that wasn't his to bear."

"Murton carries the weight of those around him like no one I've ever known. Sometimes it's a burden I honestly feel would break any other man. Other times I think in some odd way, it's his own badge of honor."

Tate looked Virgil in the eye, and said, "Is he okay?"

Virgil watched Murton for a moment, then turned back to Tate, and said, "No, not yet. But he will be."

Thank you for reading State of Life. If you're enjoying the series, then there's good news:
Virgil and the gang are back right now in
**State of Mind.**

*You felt the Anger.*
*You experienced the Betrayal.*
*You took Control.*
*You faced the Deception.*
*You accepted the Exile.*
*You fought for Freedom.*
*You understood the Genesis.*
*You held on to Humanity.*
*You braced for Impact.*
*You defined Justice.*
*You captured the Killers.*
*You lived the Life.*
*Now, it's time to master the Mind!*

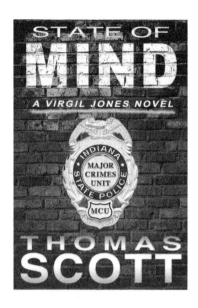

Stay tuned for further information regarding the Virgil
Jones Mystery Thriller and Suspense Series.

Visit ThomasScottBooks.com for updates.

## — Also by Thomas Scott —

Updates on future novels available at:
ThomasScottBooks.com

# ABOUT THE AUTHOR

Thomas Scott is the author of the **Virgil Jones** series, and the **Jack Bellows** series of novels. He lives in northern Indiana with his lovely wife, Debra, his children, and his trusty sidekicks and writing buddies, Lucy, the cat, and Buster, the dog.

You may contact Thomas anytime via his website ThomasScottBooks.com where he personally answers every single email he receives. Be sure to sign up to be notified of the latest release information.

Also, if you enjoy the Virgil Jones series of books, leaving an honest review on Amazon.com helps others decide if a book is right for them. Just a sentence or two makes all the difference in the world. Plus, rumor has it that it's good for the soul.

*For information on future books in the Virgil Jones series, or to connect with the author, please visit:*
ThomasScottBooks.com

And remember:

Virgil and the gang are waiting for you right now in State of Mind.

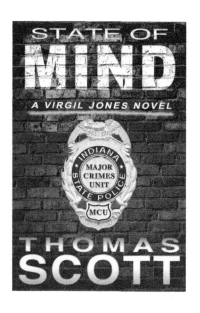

Made in the USA
Las Vegas, NV
16 January 2023